DARK
BOUND

SHADOW AND LIGHT
BOOK TWO

KIM RICHARDSON

FABLEPRINT

FablePrint

Dark Bound, Shadow and Light, Book Two

Copyright © 2018 by Kim Richardson

All rights reserved, including the right of reproduction in whole or in any form.
Cover by Kim Richardson
Text in this book was set in Garamond.
Printed in the United States of America

Summary: After narrowly surviving her encounter with the archangel Vedriel, Rowyn finds herself on another Hunt. But there's a catch. Her new employer is the faerie Queen of the Dark Court, and Rowyn HATES faeries.

ISBN-13: 978-1087067674
[1. Supernatural—Fiction. 2. Demonology—Fiction.
3. Magic—Fiction].

DARK
BOUND

SHADOW AND LIGHT
BOOK TWO

KIM RICHARDSON

CHAPTER

1

NOTICE OF FORECLOSURE.

Damn. I held the letter in trembling fingers. It didn't matter how many times I'd read the stupid notice. It always said the same thing; the bank was threatening to take my grandmother's house.

My gut clenched, and a sick feeling weaved its way into my being. I sat in my usual spot at my grandmother's antique wooden table. Suddenly cold, I stared out the kitchen window to the falling rain, forcing myself to breathe. The cool autumn wind drifted through the open window and I clenched the paper so I wouldn't hyperventilate.

This can't be happening.

"Rowyn, put the notice down before you give yourself a heart attack," commented Father Thomas sitting across from me, his beautiful voice, rich in tones and resonant. "The words won't change no matter how many times you read them."

I let the notice fall on the table and glanced at the priest. He'd been on one of his regular visits to my grandmother's when I popped in this morning to check on her.

Father Thomas was one of Thornville's local priests, but also a modern-day Templar Knight. They called themselves Knights of Heaven, and they were a team specially appointed by the church to investigate all the "unusual crimes" that happened in the city and the surrounding areas, specifically New York City. They waged a secret war against the church's enemies—demons, half-breeds, ghosts, and other supernatural baddies that posed a threat to the church.

He wore his usual dark ensemble of black slacks and a black shirt, the white square of his clerical collar stark against the deep tones. He was a few inches taller than me with a drool-worthy, athletic physique gained from hours at the gym and somewhere in his early thirties. His strong, handsome features complemented his dark, intelligent eyes, and his olive complexion framed by his raven hair spoke of his obvious Spanish ancestry.

Tall, dark and handsome. Yup. El padre had the full package. I wasn't even sure I was allowed to say or even *think* a priest was hot. Would God strike me down and send me to the Netherworld for thinking Father Thomas was a tad pretty?

Father Thomas is hot.

Father Thomas is hot.

Father Thomas is hot—yup, still here. *I guess it is allowed.*

"Father Thomas is right," said Tyrius, sitting on the table, and I pulled my eyes from the priest. "We've all memorized what it says. Now we need to figure out what we're going to *do* about it."

The chic Siamese cat looked regal with his carefully refined features, elegant black mask, and black-gloved paws. The concern in his voice mirrored my own. Tyrius loved my grandmother deeply, and this notice had us both on edge.

I glanced at my grandmother, standing with her back to the oven. The sign above her kitchen cabinets read LIFE'S TOO SHORT. LICK THE BOWL.

She wore a calf-length sweater dress with her white hair tied loosely in a long braid. Her face was paler than usual, and her eyes were a bit sunken, lacking their usual mischievous glint. The age lines in her face that I once found so comforting were deeper, making her appear tired and older. The sadness that clouded her eyes brought my heart into my throat.

"Can the bank really do that?" asked Tyrius, his deep blue eyes flashing. "Can they really take her house?"

"Yes." Father Thomas shifted in his chair. "The loan agreement was signed with the client's consent for the bank to take the necessary action should the client default on payments." I heard the frustration in his voice. "And that means they have every right to repossess the house if the payments stop."

"When does the bank take possession?" asked Tyrius, his voice carrying a new concern.

"If we don't cough up twenty grand," I said, my fingers drumming on the table, "in seven days from today."

A sullen silence descended, and I leaned over with my elbows on the table, letting my head fall in my hands. I'd been so wound up in my own affairs with the archangel's death, the deaths of the Unmarked, and my confusing feelings about Jax—I'd never even noticed the strain happening at my grandmother's. I was a fool. A selfish fool.

My thoughts were rambling now, panic making it hard to breathe. I needed to focus. I needed to figure this out.

I needed twenty freaking thousand dollars.

Since I hadn't actually *vanquished* the Greater demon Degamon, I wasn't entitled to the full ten thousand the council had originally offered. But having solved the murders, the council allowed me to keep the five thousand they'd given me upfront. Jax had explained Degamon's involvement to the council, in a lie that we had agreed upon. He told them Degamon was hunting the Unmarked because their souls were more potent and held more life-force than regular mortals or angel-born.

I don't know if the council bought our fabricated story, but the killings stopped, and so did the council's attention on me. Good. That's how I wanted to be—left alone.

Most of that five thousand had gone toward three months' rent, overdue bills and a desperately needed new wardrobe. I'd put the remaining five hundred dollars in a savings account, hoping to save up for a car. I hated having to take the bus and subway to get around. I was a Hunter. Taking the bus was bad for my image.

Screw my image. I had five hundred dollars to put towards my grandmother's debt. Now I had to figure out a way to get nineteen and a half thousand in less than seven days. Damn. How the hell was I going to pull that off?

"I say we rob a bank," said Tyrius, and to my surprise Father Thomas laughed. "What?" said the cat. "You think I'm kidding? Do you know how easy it would be for me to hack into the bank and transfer some cash to Cecil's account?"

"No one's robbing a bank," I growled, though I was tempted, just for half a second. But with my grandmother's strong moral fiber, she would never agree to it.

Jaw clenched against a New York-sized headache, I glanced at my grandmother, my heart breaking at the pain I saw. "Why didn't you tell me?" Twenty grand meant she hadn't been paying her mortgage payments for more than a year, plus interest.

My grandmother wiped her eyes, and I strained to keep my own waterworks at bay. "You had so much on your plate already, with you moving back here and then that Greater demon Degamon on a killing spree and that insufferable council meddling in our affairs again. I didn't want you to worry."

"Too late. I'm worried." Although I'd been open and honest about the encounter with Degamon and why it was after me, the memory still sent my heart pounding.

I shifted to the edge of my chair, wondering how I could have missed this. "Grandma, I thought you and grandpa had some money put away?" I said. "A pension and some lucky savings?"

"Lucky savings?" My grandmother gave me a tight smile. "I needed a new roof. Water was leaking through cracks in the foundation, so that needed to be fixed. Don't get me started on the plumbing." She sighed heavily. "It's an old house. Old houses always need repairs, just like this old body. If it's not a hip replacement, it's a window replacement. I've stretched that small pension as far as it will go. It just wasn't enough."

A knot of worry tightened around my middle. I couldn't let my grandmother lose her house. I had to do something.

"I'm so sorry, Cecil," said Father Thomas as he leaned back in his chair. "I'll make inquiries about a possible loan from the church. There has to be something we can do to help."

"No." My grandmother's expression was hard and she straightened. I recognized that stubborn pride. Guess I got it from Granny. "Stop fussing

DARK BOUND

about me." She set her coffee mug on the counter. "It's just a house. It's got a roof and walls. That is all. If that goddamned bank wants it so badly, they can take it. I just don't care anymore."

Father Thomas startled at the foul word coming from such an innocent-looking old lady, and I smiled at the hint of the badass angel-born she'd been in her younger years.

Of course she cared. I cared. "It's not *just* a house, grandma. You poured your life into this place. It's the house you bought with Grandpa. It's the house Mom grew up in. It's the place where I can transport myself into memories of her and Dad and Grandpa. Memories are all I have left of her... of all of them." I gritted my teeth until my jaw hurt. "The bank's not getting those memories," I added and blinked the moisture from my eyes.

"So, what's your master plan, then?" Tyrius cajoled as he shifted atop the table.

"I'll get a job," I announced, surprising myself. "A real, human job." God, that sounded lame to say it out loud. The thought of a human job was foreign, disturbing and even a little creepy. Could I even pull it off?

Tyrius's bark of laughter caught me off guard, and I frowned as he cleared his throat and said, "You? A real job? That's as hilarious as rainbows shooting out of my ass."

I stiffened in my seat. "What? You don't think I can?" Heat rushed to my face and part of me wanted to knock him off the table.

"Never said you couldn't." The cat's smile was brief but sincere. "It's just… well… what skills do you have? Apart from killing demons and that one, lame-ass archangel… what else can you do?"

My eyes flicked to my grandmother as she stared at the table without blinking, her expression far away and distant, and I nearly lost it.

"I *can* get a regular job," I protested, nearly shouting. "My people skills are a little rusty. But how hard can it be? I'm loyal. Dependable. Kind."

"That's great," commented Tyrius. "Now, all you have to do is learn how to catch a Frisbee and you can work as a Golden Retriever."

Father Thomas laughed and I scowled at the cat. "You've got a better idea?"

Tyrius grinned in a way that made me want to pull out his whiskers. "We could *borrow* money from the bank. They wouldn't even notice. Easy-peasy."

"No."

"It would be so-o-o-o easy, so ridiculously easy."

"Tyrius, we are still not robbing a bank," I said, watching Father Thomas smile at the cat because he thought he was joking. He wasn't. I knew if I said yes, Tyrius would probably transfer small amounts of cash from several different accounts so as not to draw any attention and then stash it into my grandmother's. But she wouldn't go for that. And neither would I.

The cat made a face. "Fine. Have it your way then. But the idea of you behind a desk is as unnatural to me as a swimming cat. It's just plain wrong. You wouldn't last a day."

I rubbed my temples. "I would." *I didn't even know where to start.* "I will get a regular job if it means I can save this house. I'll do it."

"Do you have a résumé?" Father Thomas's mouth quirked, and he touched his clean-shaven chin with the back of his hand.

If he wasn't so pretty, I would have slapped him. "No." My face warmed. Hunters didn't have résumés. We got our jobs by reputation. Not that it mattered now.

"Rowyn, be reasonable." My grandmother tilted her head, and a brief look of pain passed over her features. "Tyrius is right. You're angel-born, a Hunter. The human workplace is no place for my granddaughter. You won't fit in."

I don't fit in anywhere, I thought sourly. No big surprise there.

With a troubled look, my grandmother exhaled. "I'm sorry you're losing this place, Rowyn, but there's nothing else we can do."

Now I felt guilty. "Yes, there is." I pushed my chair back and stood. "I'm not giving up. I *won't.*" I glanced at my grandmother and I swear I saw hope flitting behind her eyes. "I'll figure something out," I said, my throat closing. "Just don't do anything rash until you hear from me. Okay?"

"Where are you going?" my grandmother called as I walked out of the kitchen and rushed down the hallway.

"To get the money," I whispered to myself. My head throbbed as I pulled open the front door and stepped out into the morning rain onto Maple Drive.

Yes, my life was a bag of disasters, but it needn't be for my grandma. She was all the family I had left, if you didn't count Tyrius. And I sure as hell wasn't going to sit back and do nothing.

I *would* get the money. Even if I had to hurt a few people to do it.

CHAPTER

2

I picked my way through the crowded West 42nd Street in New York City, cursing at the human elbows that kept slamming into me as I followed the shifter demon. Even on a Monday night, the street was alive and noisy with tourists posing to take photos and New Yorkers hurrying back and forth from work and restaurants. The giant screens and billboards glittered like starlight. Cars and cabs honked, their exhaust fumes making me dizzy, but my keen angel-born senses could follow the stench of demon anywhere, even amidst the throng of humanity.

I smiled, remembering my first experience as a Hunter. On a cool night like this I killed my first demon. I was fifteen at the time, totally unaware of the demon that had followed me home from a night at the movies. I'll never forget the surprise on its face when I slashed its neck with a swipe of my blade and killed it. That night was the first time I felt alive, normal, with a sense of purpose. And I was damn good at it.

But as it turns out, my ability to hunt and track demons so easily also came from my demon heritage. My senses were turbocharged because I had demon essence flowing in my veins.

I'd always known I was different from the other angel-born. Without an archangel sigil, which all Sensitives were born with, I stood out like a zebra among mustangs. I was a different breed.

Okay, so I had angel *and* demon essence flowing in my veins. Whoop-de-freaking-do. It didn't make me bad... or did it?

It all made sense now, when I thought about it. It was why I could heal from a vampire bite and why I could handle a death blade when just the touch of the black metal could kill an angel and angel-born— because *I* was part demon. It was the darkness Tyrius had been curious about when we'd first crossed paths and the reason why he'd followed me home when I was a kid. He'd sensed it too.

Ever since the archangel Vedriel had made the declaration of my true heritage, Tyrius was like a cat on catnip—bouncing off the walls and rolling around in papers on the floor. He was a vigorous, frenzied furball, and he was ecstatic. Go figure. Maybe because he felt we were even more alike than before.

Although admittedly I couldn't Hulk-out into a giant black panther when danger arose, I still had skills, demonic skills.

I couldn't help but wonder if my parents had figured it out. Vedriel had them killed because they were getting too close to discovering to the truth. But what if they had already found it? What if they had known their only daughter was a freak?

I was both angel and demon-born—a gift from the Legion of angels, or a curse. According to the archangel Vedriel and his cronies, the other Unmarked and I were an experiment, a new race of Horizon soldiers. And for whatever reason, they wanted us terminated.

They had almost succeeded, but I was *still* alive.

However, my survival came at a steep price—the death of the archangel Vedriel.

Yes. We killed an archangel. I cringed whenever I thought about it. The feeling of helplessness, of being trapped and forced to kill or be killed, swept through me. I hated that he'd made me into an angel killer.

The blessed, sacred, perfect archangels were supposed to be righteous and protect us mere mortals from evil. But it was like Tyrius had said; not all archangels and angels were good. Turns out Vedriel was very, very bad. And his bad-ass self had ultimately been his demise.

No one else knew we'd killed the archangel Vedriel. Only me, Tyrius, Jax, Danto and the Greater demon Degamon were there. We'd made a pact that early morning not to tell a soul about what we'd done.

We needed to keep this quiet. The angel-born council would never understand, and it would just complicate matters.

I doubted Degamon would tell the council, but we still didn't know all the details of Vedriel's plans to eliminate the Unmarked. Who else was involved? He had said other archangels were part of this scheme. Maybe Vedriel was just the errand boy and the real architect was still out there.

Sooner or later, the Legion would figure out what happened to their archangel and then they would come after us... after me.

In the few months since, I'd slept poorly. I'd been on edge, thinking a legion of angels was about to pound me. And yet, I was still here, back at my old job, hunting demon scum.

Father Thomas gave me this new mark after a series of unexplainable deaths at a New York City law firm. The eyewitness reports of strange slops of skin-like substances at the crime scenes had caught the priest's attention—demon goo. A shifter always sheds its skin after it killed its victim and took its shape.

To a Hunter, it was an easy red flag and stupid, but hey, most demons were stupid.

I sighed through my nose and pivoted around a smiling Asian couple. I couldn't refuse any work. I had five more days to come up with my grandmother's debt or the bank would take her house. I'd been working nonstop—day and night— for two days since I found out about the bank's threat. Since then, I'd taken every job the priest threw at me and a few jobs from my own personal website—two closet demons cases (yes, closet monsters were real) and a gremlin that had been terrorizing an elderly couple by smashing the pipes in their basement and causing it to flood. I'd even drafted a résumé with Tyrius's help and applied to fifty different human jobs online, from data entry clerk to housecleaning.

But I'd heard nothing yet. Without experience or the education to back me up, the humans weren't interested. Hell, I didn't blame them. Even *I* wouldn't hire *me*.

Hunting was my only option. And I would take every goddamn job that came my way, and then some. Whatever it took.

Still, it wasn't enough.

I'd barely made seven hundred dollars. And with my five hundred in the bank, I was still over eighteen thousand dollars short.

Damn. At the rate the priest was paying me, I needed to hunt fifty more shifter demons. Double damn.

The shifter demon took a sharp left on 8th Avenue. After sliding my hand on the hilt of my soul blade, I headed across the street after it. Show time.

The shifter demon had taken on the shape of a beautiful young black woman, Claire Beaumont to be exact. The body of the lawyer had been found yesterday morning in her apartment, next to the slop of skin. The shifter demon would keep the shape of the young lawyer until it began to tire and needed to replenish its demon energy with its next victim.

Demon-Claire sashayed her way towards a pizza joint. Men turned at her approach, their eyes on the pretty woman. My skin pricked as the demon flicked its black eyes across the mass of men still staring at it. Crap.

The demon smiled seductively as it approached a tall, handsome dark man in a suit that barely contained his muscles. He smiled back and stood, breaking apart from the others, too close to the dark alleyway behind the restaurant.

My heart pounded in my ears. I walked faster.

The demon stroked the dark man's arm and leaned over to whisper something in his ear. I didn't need to hear the exchange. I saw the desire flicker in the man's face and knew exactly what the demon had said. The shifter smiled as it pushed the mortal man back playfully towards the alley, back into darkness—

"Claire! There you are!" I grabbed its left arm while pressing my soul blade against its side. "I've been looking all over for you," I said, pushing my blade a little harder. Seeing the ire in the man's face, I added, "Sorry, my friend's had a little too much to drink. Bye now."

I hurled the demon with me into the alley. I'd barely made five steps before it feigned a trip, taking me by surprise.

"Angel bitch!" The demon elbowed me in the ribs and leaped away, sprinting like an Olympian.

16

"Oh, hell no." My boots scraped the pavement as I shot after it into the dark alley. "Come back here!" I yelled, stunned that the shifter could run that fast in six-inch heels. That took some serious skill.

It pulled right and disappeared behind a metal garbage bin. Adrenaline spiked through me as I pushed my legs faster. There was no way I was letting my mark get away. Especially now that it had seen my face. It might take on my shape just to piss me off. I wouldn't take that chance.

The stench of spoiled meat and rotten fruit hit me like a slap in the face as I dashed past the bin—

A leg darted from under the container. It caught me on my shin and I pitched forward onto the hard pavement, scraping my knees and the side of my face. *Ouch*.

Demon-Claire was on me before I hit the ground. A sudden blow slammed my back as human teeth sank into my neck. Before I could catch my breath, the demon grabbed a fistful of my hair and smacked my head against the ground. Black spots exploded behind my eyes as I cried out in pain. This was not going well at all.

In one smooth, mighty movement, I bucked wildly and felt it release my hair. Without stopping, I rolled over and kicked out hard, my boot connecting with the demon's chest, and it stumbled back.

I shot to my feet and felt my forehead. "Great. Now that's going to bruise. Do you know how hard it is to hide a bruise with makeup without making it look caked on? VERY HARD."

The shifter demon spat, its black eyes wild and consumed with hatred. "I'm not going back. I'd rather die than go back to the Netherworld."

"That's the point." I pushed my jacket back, showing off my additional blades. "You know, the part of you dying. It's why I'm here, demon." I grinned when I saw the shifter's eyes locking with the death blade on my weapons belt.

What can I say? I got the *feels* whenever a demon spotted the death blade at my hip. It made me all warm and tingly inside to see the confusion cross their marred features. It was almost as exhilarating as the thrill of the hunt. Almost.

I gave the demon my best pageant smile. "Yes. That's a death blade. And before you ask, no, I'm not a demon. I'm something else. But I'm feeling super generous tonight. I'll give you the choice." I cocked my hip. "Soul blade or death blade? Which one do you want me to use to kill you? Hmmm? What will it be, demon?"

The shifter snarled, twisting its human guise to look more and more animal than human. It stood with its fists at its sides, glaring at me. "I'm never going back. Never!"

"Then you should have thought about that *before* you started killing the innocent. You did this to yourself, shifter. I *am* going to send you back."

The shifter hissed, its black eyes wild, and lunged.

It came at me in a whirl of limbs, spit, and hair. But I was ready.

With my muscles locked tightly, the night air whistled as I gave a mighty swing of my blade. Without pause, the demon spun, evading the killing thrust of my blade. But as it came around, closing the distance to deliver its own strike, I drew my weapon back, slicing across its neck.

With a howl, the demon stumbled back, black blood spilling down its neck and over its chest.

I smiled at the fear in its eyes. "See? Told you I was going to kill you. Stop fussing and let me just do it. It'll be quick. I promise."

"Help!" screamed the demon in a perfect imitation of a human female in fear. It looked at me and smiled before yelling again. "Help me! Please! Someone help me!"

"Shut up." I looked over my shoulder to the street and my stomach churned. A silhouette of a man had stopped at the sound of the shifter's screams and turned his attention to us.

Shit. Was it the same man the shifter had spoken to before? Was he looking for it? There was no way I could kill the demon now, not with the human staring. There were rules about this sort of thing. Not that I cared for rules, but I knew I couldn't kill the shifter with a human watching. If he called the cops, I was in for it. I'd have to leave—without my mark or my money.

"Help! She's trying to kill me!" wailed the demon, tears now spilling down its face and adding to the dramatic effect.

"Damn you, demon." I looked back over my shoulder and a mixture of surprise and relief coursed through me when I noticed the man was gone. "Ha. It didn't work. Better luck next time."

The shifter lost its smile and threw itself at me in a fit of rage. It moved faster than I'd thought possible, and before I could raise my blade, it crashed into me. The two of us tumbled to the ground. My blade was still grasped in my hand as we rolled over, each trying to gain the advantage.

"Not going back! Never!"

The shifter began biting me with its human teeth. Bile rose in the back of my throat and I was surprised at the pain I felt. With its superhuman strength, it tried to muscle me onto my stomach, and I winced at the fetid breath on my face. I struggled to get an opening with my blade, but the demon lashed out and scratched at my face and eyes. It was like wrestling a crazed cat, the demon hissing and spitting as it bit and scratched at me in a fit of demented panic.

This demon was really starting to piss me off. Anger spiked in me. With a surge of strength, I heaved the demon back and staggered to my feet.

"It ends now." Raising my soul blade to the creature's chest, I moved forward, angling my weapon for the killing strike—

Bone popped. Muscles tore. An arrowhead perforated the demon's chest. A look of surprise warped its features and I stopped cold at the sight of blood I hadn't put there.

"Not going back," said the demon as it cupped the arrowhead with its hands. "Not going—"

The rest of its words died at the impact of another arrowhead bursting through its mouth from the back of its skull. The demon teetered on the spot, its black eyes fixed on me, and then exploded.

Not ash that could easily be wiped off with a brush of a hand like the rest of the demons, but a spill of wet, putrid bits of skin and yellow liquid.

I gagged as the slop hit me in the face, neck, and chest, and I shivered as I tasted carrion. I was covered in its wasted slime, its demon goo. I spat and kept spitting until I thought I'd gotten all of it out, hoped I'd gotten it all out. That was truly disgusting. I almost threw up when I saw the slime on my jacket steaming in the cool air.

Just as I heard the shifting of feet, someone stepped out of the shadows, a bow in his hand. No. Not a someone. A faerie.

CHAPTER
3

I hissed under my breath. Damn. I never felt him coming. I was either losing my touch or the shifter guts were affecting my demon senses. Or maybe I was just having a *really* bad night.

Every time I spotted a faerie, images of Tyrius skewered on a stick being barbecued flicked in my mind's eye, and I hated them even more. I couldn't help it. Any creature that ate cat or dog was my enemy. Period.

I'd always felt something viler and more sinister whenever I was in the presence of a faerie, a darkness I couldn't explain. There was a wild, demonic energy about them, unlike any other half-breed, and it always made my pulse quicken and my creep-o-meter shoot sky high.

This one was tall, very tall, making my five-foot-nine-inch frame look petite next to the gangly bastard. Faeries and vampires were distant cousins in the half-breed world, having a similar demon heritage, but where vampires were gifted with good looks, charm, and sensual grace, faeries were cold and gaunt-looking, like starved heroin addicts.

The male faerie attached his bow to the quiver strapped behind his back. His long legs moved with a business-like purpose as he deliberately stalked toward me, his steps as silent as a cat. How ironic. I'd always hated that about faeries, the way they could sneak up on people without being heard.

The smell of candy canes and rotten eggs clogged up my nose. Perhaps thirty years old, his blond hair was tied back from his face, making his cheek bones stand out sharply against his pale skin and revealing his pointed ears. He wore a long, black coat with matching shirt and pants and carried two curved daggers sheathed along his baldric, each long and deadly like a beast's claw. A series of tattoos peeked out from the collar of his shirt, up and around his neck—faerie symbols. His eyes were deep brown and dangerous, surprisingly dark for a faerie with such pale skin and fair hair. He carried his weight with a pompous sort of dignity.

I hated him on the spot.

His gaze traveled over me to the death blade at my hip. I would have smiled at the arch in his brows, but I was too pissed off. When his eyes met mine, he gave me a look like I should be thanking him. Hell no.

I straightened my shoulders, gripped my soul blade, and pushed myself onto the tips of my toes, trying to look taller. "You just stole my mark *and* you ruined perfectly good clothes. Who's going to pay for that? You?"

"I did you a favor, Hunter," the faerie intoned, its voice scratchy and annoyingly high pitched for a male. "Looks like the shifter would have finished you off if I hadn't intervened. I saved you."

Peeved, I almost snarled. "You had no business intervening, *faerie*." His eyes narrowed at my tone. "As I recall, faeries don't do favors for non-faeries. And they don't mix with Hunter business either."

I threw out my senses, scanning for any familiar, cold, demonic energies. My skin pricked at the shift in the air, like tiny electrical currents. More faeries. I was willing to bet there were four or five more hiding in the alley, no doubt pointing their arrows at me. They always moved in packs, like werewolves. Did I mention how much I hated them?

Cold rain fell around me, light but steady, and my pulse quickened. "Quit staring at me like you're about to ask for my number, 'cause that's *never* going to happen." I gritted my teeth. "What do you want?" The faerie's dark eyes were starting to creep me out. I just wanted him gone so I could go home and shower before the demon goo penetrated my skin like a cream. I'd never get the smell out then.

The faerie's pompous expression never changed. "I'm here on behalf of Queen Isobel. She requests an audience with you, Rowyn Sinclair."

"Ha-ha." I laughed, but inside I flinched. I didn't like this faerie knowing my name. I shifted my weight, my eyes never leaving his. Now this was getting interesting. "What does the queen of the Dark Court want with me?"

I'd never met or seen the faerie queen of the Dark Court, but I'd heard the rumors, just like everyone else. She had acquired her throne by removing the dark faerie king and taking his place. She *ate* him, or so the story went. Yikes.

The queen of the Dark Court's story was legend and nightmare among our kind. She was the most lethal faerie on this side of the northern continent. She was powerful and held more magic than most faeries, which she used to slaughter humans and any half-breed who dared defend them.

I knew she had set up her lair in Mystic Quarter with a legion of vicious faeries by her side. Blondie here must be one of them. I'd also heard that she liked to keep human men as her sexual slaves, their minds too weak and corrupt to know the difference between glamour and the real world.

But the Gray Council had put a stop to her slaughtering humans five hundred years ago. After centuries of conflict, a truce was forged between the half-breeds and the angel-born, and the Gray Council was created. It consisted of one member from each half-breed court—vampires, faeries, werewolves and witches—and it also includes the leaders of the angel-born.

All half-breeds were allowed to live in the mortal world and govern themselves if they followed one strict rule—never harm a human. They forged their own councils and their own courts. But a truce was a fragile thing, some longed for the return of the old ways, the dark days before the angels interfered and created the angel-born to keep the peace and watch over the mortal world.

And when any of these half-breeds stepped out of line, it was my job to hunt them.

"The queen requires your services, Hunter," said the faerie, his face twitching into something between a smile and a grimace.

I raised my brows. "Really? A job? Bull."

The faerie snickered. "I wouldn't be here wasting my time talking to a Hunter otherwise," he said belligerently. "Trust me. I'd rather be anywhere else but here right now." His voice was dripping with indignation at having to deal with little moi.

My pulse quickened. I didn't like to be cornered and surprised by half-breeds, even less by faeries. Worse, I smelled like a week-old garbage bin left in the hot sun.

If he'd wanted to kill me, he and his goons would have tried putting a few arrows in my chest already. Maybe he really was here on the queen's business. Curious, I gave him another once-over. He looked like he despised me about as much as I despised him, but I wanted to know why the queen of the faeries had sought me out.

"What kind of job?" I asked, shoving my jacket back so that my weapons were in full view, just in case he wanted to admire them again.

The male faerie kept quiet and I could tell by his stern reserve that he wouldn't tell me. He just stood there, eyeing me like I might be tasty to eat. Swell.

"Listen," I said, brushing a strand of hair out of my eyes. "If it's not a paying job, I'm not interested. As you can see—" I lifted my arms in a show of demon guts, "—I'm quite busy at the moment. I don't do freebies. You can tell your faerie lady to forget it—"

"Isobel is *queen* of this land." The male faerie did nothing to hide the ire in his voice, pulling my stomach tight. "She is the Dark Queen of New York," he breathed, his eyes wide with some admiration and possibly a little fear.

"Right, well, she's not *my* queen," I said, loudly enough for the other faeries to hear. "What does she want?" I was beginning to regret not accepting Tyrius's offer for backup. I never worked with a partner, apart for that one job with Jax, but I was wondering if I should start to seriously rethink that. His alter ego black panther might have been handy right now.

The faerie watched me for a moment. "Perhaps one day she will be your queen, and then you will show some respect."

I scowled, not liking where this conversation was going. "Listen here, you skinny-ass faerie. I don't have time for this. Either you tell me what she wants… or get the hell out of my way."

A flicker of anger set the faerie's eyebrows high. "I'd kill you right now, if my queen hadn't commanded me not to harm you. Pity. I could have added Hunter to my list of kills."

My mouth fell open. Torn between anger and shock, my face went cold. "You know," I said as I felt a piece of the shifter's remains slip down my forehead and wiped them away with my hand. "I've got a lot on my plate right now. I'm booked for the month. Sorry, but you'll have to tell Her Highness no." There was no way I was going to do a job for any faerie. I didn't care if she was a queen or a princess. That meant diddlysquat to me.

"The queen is prepared to offer you twenty thousand dollars." The faerie wrinkled his face as if carefully considering what I would say.

Twenty thousand? My heart leapt as I struggled to keep my face blank. "Sounds like something serious. And you still won't tell me what it is?" That was more than a whole year's pay, even as a freelancer.

A chill hit my guts. Typically with hunting, the higher a mark was priced, the more dangerous it was. It could be anything from a Greater demon to a mass of lesser demons. But with that kind of cash, my grandmother could keep her home.

My heart pounded. "Why me? Why not have—"
I waved my bladed hand, "your own kind handle the
queen's affairs? Why seek me out?"

"The queen requires someone with your... *unique*
skills," replied the faerie, sounding both bored and
irritated at the same time. His eyes were full of an
amused disbelief as he took in my casual jeans and
leather jacket. It was obvious he wasn't comfortable
with the idea of his queen requesting *me* for a job.
Maybe he was jealous. Maybe that was just his normal
face. And it made me all tingly inside.

Still, I'd never heard of any faerie—queen or
common faerie—ask for help. Perhaps this was a trap
and they wanted to lure me in with the promise of so
much cash... then kill me... then eat me.

The faerie must have read my mind. His face
pulled into a smile and my blood turned cold. His
yellow teeth were filed down into sharp points, like
the teeth of a fish.

Damn, maybe *he* wanted to eat me.

The faerie shifted and reached inside his jacket. I
tensed, lowering myself in a crouch, only to find the
half-breed flipping me a coin. A gold coin.

I caught it easily and flipped it over. Yup. It was
gold. I rubbed my thumb over the portrait of a man's
face with a large hawk-like nose. The coin was from
Spain. I couldn't read the inscription around the
edges, but I could make out the year 1822 engraved
on the bottom. Who pays anything in gold these days?
The stinky, filthy rich, that's who.

"Please accept this gift as a token of my queen's good faith." The faerie's dark eyes searched my face.

With my fingers, I moved the coin around in my hand. Damn, gold felt good. "I don't even know what the job is. How can I say yes to something I don't know?"

The faerie raised a brow, seemingly knowing I was going to say that. "It's not my place to say. The details will be explained to you at the meeting. Do you accept an audience with the queen or not? A simple yes or no will do." The faerie sighed, visibly biting back his annoyance.

I felt marginally better knowing that I was annoying him. Clasping the gold coin in my hand, I answered, "Fine," surprising myself as I pocketed the gold coin before faerie-boy asked for it back. Tyrius was going to have a field day when I told him about this encounter—and possibly cough up a furball at what I had just agreed to do. Just the thought of his tantrum had the corners of my lips twitching.

"I'll meet your queen," I told the faerie. "But I'm not making any promises. I want to hear what she has to offer first, *before* I make my final decision. I'll meet her… but it doesn't mean I'm taking the job. Got it?"

A flicker of surprise moved over the faerie's tight features. "Yes. That's fine."

"Okay then," I said, tension tightening my shoulders. "When and where?"

The faerie met my gaze, his expression blank. "The queen wishes to see you at midnight tomorrow night at Sylph Tower." He eyed me, his eyes suddenly bright with amusement. "Do you need directions?"

"I think I can manage," I said, bristling. Sylph Tower was in Mystic Quarter.

A lump of fear settled heavily in my belly as a wicked, contriving smile spread over the faerie's chiseled face. "Don't be late," he said. "My queen won't tolerate tardiness." And with that, the faerie spun on his heels and bounded back up the street.

I opened my mouth to tell him to shove his attitude up his ass, but my breath caught at the sudden shift in the air.

My skin erupted in gooseflesh as my heart thumped against my ribcage. From the shadows of the alley came a low hissing sound, and I felt another, stronger slither of vile and cold demon energy. Four Dark Court faeries appeared in the alley as though formed from the shadows. They all came together to form a line behind the blond faerie. Darkness cloaked their faces, but they were all tall and gangly like him and wearing similar black clothes with matching arrow-filled quivers—the very arrows that had been pointed at me this whole time.

I stood in silence watching the faeries disappear into the night until their foul scent had vanished and all that was left was the eye-watering stink of shifter demon guts on me.

I slipped my hand back into my pocket and pulled out the gold coin. What was this job? And why did the faerie queen of the Dark Court wish to hire *me*?

Unease tightened my chest as I rubbed my thumb over the Spaniard's face. Nothing good would come from accepting a job from a faerie. And things could always get worse.

What did I get myself into?

CHAPTER
4

"**C**an't you just give the damn faerie his golden coin back and call this whole stupid thing off?" argued Tyrius as we walked along the sidewalk, his tail twitching nervously behind him. The light of the moon cast a silvery radiance over his tawny-colored body, making him glow. "I mean… you haven't made a deal with the queen yet—so there's no harm in not going. Call this off, Rowyn. You can't trust the fae. I don't care what comes out of their mouths. Tricksters, the lot of them. Nothing good can come from this meeting. Trust me. The fae are rotten to the core. It's in their DNA. I don't like it."

"I don't like the idea of working for any faerie," I said. "But I can't turn down twenty grand. Not when

I'm desperate to save my grandmother's house. And not until I know what she wants."

"To eat you?"

I rolled my eyes. "She doesn't want to eat me." *I hope.*

"How would you know?" asked Tyrius incredulously. "You've never met her."

"Neither have you."

"Yes, but it's my business to know things. And I *know* the queen is a monster in mortal flesh."

"She's a faerie, not a mortal—"

"She *eats* CATS!"

I sighed through my nose, my body tightening with anxiety. I didn't want to argue with Tyrius on my way to meet this queen. His deep hatred for the fae was totally understandable, seeing as he was one of their preferred dishes. Faeries were a baal's natural enemy, which made them my enemy. Besides, I had a feeling he was right. The queen was a monster.

Tension pulled my shoulders. The idea of meeting the faerie queen in her lair, surrounded by God knows how many, pointy-eared, cat-eating faeries, had me wire tight. Fear made my heart pound, and as a precaution, I'd doubled on my weapons, adding all the daggers and blades that would fit on my weapons belt. Just in case.

I was glad when Tyrius offered to come with me, but his being a baal demon—a Siamese cat—was a problem. The fae would see him as a meal rather than backup. Maybe that was a good thing. Maybe it wasn't. I clenched my jaw as sweat broke out along my skin making me cold. I'd slaughter them all before they laid a finger on one of his whiskers. Not my Tyrius.

The Dark Court faeries were notoriously wicked, evil, and entirely without remorse. I'd never met any faeries from the Light Courts, so I had no idea if they were any more wicked than the Dark Court faeries. Still, only a fool would willingly associate with them. Apparently that fool was me.

"You don't have to come, you know," I said, my boots clanking loudly on the uneven sidewalk. The sound was dull in the heavy air from the evening's rain. "I won't be mad or anything if you want to leave. I can do this alone—"

"Not on your life, woman." Tyrius's tail bristled. "I'm coming with you. Besides, I want to see this witch of a queen with my own eyes. See if she's as mad as the rumors say she is."

"If she likes to eat fae kings," I said, "I'd say she's quite mad."

Tyrius flashed me a smile, the only way a cat could smile. "Right you are, angel-born—or is it demon-born now?" His ears swiveled back. "I never asked you this but... do you feel more like an angel or a demon?"

I bit my lower lip. I'd been asking myself that question for months; did I identify myself as angel-born or demon-born?

"At this very moment... neither," I answered. "I feel like me. Both I guess? I don't know what it is to feel like more angel or demon. I only know what it is to feel like me."

"Hmm. Perhaps you're the perfect balance of both," commented the cat, his tail high in the air as he padded next to me. "The yin and yang of angel and demon. The two halves that complete each other."

That brought a smile to my face, but it disappeared as I pulled out my phone and checked the screen. Eleven forty-five. Still plenty of time to make my midnight rendezvous with Her Highness on time. I switched my phone to vibrate and dropped it in my pocket.

All around us, Mystic Quarter was just as flamboyant and strange as the last time I was here a few months ago, but without the Seal of Adam dragging me down. In this secret district, the paranormal lived and mingled freely—the only place where goblins sold jewelry at their night market, witch shops crowded the streets, werewolves tried to pick fights with opposing packs, and vampires out for a stroll displayed their hypnotic and cold beauty.

The stench of sulfur seared my nostrils, sharp and tainted with the thick smear of demon magic. It was everywhere in the air we breathed, and I tasted rot in my mouth.

As we passed another block, I caught a glimpse of a beautiful faerie girl running her hand along the muscled, tattooed chest of a male faerie. I pulled my gaze away as he turned his dark eyes on me.

We were moving swiftly through the streets and I was aware of every glance between the faeries. I could make out crowds of vampires gathered on the many balconies and windows of elegant brownstone apartment buildings and heard the clink of their glasses and low chatter as we passed them. From the calculating looks on their faces, it was almost as though they were expecting to see us.

A chill from the wind pulled my head up. The night was awake and damp, and the hum of humanity was far away and distant, oblivious to the lively quarter filled with paranormals. The moon was trying to break through the light fog, giving everything a silver sheen.

And I was going to see the faerie queen of the Dark Court.

Tyrius looked up at me, his blue eyes a stark contrast against his black mask. "You look like crap."

Lips pursed, I glared down at him. "Always so gallant, aren't we?"

The Siamese cat tottered gracefully next to me, tail held high in the air like a show cat. "I'm just stating the obvious. Are you sleeping okay? Too much on your mind? A particular *someone* on your mind?"

Blood rushed up to my face. "Shut up." I hated how perceptive the tiny baal demon was and how easily I flushed at the thought of Jax. I hadn't been able to get his kiss out of my mind since he'd planted it on me. My heart raced just at the memory of his lips crushing mine. A shudder went through me as I recalled how soft they'd felt, and the eager, unashamed desire in his eyes.

"Hmmm," came the cat's voice, pulling me out of my reverie. "Still haven't heard from him, huh?"

I shook my head. "It's fine. There's no reason he should call. It's not like we're a *thing*—because we're not. He has his own life to live." I shrugged. "We're just friends—"

"Just friends?" drawled Tyrius. "I seriously doubt that. Jax and I are *just* friends. The mailman and I are *just* friends. But you two are *not* just friends and you know it."

Feeling my chest clench, I swallowed hard. Jax's absence had put a damper on my mood lately. I couldn't pretend that his lack of communication didn't hurt a little. Just a little. The last time I'd seen him was on the morning of Vedriel's death. That was more than six months ago.

Maybe he was too busy with Amber, the voluptuous redheaded angel-born, to remember who I was. Jax was too pretty to be single, and it wasn't like he owed me anything. We'd only just met for a job from the council and then had parted ways. Perhaps it was just as well. Love, feelings, relationships—they complicated matters. My life was complicated enough, thank you very much.

"What about that kiss?" said Tyrius.

"That was nothing," I said, my voice flat. "It was just a kiss."

"I saw the way the two of you were looking at each other," said the cat, and I heard the dismissal in his voice. "If we weren't about to kick some demons' asses, you would have ripped each other's clothes off and done it right there and then."

"Tyrius!" I hissed, my eyes widening in shock.

The cat raised a brow. "You know it. And I know it."

"I do not."

"Admit it," the cat drawled. "That was *not* just a kiss."

My face flamed like it was on fire. Knowing Tyrius had witnessed the kiss made it worse. "I don't have time for romance," I said, aware of about a dozen faeries eyeing us from the street corner. A male with bright red hair licked his lips as he smiled at Tyrius, revealing his pointed teeth. "I'm not a romantic person either," I voiced, walking faster. "And I'm definitely not girlfriend material. I need to get my life in order first. Then… who knows."

Tyrius was silent for a moment. His graceful trotting turned into a guarded progression, like he felt something was about to jump him. "Is it me or have all the faeries from Mystic Quarter decided to grace us with their faerie presence tonight?"

Glad for the change in subject, my skin prickled as more and more fae stepped from the shadows and into the light of the moon, their hungry eyes on us. "They must know we're meeting with their queen. Maybe they're just curious," I said, but I pressed my palm into the pummel of my soul blade.

"Yeah. And maybe they're just hungry." Tyrius's fur stuck out on its end, giving the impression of more bulk. "Remind me why we're going to meet with the faerie princess again?"

"I've got twenty thousand reasons why." I looked down at the Siamese cat as we walked. "You've been in a bad mood all day. What's with the pissy attitude?"

"I broke a nail." Tyrius hissed at a faerie female with pigtails as she slipped from her group and tried to get closer. She made a face at the cat's reaction, causing her pretty features to warp and twist into something grotesque and animal-like. Strange how fast their beauty disappeared. Made me wonder if it was just a glamour.

"It's this fae business," said the baal demon. His eyes narrowed into slits. "I hate those pointy-eared bastards." He eyed the faerie girl, his eyes like tiny moons in the semi-darkness.

I opened my mouth to remark that he too had pointed ears, but then I decided it would just make him angrier. I was glad he was here. I didn't want him to get pissed at me too.

So, instead I said, "Get ready for more of these pointy-eared bastards." I motioned with my head towards the tall, gleaming black building. "There's Sylph Tower."

Across from us was a three-story building, the sort of place you could never look away from even though it gave you the creeps. It was a peculiar building, rumored to have been built by the faeries themselves in the likes of their demon forefathers' homes.

The building consisted of ridged, painted stucco on a cylindrical cement frame with rusty rain smeared on the outer walls so that gobbets of orange ran down the walls in streaks like blood. Strands of stucco stuck out, molded into points like big clumps of wet fur. It looked like a silo wearing a black fur coat.

I grimaced. It was the ugliest building I'd ever seen, and I'd seen my share of butt-ugly buildings.

"Thank God it's not too obvious or anything," I muttered. Pulse quickening, I crossed the street, squinting at the building as I headed toward it.

I'd crossed paths with Sylph Tower before, but I'd never actually been inside.

And now I wasn't sure I wanted to.

CHAPTER
5

"**T**he uglier and gaudier it is, the more the fae will like it," said Tyrius as he padded beside me. "Twenty bucks says it's even tackier on the inside."

A dark figure emerged from the shadows of a lamppost, and a spike of fear shot through me as it headed towards us. Heart pounding, I pulled my soul blade from my weapons belt—

"Oh, swell," said Tyrius, sounding a little bored. "It's the brooding vampire."

Sure enough, from the shadows rushed Danto, head of the Vampire Court here in New York City. Yes, he was a brooding vampire, but he was still gorgeous.

I sheathed my blade as I took him all in. He was barefoot, as always, and dressed in black slacks. His unbuttoned black shirt billowed behind him like a cape as he went, revealing his muscular bare chest and porcelain-like skin. He moved with a predatory grace, but he also had the traces of gentle elegance of the high born. He was ambitious, clever, beautiful, bold—and lethal.

He angled his head, his long black hair shifting with the movement and gleaming like oil, counterbalancing his pale skin. Those gray eyes sparkled in the moonlight as they fixed on me, making my pulse quicken. I couldn't help it. The vampire was just *way* too pretty.

Danto gave me a tight smile, nothing like the playful way he'd smiled at me before, with his full and very sensuous mouth. The pain of losing Cindy was still visible in the lines around his eyes and the tightness of his lips. His chiseled face looked older, and her death clearly still haunted him.

My chest clenched when I thought of Cindy and how she died. Guilt and regret still pulled at my heart that we couldn't save her. But it was nothing compared to the visible pain and suffering on the vampire's face. He wore it raw.

Still, a flutter of disappointment washed through me. It wasn't Jax. I'd sent Jax a text from my phone last night to tell him about my meeting with the faerie queen of the Dark Court, but I hadn't heard back. In fact, Jax hadn't returned my one phone call a week after Vedriel's death. I wasn't going to be that girl who kept on calling. I called and left a message. If he didn't call back, well, I could only guess at the reason why. He'd gotten what he wanted out of me, and that was solving the angel-born murders. It was a one-time-only, and now he was gone from my life. Perhaps forever. I had to start getting used to the idea.

Now I felt stupid that I *had* actually texted him. Great.

I watched the vampire as he closed the distance between us, wondering how he'd known we'd be here.

Danto's gray eyes met mine. "I heard you were coming to Mystic Quarter to meet with the faerie queen of the Dark Court," he said, as though he read my mind. Creepy.

I thought of the group of vampires I'd just seen watching us. "Nothing gets past you, huh?" Had his vamps been tailing me?

Danto shook his head, a hint of a smile on those perfect lips. "Not in Mystic Quarter, no. I have eyes and ears everywhere." His gaze turned intense. "I'm coming with you."

"Thanks, but there's really no need," I said, feeling the warmth of gratitude spreading around my chest. "I've got Tyrius for backup."

"Damn straight," said the cat, looking smug.

Danto kept his eyes on me, making me a little uncomfortable. "No." His voice was final. "I'm coming with you." He raised his hand and my protest died in my throat. "You'll be the first angel-born to ever set foot in that... that place. Whatever job she'll offer you is not just a job. It never is. You can't trust her. You can't believe anything she says."

I stared at the vampire, wondering how he knew about the job offer as well. "I thought faeries couldn't lie."

"That's a load of BS," laughed Tyrius. "It's more along the lines of they can't tell the truth."

"I know her," continued the vampire. "She has a way of twisting her words to make you do things you never wanted, never thought you could do. She's evil, really evil."

Frowning, I thought it strange that this old vampire would call another half-breed evil. I mean, he drank blood, for God's sake. And I'd heard and seen some of the wicked things Danto had done in the past. If he thought she was evil...

"Isobel likes to play her games," Danto said simply. "She gets rather bored in her tower, day after day. She likes to be entertained."

I scowled. "Well, I'm not here to entertain her." My thoughts of the queen coalesced into irritated anger.

"There's something in it for her. Always is." Danto's gray eyes darkened, as though holding on to some distant, horrific memory. I wondered if it was because she had vexed him somehow. "Don't think for a minute this is just another mark, another hunt. It's not." The vampire's hands were clenched into fists. "But know it's something else."

It was an odd thing to feel such warmth and coddling from a vampire, when my blood could be his meal. No doubt, it was even stranger for me to sense any affection, loyalty, and friendship. Because it was creeping up on me.

After killing the archangel Vedriel together, we had all bonded—the four of us. It was inevitable after sharing an experience like that. We couldn't just kill a lieutenant from Horizon's army and go home afterwards for some afternoon tea. Something had sparked in us, and I knew at that moment we'd be changed forever, marked with the blood of an archangel on our hands.

Wisps of his hair moved in a sudden breeze, and his face was shadowed, but real concern shone in his eyes.

Damn. I was starting to like this pretty vampire—in a platonic way, of course.

I shrugged. "But why? You don't owe me anything. You don't have to come."

The vampire looked away. "You're the closest thing I'll ever have to Cindy again."

Awkwaaard.

He was silent for a moment and then turned his attention back to me. "We're friends. As strange as it sounds, we are. Sylph Tower isn't safe. You need me with you both," he glanced at Tyrius.

The cat turned his face up at me, blue eyes gleaming. "I agree with the vampire. Three of us going to meet her royal-faerie-ass is much better than just the two of us. Danto says he knows her, and that could turn out to be handy… if she tries to stiff us."

"Okay then," I agreed. "Let's go." Tension crept along my spine as the three of us made our way towards the black tower. Danto's sudden appearance was flattering, but it also ticked me off a little that he thought I couldn't handle Her Highness on my own. We'd see about that.

Tyrius made an ugly sound in his throat to get our attention as he sauntered between Danto and me. "Vampire. What's up with you and the not-wearing-shoes part? I don't think I've ever seen you with something on your feet."

I stifled a laugh at the shocked expression that crossed Danto's face. He looked down at his feet as he walked. "I don't like having my feet confined. I prefer to feel the earth under my feet." He raised an eyebrow. "I don't see you wearing shoes either."

Tyrius's mouth fell open. "I'm a cat."

"You're a demon."

The cat's shoulders rose and dropped. "Same difference."

I pushed my nerves and my discomfort down and replaced them with the semblance of calm as we came up before the heavy wooden door. Silver and gold symbols were etched into the door, framing it like artwork in the language of the fae.

I looked at Danto. "How do we get inside? There's no handle."

"The non-fae can't enter without permission," said the vampire, and a muscle from his jaw feathered as though he was struggling with something. "The door is spelled. Only those who were invited can enter. You knock. And then you wait."

"Faeries," grumbled Tyrius as he sat back and curled his tail around his feet. "Always feel the need to make things overly complicated."

I sighed long and low. "I'm starting to regret coming here." Raising my fist, I noticed that it was shaking lightly. I pounded on the door, harder than I had intended.

We didn't have to wait long. Less than twenty seconds after I'd knocked, the door swung open to reveal a male faerie as tall as Danto with gangly limbs, pointed ears, and long raven hair. Green skin peered through his fae tattoos. I could smell the stink of rot and sweet candy rolling off of him, making my stomach churn. His cruel, pitch-black, depthless eyes met mine and held them.

A curved crossbow was pointed at my face, which really ticked me off. If he thought he was intimidating me with that thing, he was wrong.

I flashed him a smile that would make Amber proud. "Get that crossbow out of my face before I make you eat it." The male faerie's face was expressionless as he stood there without moving, gazing at me stonily, so I continued. "Put that damn thing down," I said again. "I'm here to see Isobel your queen. Rowyn Sinclair? She's expecting me." I looked over his shoulder, but all I saw was a corridor that ended in shadows.

The green faerie's eyes moved between Tyrius and Danto. "Just you," he said to me, his voice deep and rough as he lowered his crossbow.

Tyrius jumped to his feet and growled. "Whoa— wait a faerie-flipping moment! Rowyn is not entering this fae-infestation without us. You can just forget it."

"Uh, right, what he said." I gestured towards the Siamese cat as I crossed my arms over my chest and tilted my head. "Your choice. Either my friends come with me… or you can tell your little queenie that you turned me away. Not sure she'd like that since *she* invited me."

The faerie smiled at me, revealing slightly pointed teeth. "Angel-born female," he murmured, running an eye over me. "We've not seen one of you in Sylph Tower before."

I grinned. "Lucky me." Tyrius snickered as I uncrossed my arms and stood with my hands on my hips. "I don't have all night. Are we in or not?"

Without another word, the faerie gave a nod of his head and motioned for us to follow him.

I tapped the hilts of my blades with my fingers. I might have been going to my death, but I wouldn't arrive weaponless.

As soon as I crossed the threshold, I felt the cold, demonic energy from the faeries coursing into the room and throughout the tower. I could sense the intensity of their presence much more sharply than when I had wandered through the streets of Mystic Quarter. It was as if the energy had somehow become more concentrated, filling up the air, the ground, and even the walls surrounding us.

I felt like I was walking through a cave with low ceilings and tight spaces. Even the cold air had a faint moldy smell. Sconces lit with the green flames of demon fire lined the walls, casting hues of green throughout the corridor. The passage was deadly quiet except for the soft tread of our boots, feet, and paws, and the relentless pounding in my ears. We moved silently through a smooth-walled hallway etched with more of the same ornate fae writing along with images that portrayed faeries and demons in various scenes of battle. The same female fae was depicted over and over—battling a giant winged demon, cutting the head off what looked like a short-legged and squished face goblin, and lying in bed with many human men. Queen Isobel, no doubt, but I couldn't get a good look at her face without better light.

I had the feeling we were moving in a circle, a very big one. The floor was hard-packed dirt, and I thought it strange that it wasn't marble or some other elaborate polished stone that shimmered like jewels. Faeries loved to show off.

The male faerie never looked back as he led us through the cave-like maze. He had the same superior strut as the other male faerie who'd stolen my demon shifter mark.

I wonder if he'd get mad if I tripped him?

"Smells like regurgitated food in here," said Tyrius. "Or maybe it's Spam?"

"No, I think it's just the way faeries smell—like vomit." I smiled as I saw the faerie's shoulders tense, but he never looked back.

After a minute, a crack of brighter green light spilled through the semi-darkness. Two enormous stone doors rose before us, ancient, and etched with the same silver and gold faerie language that was painted on the front door. A cacophony of voices came from beyond the doors.

My pulse quickened, and I was beginning to regret my decision to meet with the fae queen. We strode through the doors and into a vast, circular chamber of carved limestone supported by four pillars whose tops disappeared into the darkness above.

Dark green vines with roses bursting in whites, reds, and pinks twined around the pillars. The male faerie led us down a path lined on either side with crabapple and apple trees in full blossom. Daisies, purple cone flowers, lavender and countless more roses were interspersed with the trees. The room was filled with green light, and I felt like I'd just stepped into a lush garden, not some cylindrical, butt-ugly tower.

Through the trees, I spotted crowds of faeries, some of them dancing to a low beat of drums, some milling about chatting, some sprawled on the ground—but all had their eyes on me, on us. There must have been at least a hundred faeries. I felt a spike in my blood pressure as I forced myself to keep my pace even. There was no way in hell I would show these faeries the effect they had on me.

Everything was a blur of black eyes, pointed teeth and fine clothing. Their faces were lovely, yet feral and thin, always too thin.

A dais stood before us, and lounging on a red couch surrounded by an assortment of lanky male and female faeries was a woman. No. Not a woman. A faerie queen.

"My Queen," said our escort, bowing low. "I have brought the Hunter and her… companions."

Our escort seemed to shrink back, as though he wasn't worthy to be in his queen's presence. But the queen didn't even look at him. Her eyes were on me.

Slowly, the queen slid up straight. Both sides of her head were hairless, and from the middle part of her head spilled tresses of raven hair down past her waist, like a Mohawk. She was nothing like I'd imagined. She was far, far worse.

Though parts of her face could be considered lovely, her snow-white skin was pulled and stretched too tightly over her sharp features, making her more petrifying than beautiful. Maybe it was the look she was going for—queen of the walking dead.

Her neck was just a little too long—as were her arms, legs and fingers—to pass for a human, almost insect-like. She wore a black gown that slipped and shifted with her movements like oil but no jewelry that I could see. A pale crown was woven through her hair above her head, and the more I stared, the more the crown looked like teeth. Flat *human* teeth. Damn. She was insane.

Her ebony eyes shone with a calculated coldness, and they were still fixed on me.

Fear slithered through me, but I pushed it down at the starkness of her expression. If she saw, smelled, or even just sensed my fear, I was a goner.

The air shifted behind me as I felt Danto's shoulder brush up against mine. I exhaled slowly. Never had I been happier to have a blood-sucking vamp so close to my jugular before.

The queen's eyes fell on Danto, and for a moment, her bulging red lips lifted into a sneer that was truly terrifying. Her dark eyes flashed with the hatred of some past history before her attention flicked back to me. Then just as quickly, she smoothed her features back into that brash, aristocrat demeanor.

"Rowyn Sinclair," purred the faerie queen, her voice silky and venomous like a snake's. "Glad you could come."

CHAPTER

6

I stood there, momentarily silent, holding the queen's gaze. There was no way in hell I would look away first. I knew how to play this game.

The corners of her mouth twisted at my defiance, her gaze shifting to the assembled faeries at the sound of boots treading against earth. I pulled my attention to my left as six male faeries stepped from the crowd and came to a collective halt before the dais, bows in their hands.

I recognized the tall, pale faerie male that killed my shifter demon. Bastard. He stood with his bow clasped in his hands before him, no doubt waiting for a sign from his beloved queen to shoot an arrow through my chest. I tried to get his attention, but he wouldn't meet my eyes.

The queen caught me looking and her ruby lips stretched into a terrifying smile.

That pissed me off. Tendrils of tension squeezed my chest, and all my warning flags went up as I heard Tyrius's deep growl.

I cocked an eyebrow at the queen. "I thought I was a guest here," I said, glad my voice came out leveled and strong, even though my stomach was in turmoil. "Is this," I gestured to the armed faerie males, "how you treat your guests? If so, you can kiss your job goodbye." I pulled out my gold coin, and after inspecting my Spaniard one last time, I tossed it in the air. It made a loud clang as it landed at the queen's feet. I had good aim, one of the many perks of having supernatural essence.

"Nice throw," whispered Tyrius as the fae that surrounded the queen hissed their outrage at what I had just done. I bit my tongue to keep myself from laughing—because *that* would get me in some seriously deep doo-doo.

The twinge of indignation on the queen's pallid face almost made me smile. Hell. It felt good to piss off a queen. I should have done it sooner.

The queen turned to the armed males and said something to them in a language that sounded both guttural and musical. As a collective, five of the six males broke away and disappeared under the crowds of faeries. That left only my blond faerie friend.

"Daegal is the commander of the Dark Arrows, my personal guard and trusted advisor. He will stay," said the queen, her lips curling to show pointed white teeth. "Better?"

Better? We were outnumbered about fifty to one, and she knew we could do nothing against all of them. Still, not having all those bows staring me in the face did loosen some tension.

I gave the queen a tightlipped smile. "Better." *What the hell am I doing here?*

The queen's eyes dropped to my hip and widened. "A death blade. So, the rumors are true," she said, a mixture of irritation and slight coating her voice. "You *are* part demon. How interesting."

Interesting? "So it seems." I matched her smile, not liking how she was looking at me as though wondering how my flesh would taste in her mouth.

Tyrius pressed his body against my leg and whispered, "Did you spy that crown on Her Majesty's head?"

"Yup." I stifled a shiver as I pulled my eyes from the creepy human-teeth crown and looked straight at the queen. "Why am I here? Your guard—Daegal—said you had a job for me. What is it?"

The queen looked slightly taken aback that I was speaking to her so directly instead of formally using her title of queen. She might have been queen of the faeries, but she was not my queen. I wasn't about to submit to her court or bow to anyone who wore a crown of human teeth.

"Yes," said the queen. "I have a job offer. Apparently one that pays well enough, or you wouldn't have bothered to come." She smiled knowingly at me, like she knew I was broke.

I was desperate. Not stupid. How could anyone trust a word that came out of those sausage-like lips?

As the queen tilted her head gracefully, the light of the demon fire pierced through the trees and sparked off the circlet of human teeth above her head.

"I need you to find a faerie for me," said the queen.

My mouth opened in shock. I was not expecting that.

Tyrius spat. "A faerie? Is she freaking kidding?" A row of hair spiked on his back. "We came to this stinking fae-fest for a freaking faerie?"

Queen Isobel leaned forward on her couch, her eyes on Tyrius. "And who might you be? Dinner?" Her eyes sparked. "Oh, you look delicious. Purebred meat is always more tender." At that the queen's courtiers all laughed, their eyes on Tyrius and their mouths open, salivating as though they had already fixed him on a plate of baal fillets.

Tyrius pulled back his lips in a smile and said in a clear voice, "I'm your faerie godmother. Hang on a second while I pull my magic wand out of my ass—"

"Tyrius!" I hissed under my breath, my eyes on Daegal as he shifted and his bow appeared in his hand. That damn faerie was quick.

"What?" Tyrius's blue eyes flashed as he looked up at me. "The Tooth Faerie just threatened me, Rowyn. I'm not going to just bend over and take it."

Heat rushed to my face as I felt a spike in my adrenaline. I hated faeries. But I *loathed* this queen with every fiber of my being.

The queen pressed her ruby red lips into a thin line, her face shining with a sudden terrible beauty. Isobel drew herself up, her eyes dark with murder. The energy in the room iced. The tension continued to build, and the seething gasps of the fae grew.

Shit. My heart pounded hard and my breath came fast. "Tyrius. Stop talking. Not a single word. You're going to get us killed." My fingers graced the hilt of my blade. If Daegal nocked an arrow, my soul blade would meet his neck first.

"Rowyn's right," came Danto's voice. He was close enough that I could smell old blood rolling off of him like cologne, a scent that made my stomach churn. Tension pulled his jaw tight. "This is not a fight we can win."

"Nonsense." Tyrius never stopped sneering up at the queen. "She won't kill us. She needs us. If she's desperate enough to call upon the services of a Hunter to find her missing faerie, she will do no such thing."

Sighing, I looked up and met the queen's glare, hoping Tyrius was right. "I'm going to need more details before I make my decision," I said to the queen.

Isobel gave an irritated glance at Tyrius before returning her eyes to me. "The faerie's name is Ugul." She pronounced his name like it tasted bitter in her mouth. "And he killed my son."

Now I was really curious.

The queen stiffened in her chair. She stared at me for a second, anger and pain on her face. Then they vanished, and she smiled. "I want you to find him and bring him to me. Alive."

I studied the queen's face. She must really want this faerie if she sought the help of little ole me. But there was something off with the way she was speaking to me, enunciating every word carefully like it was rehearsed. Even as her lips moved, her eyes spoke of something else.

"Do you have any idea where he is?"

The queen's face was blank of emotion as she said, "Elysium."

My eyes widened. Elysium in Greek mythology is the concept of afterlife, but to us paranormals, it was also an underground world in New York City, under Manhattan.

The truth was, the New York City legendary Mole People and Tunnel Dwellers were actually half-breeds living under Manhattan's abandoned tunnels, caverns and old subway systems. Most of them were castoffs from their clans, the sick and diseased, but some just preferred to live like moles. Elysium was gargantuan, with thousands of places to hide. No wonder they couldn't find this Ugul.

The queen's face was expectant but her eyes were hard, leaving me with the feeling there was something more she wasn't telling me. "That's it?" I asked. "You've got nothing more to give me?"

The queen gave me a level stare. "That is all you need to know."

I looked down at Tyrius and raised my brows.

"There's no lie in her words that I can sense," said the cat, reading the question in my mind.

Danto angled his head and I tried hard not to wince as I felt his hair brush against my neck. "But it doesn't mean that she's *telling* us *everything*."

The vampire leaned back and straightened, his eyes fixed on the queen. "Why did you summon Rowyn? Why not ask one of your Dark Arrows to search for this faerie?" His voice was now clear but filled with deep loathing, as though it took great effort just to speak to her. "Faeries never seek the help of outsiders because no one would ever trust you, and for good reason."

Queen Isobel sneered, her features pulled back and making her look feline. "Why are *you* here, vampire?"

The faint tightening of Danto's jaw was the only sign of his resentment. "I'm here to make sure you don't screw Rowyn over with this *request*. I know you. I know what you've done… what you're capable of. I won't let you harm her."

Heat rushed to my face, and I prayed to the souls no one had noticed. My nerves stretched as tightly as a piano wire.

The queen's face twisted in a wicked smile. "And I know you, Danto de Luca." Danto had gone very still. "You are no leader. You don't deserve the title of Head vampire. It was never yours to take."

I sucked in a breath and looked at Tyrius, who gave me a hell-if-I-know shrug. What the hell was this? When I looked at Danto, his face was rigid with frustration, but he wouldn't look at me.

Isobel's smile widened at Danto's discomfort. "The title was only granted to you because you were the Elder vampire, Oros's, favorite. We all know what that old fool did. We know Oros changed the votes in your favor." Isobel clicked her tongue. "The vampires don't support you. They felt cheated out of their vote." She bared her teeth. "Stefan is the true Head vampire in the New York Court. Not you. He had the support, and you stole the votes from him. You will never have the support of the other Vampire Courts."

Damn. I felt like I'd just stepped in a vampire-faerie soap opera. I thought I knew Danto from working as a Hunter. We'd crossed paths many times over the years. Turns out, I didn't really know him at all.

"I wish I'd brought some popcorn," said Tyrius, his mouth twitching. "This is some pretty heavy stuff."

I didn't feel like being drawn into the faerie-vampire drama, but I couldn't just turn around and leave. I hadn't decided if I wanted to take the job or not. If nothing else, it might provide me with some valuable insight on the vampire's character and the queen's.

"Stefan is one of yours. Isn't he? One of your pawns?" accused Danto, leaning slightly forward, his toes splayed in the dirt floor. "How many Vampire Courts have you been bribing over the years? Corrupting and manipulating their minds with your lies? Ten? A hundred? Your efforts to kill and pollute lives have always been to acquire more power for yourself." Danto's jaw pulled tightly, his hands in murderous fists. "You wanted to sink your claws into the Vampire Courts. You wanted to control them. Oros knew this. He knew what you were trying to do. It's why he changed the votes and made me Head vampire."

"You're not the leader of anything," hissed the queen. "You and that angel-born whore you flaunted around. You are a disgrace to your race. You bring shame to the New York City Court."

Danto's features darkened, and without warming, his eyes blackened. Shit. He was going to vamp out. My blood pounded in my veins. If he did anything, if he lashed out, we were all dead.

"Danto," I pressed, and added calmly, "don't do anything stupid. It's not why we're here, why you came. Remember? You came for me. Danto?"

Isobel laughed. "Give me one reason why I shouldn't destroy you where you stand, vampire. No one will care if I end your life. I'll be doing the Vampire Courts a favor." Her pointed teeth gleamed as she gave him her snake-like smile.

"Uh, Rowyn." The panic in Tyrius's voice pulled my attention to him. "The vampire's about to blow."

Sure enough, Danto's fangs and claws were out. I couldn't trust that he'd keep calm in this situation. If I didn't do something now, we'd all end up as meatloaf for the faeries.

I took a deep breath and looked up to address the queen. "This is all very informative, but I didn't come here to hear about your drama." My voice echoed throughout the whole chamber as clearly as if I'd been shouting. "I have to agree with my friend the vampire," I said, looking at Danto. His eyes were still black but I saw fingernails, not claws at the ends of his hands, and some tension had left his body. "You are fae," I said, as I flicked my eyes back to the queen. "Why not have your faeries take care of this? Why me?"

The queen leaned back into her sofa and crossed her legs very slowly, her clash with the vampire forgotten as her full attention focused on me. "Because they failed." The queen gave a dark glare in Daegal's direction. "It's why you're here, Rowyn Sinclair. Why I need you. You're my last hope at finding my son's killer. Come now, Hunter," Isobel said. Her lip curled back, revealing too-sharp canines, which gave me the creeps as I stared into her black eyes. "Do we have a deal? Will you help me find my son's killer?"

A band tightened around my chest, squeezing me as I turned her words over, looking for traps and loopholes within her wording. But it all sounded right.

"What do you want to do, Rowyn?" asked Tyrius. His worried expression pulled at my chest. "You want this or not? You don't have to say yes. We'll find another way to get that twenty grand. We can all leave now and forget we've ever met the Tooth Faerie," he added loudly enough for Her Majesty to hear. I loved that stupid cat.

No, I didn't have to say yes, but with the due date approaching I knew this job was my best chance at saving my grandmother's home. Looking for a single faerie didn't seem all that bad. Hell, it was almost too easy.

"What about payment?" I wasn't about to go hunting a faerie for Her Highness without some sort of payment. I wasn't stupid.

The queen lifted a hand and gestured to her Dark Arrow commander. "Give Daegal your bank account details and we'll wire you ten thousand tonight. I'll keep ten thousand as a security deposit, which you will get when you bring me the faerie."

"And what if I can't find your faerie... will you send your Dark Arrows after me?" I said, remembering stories my grandmother told me about angel-born going into Elysium to never be seen again. I'd also heard that it was plagued with Rifts, demon portals that would open up and suck you away to the Netherworld.

The queen sighed, visibly biting back her annoyance. "I would never do that, silly Rowyn," the queen purred and sent goose pimples all over my skin. "And before you ask, you can keep the ten thousand for your trouble."

"It's never that easy," I countered, having suffered my share of unhappy clients when things didn't turn out the way they wanted—usually asking for their money back.

"It is," said the queen, "you have my word."

Right. Like that meant anything to me. How could I trust a faerie with a crown of human teeth on her head? I didn't. But I trusted Tyrius with my life, and when he gave a slight nod of his head, I knew the queen was truthful—or at least she thought she was.

"You'll get your money," said the queen. "I'll trust you to fulfill your end of the deal, Hunter. You come highly recommended in the community."

My eyes fell on Daegal and I flinched when I realized he'd been staring at me this whole time. His tiny smirk sent a new wave of heat to my face. The bastard was daring me to say yes, like he thought I was afraid to take the job. Hell no. I was not afraid of some faerie.

"Well?" Queen Isobel demanded as she picked at her nails, and warning bells resonated in my mind. "Do you accept? Will you bring me Ugul?"

My pulse quickened at the thought of what I was about to do. Me? Hunting for a faerie? I hated faeries.

I glanced at Tyrius one last time before I said, "You have a deal. I'll find your bloody faerie."

CHAPTER
7

Tyrius lay on my bed on his back, legs splayed on either side of him exposing his belly. We'd been going over the Manhattan subway and Amtrak maps for most of the night and early morning, looking at some points of entry that we both knew existed, specifically an entrance at the Riverside Drive viaduct. Elysium was a massive network of passageways, and we were both tired and grumpy by the time the sun was up and spilling yellow rays through my kitchen window over the empty pizza box.

And then Tyrius started moaning.

"What's wrong now?" I asked, pulling my eyes from the maps on my laptop's screen and blinking back the eye-burn I always got from staring too long and too close at a computer screen. "Hairball?"

The Siamese cat's head lolled to the side. "I feel fat."

I let out an exasperated breath and shook my head. "You should have thought of that before you ate four slices of pizza. I mean... in that tiny body... where does it all go?"

The cat sprang up on his feet, tail in the air. "Do you want me to tell you?"

"You're a pain in my ass. That's what you are," I grumbled, wiping my eyes and feeling an ache at the back of my neck. "Where do you want to start looking? This Ugul character could be anywhere."

After leaving Sylph Tower and her royal faerieness, Tyrius had made me promise to take him with me on my hunt for the faerie. But when I had turned expectantly to Danto, he seemed only to want to put some distance between us and had left without saying goodbye. No doubt, he was embarrassed that we had heard the queen's words. It painted a very different picture of my vampire friend, a more mysterious one.

Unease had welled in my chest as I had watched the vampire disappear into the night. Strange how things had changed. I actually gave a damn about a blood sucking vamp. Who knew I was so sensitive? Maybe I was losing my mind. Or perhaps my perception had changed now that I knew Danto and I had something in common—we both had demon essence flowing in our veins. But something in the way his eyes shone with betrayal and pain had left me concerned.

I knew about the Vampire Courts and how they governed themselves, but I'd never heard of the vampire Oros. Guess that was before my time. If anyone could get bored to death with angel-born or half-breed politics, it was me. But if what the queen said was true, Danto was an outcast among his own kind—just like me.

Vampires never stayed that way for very long, especially if his fellow kin felt as though he'd cheated them. Sooner or later Danto would be hunted and killed.

"What do you know of this vampire Stefan?" I asked as I leaned back in my chair.

Tyrius stopped washing and looked across, eyes narrowing to frowning slits. "That he's a nasty piece of work. He gets off by drinking the blood of virgins, right before he snaps their necks."

"Nice," I said, stifling a shiver.

"And if he's in bed with the sweet faerie queen of the Dark Court, he's even worse. Only the truly evil would take sides with that crazy half-breed bitch." The cat's tail quivered straight out behind him. "If I were to guess, I'd say she tried and failed to get Stefan the vote. She's probably planning on Danto's replacement with Stefan as we speak. It sucks, but the brooding vampire's days are numbered."

"Why?" I asked, feeling suddenly awake. "What's in it for her?"

Tyrius shrugged. "Nothing good. The fae and the vampires have always been sworn enemies. I've never heard of any coven or clan from the different races working together. I think we're missing something here."

"I agree, but we don't have time to get into all that right now." I slumped in my chair thinking of coffee and how good it would taste down my throat. "Aren't there maps of Elysium?" I said between yawns. "Maybe Bemus and Mani might have one?" I pushed my chair back and went in search of coffee in my kitchen.

"Maps of Elysium don't exist," mewed Tyrius, his pink tongue darting as he cleaned his front right paw.

"Why not?" I whirled around with a scoop of coffee grounds in my hand. "That seems a little weird... even for us."

"Personally, I think it's because no one ever bothered to make one," said the cat. "But it could have something to do with the fact that the place keeps changing. New tunnels keep popping up. Doorways appear and disappear. It's cursed. It's like a living maze."

"Great. Why do I get the feeling I got screwed?"

His eyes widened. "You're making coffee?" With a single bound, Tyrius leaped on the kitchen counter and padded over to me. He raised a questioning brow as he sat next to the coffee machine. "Is it organic? You know what pesticides do to my coat."

I shook my head. "Yes—I mean—no. Tyrius. You know what happens when you have coffee. You're... not yourself. I've seen cats on catnip, but you on coffee... you're like *a hundred* cats on catnip combined. Remember what happened the last time? Father Thomas had to hose you down to keep you from ruining his garden."

"How can I forget," mumbled Tyrius. "The priest had me nailed to the wall with his hose—that sounded dirty. Oh, come on. Just a sip. I promise I won't spaz out." He put his right paw to his forehead. "Baal's honor. Besides, I need a little kick. We've been at this all night. I. Deserve. Some. Coffee."

"You are a spaz. But a cute one," I laughed as I poured the water into the coffee machine and then added the coffee and pushed the on button. The smell of the beans was intoxicating, rejuvenating me with only its aroma.

"They say Elysium is the closest doorway to the Netherworld," continued the cat, as he eyed the coffee dripping into the glass mug. I swear I could see drool forming at the corners of his mouth. "And by closest I mean like right next to it, where the planes from the two worlds meet. That's why if you open a door, it could very well be your last door since demons of the Netherworld might be waiting on the other side to pull you in."

Yikes. And I was going there.

I wasn't claustrophobic, but the idea of being underground in tight spaces, not knowing where we were going in the cursed maze, with demons and half-breeds lurking in the shadows had my blood pressure rising.

After I'd poured a small amount of coffee in a small bowl, I placed it in front of Tyrius. Glancing at my phone on the counter, my thoughts drifted to Jax and my heart seemed to fall to my gut. A tendril of heat rose from my neck to my face as I remembered his kiss. His square jaw and nearly hairless, muscular chest. Back to those damn lips again…

I was being an idiot. And then I got mad at myself for *letting* myself think about him.

"Stop sulking. It doesn't suit you."

I pulled my eyes from my phone to find Tyrius staring at me, his white whiskers stained in brown.

"I'm not." *Liar. Liar. Liar.*

Tyrius made a strangled sound in his throat, and his eyes were full of amused disbelief as he licked his lips. "Right. You're just mad because you like him and he hasn't called you back."

"I don't like him." I wanted to kick myself. Not hearing from him had left an aching emptiness in my soul that had never been there before. I never got torn up about guys, never let my guard down, never let myself get attached because when I did, things got complicated. I hated complicated. I didn't have time for complicated. My life was complicated enough as it was. No need to add drama. So, what was happening to me?

"You like him," repeated Tyrius. "And I don't even have to be a baal demon to know you're lying. I just have to look at your face. It's all red."

I bit my lip as more waves of heat splashed all over my face, knowing I probably looked like a freaking tomato. "Drop it, Tyrius. I'm too tired."

"And he did kiss you. That's got to be messing with that head of yours." Tyrius's eyes flashed. "I'm getting a buzz."

I shook my head. "I just thought he was my friend. That's all. Now, I'm not so sure—"

A knock pounded on my front door.

I flinched. Heart pounding, I spun to look at the door while I pulled slowly away from the counter.

"You expecting company? Father Thomas, perhaps?" whispered Tyrius. When I looked back at him, he was starting to shake from the effects of the coffee, making him look like he was about to Hulk-out. *Great. That's all I need now, a giant baal high on coffee.*

I mouthed the word "no," and pulling out my soul blade, I tiptoed to the door.

The door shook on its hinges as someone pounded on it again and again. I doubted it was a demon or a half-breed. They never *knocked*. And whoever this was, it was clear by the thunderous door-beating they were impatient.

Wrapping my hand around the handle, I yanked the door open and pointed my soul blade at a pair of pink bejeweled glasses attached to a plump, twenty-something woman. Her blue eyes were round and full of fear.

I lowered my blade. "Pam? What are you doing here?" I stepped aside to let her in and closed the door behind me. I had no idea the angel-born knew where I lived. Pam wore an r-shaped birthmark on her forearm, marking her as being from House Raphael, the angel-born house that formed healers and doctors. She was as clever as they came.

"I know. I know. I'm sorry to show up so early at your front door like this," said Pam, slightly out of breath as she stepped into my living room. "I just... didn't know what else to do."

I frowned at her flushed face and the worry in her tone. Her red hair was pulled back into a messy bun, showing off her rosy cheeks. A white lab coat was stretched around her thick middle, making me wonder if she'd left in a hurry or if lab coats were her usual apparel of choice.

"Pam!" Tyrius leaped from the counter and raced over to Pam, his tail in the air as he rubbed his face over her legs repeatedly. "Ah... the smell of formaldehyde."

Concern flashed over Pam's face. "What's the matter with him?" She knelt down and began examining the cat's head and eyes, even opening his mouth and checking his teeth.

I sheathed my blade. "Coffee."

Pam just looked at me but said nothing as Tyrius toppled over and exposed his belly. He began purring loudly as soon as Pam's fingers raked his fur. Her face broke into a smile. I wasn't sure who was enjoying themselves more, Pam or the baal.

An exasperated sigh shifted from me. "Pam? What's going on?"

"It's Jax," she said, her fingers gently stroking Tyrius's fur as though he was the last cat on earth. "I haven't heard from him in over three weeks. We always keep in touch. We'd made a promise when we were little that we'd always look out for one another, no matter what."

"What gives you the impression something's wrong?" I asked, hearing a tinge of fear in my voice that I hoped Pam didn't pick up on.

With some effort, Pam straightened, leaving spread-eagle Tyrius at her feet looking like a dead cat. She pushed her glasses up her oily nose with a trembling finger.

"Because," she said, her face flustered, "he hasn't returned any of my phone calls or texts. That's never happened before."

A feather of tension loosened from me, knowing Jax wasn't just ignoring me. But it was immediately replaced again, tightening my gut, by the shifting fear and worry on Pam's face. When I moved my gaze over her clothes and her hair, she looked like she'd slept in her clothes for the past few days or hadn't slept at all.

Pam's gaze turned intense. "Something's wrong. I can feel it in my bones."

"So what do you want me to do?" I said, not fully understanding what she expected from me. "I haven't heard from him either, and you're one of his closest friends." A glimmer of hope flashed in her big round eyes, and at that moment I knew what she wanted from me. I moved to the kitchen and leaned my back against the counter.

"You want me to track him. Don't you?"

A loud sigh of relief brought Pam's shoulders down. "Would you, Rowyn?" Her eyes were bright and shimmering, and she blinked fast. "It would mean so much to me."

How could I say no to that? "Sure." I looked at Tyrius who was ignoring me completely, his full attention focused on Pam.

It was going to be tight. I couldn't sacrifice more than a few hours to find Jax. The bank thing was coming up in five days, so waiting just a day more would be problematic. But I also wanted to find out what was going on with Jax. Now I had an excuse. I wasn't doing this for me. I was doing it for Pam. *Yeah, right.*

"Well, since you know him better than all of us," I began, "where do you suppose I start looking?" I was a Hunter, a demon and half-breed Hunter, not a private investigator. I killed demons for a living. But was there really a difference between tracking a faerie and tracking an angel-born?

"Try his parents' place." Pam's shoulders tightened, and her sudden relief was replaced by a sullen expression. "I would go myself but…"

That got my attention. "But what?"

Pam's face went ashen as she pulled her gaze from me and looked at the floor. "His mother hates me. The last time I went over to see Jax, she shut the door in my face."

I watched the pain and embarrassment on Pam's face and I felt my anger rise. I couldn't imagine anyone being that nasty to Pam. She was such a kindred spirit, a good and kind soul. How could anyone treat her that way? Now I really wanted to meet this woman.

"She sounds like a bitch," mewed Tyrius, who seemed to have recovered from his caffeine-induced coma as he sat.

"Jax lives with his parents?" I thought it strange that a man his age, albeit still young, would still be living at home, but then again the angel-born weren't like regular humans. I'd heard of families that shared their homes with their children and their grandchildren—given that they were large enough to fit them all.

Shaking her head, Pam pinched her lips and said, "No. He has a place of his own in Parks Hollow but I've already checked there. The doorman says he hasn't seen Jax in weeks."

"Maybe he's vacationing in Europe," I offered. "Doesn't he have family in France somewhere?"

Pam's glasses slipped further down her nose as she shook her head. "He always answers my calls, even when he's overseas or just out of town. This is different." She pulled off her glasses and rubbed her eyes. "Sometimes when he thinks about his sister," she added, putting her glasses back on, "when he's in that state of mind, he goes there, to his parents' place."

Suddenly, Pam's face reddened two shades darker. "I'm sorry. You must think I'm an idiot. I know. I know. I'm overthinking this. Jax is a skilled warrior. I'm sure he's fine but... but it's just... I'm worried about him. That's all." She met my eyes. "Something's wrong, Rowyn. I know it."

I reached out, grabbed her hand and squeezed, surprising myself. "Don't worry," I said, feeling Tyrius's eyes on me as I let her go. "I'll find him. And I'm sure it's nothing. Maybe he just needed some time to himself to clear his head after all that's happened."

"Cindy's death probably brought up some dark and painful memories about his sister," said Tyrius. "That's got to do a number on anyone."

Pam nodded, her eyes growing dull and her face paling. "That's what worries me." She swallowed, as though bracing herself for what she was about to say next. "The last time we spoke he said he knew... knew who killed Gillian." Her eyes lingered on my face, her lips trembling as she asked, "Is that true?"

Crap. I could see she wished it wasn't. I'd seen how desperate Jax had been to find his sister's killer, and now with the demon's name, I knew he'd done something stupid. Something very, very stupid, like go after it. *Alone.*

Tyrius shifted nervously on his feet, his tail twitching behind him, and I knew he was thinking the same thing.

Jax had gone after the rakshasa demon. Damn.

"Yes, it's true," I said softly, straining to continue looking at her as I saw the panic shifting in her eyes like a storm. "The demon Degamon gave us its name. Strax. And it's a rakshasa demon, just like I thought."

Pam's face blanched as she nodded solemnly. "I remember. The ones that shape change and feed on the souls of the young and offer their victims' hearts as a sacrifice to their master."

"That's the ones," said Tyrius.

Pam had gone still, too still. Real pain and fear shone in those blue eyes. She swayed on her feet, and for a horrible moment I thought she was about to pass out.

Pam threw her hands in the air making Tyrius jump. "He's gone after it! The idiot has gone after it!" She leaped forward and grabbed my shoulders faster than I thought possible for someone her size. "Rowyn!" She shook me. "You have to find him."

Her eyes were brimming with tears, and I could tell she was trying to keep her emotions under control. But her fear was slipping through. "He's not thinking clearly. I'm afraid for him. I know what he's capable of when he's like this. I'm afraid of what he might do."

Fear coiled in my stomach as I remembered how crazed Jax had been at the vampire club, V-Lounge. I knew how easily he could lose control when it involved demons and half-breeds, how he'd lose himself to that hunger of revenge for his sister's death.

Rakshasa demons were slippery bastards, and very deadly. I'd never killed one myself, but they were rare and extremely hard to track and kill.

A chill scurried down my spine. It had been months since I'd last seen Jax. But it wasn't just the rakshasa demon that had my insides tightening into a ball until I forgot to breathe.

There was also the Greater demon Degamon's claim on Jax's name. My blood went cold. With Jax's name, the demon would have total control over him. Without the proper protection spells, charms, and pendants, Jax was a demon puppet. I'd read how to do it in the dark witch's grimoire, but I'd never even had the chance to tell him how to protect himself since he'd never returned my call.

What if Jax wasn't Jax anymore?

Jax... what the hell have you done?

I took a breath, exhaling long and slow, and I felt Tyrius's eyes on me. He probably knew what I was about to say even before I said it. Being soft got you killed in my line of work. When I started the hunting business, I'd made a promise to myself to never mix personal matters with the job and never get personally involved with anyone on the job. Deaths were common in my line of work, and I couldn't deal with having someone I cared about die without getting emotionally compromised. Not after losing my parents. I wasn't going to go through that again. Ever.

I might not be involved, but I was attached.

Damn it. I cared for the idiot. The faerie queen would have to wait. I wasn't about to abandon Jax to some unforeseen future as a demon's pet—or worse.

Panic fluttered at the edge of my mind and I forced myself to breathe. "Don't worry, Pam," I said, seeing a slight release of tension in her shoulders. "I'll find Jax. I promise."

I just hope I'm not too late.

CHAPTER
8

It was safe to say that the rich *never* took the bus.

Tyrius and I had to make the long hike up Maplehurst Road since the closest stop to Jax's parents' house was two miles away. Well, I walked while Tyrius rode on my shoulders, commenting on the foliage, the flowered gardens, the paved walkways and the manicured front lawns.

"OMG. Look, a hedge of New Dawn roses! They must have cost a fortune. Don't they smell divine," exclaimed Tyrius, his whiskers tickling my cheek.

"Not really." I liked roses, truly I did. I just wasn't in the mood to talk gardening with a baal demon.

I was tired, cranked up like a top. I hadn't been able to stop my heart from hammering in my chest since Pam had left my apartment two hours ago. My mind was a constant battle. There was so much pain, despair, guilt and fear. I gnawed on my lower lip, weighing the risks of what I was about to do by getting so involved and waiting to feel any kernel of fear or emotion.

I'd tried to get some much-needed sleep once Pam had left earlier this morning, but I was so wired with the thoughts of Jax and the demon Degamon that sleep wouldn't come.

It was my fault Degamon had Jax's name. *I* had summoned the demon thinking I was cleverer than it, believing I had the upper hand with the name of its summoner. Turns out I was wrong. The dark witch Evanora Crow hadn't summoned the demon. The archangel Vedriel had. I never saw that coming. And in my foolishness, I had probably ruined Jax's life. I had probably signed his death warrant and had probably killed him. Swell.

Gritting my teeth, I walked faster and climbed harder, my thighs pulsing with stamina fed by fear and guilt. Fear was the mightiest weapon of all… and I hated it. I had to make things right.

The fear fed me with a surge of adrenaline, easing my way up the hill as though I were skipping all the way down instead.

My face burning, I cursed Jax for the kiss he'd slipped past my mental shields. I reinforced them as I hurtled up the hill.

"You okay?" Tyrius's warm breath rubbed the side of my neck. "You're not talking. When you're upset about something, you shut down. What's on your mind, Rowyn? Green eyes... strong shoulders... full lips?"

"I'm fine," I lied. "I just want to get this over with so I can concentrate on finding the faerie—you know, the paying job. The one that's going to save grandma's house?"

"Right. And I'm a furry cupid."

I made a face, trying to erase that image from the inside of my eyelids.

Tyrius shifted his weight on my shoulders. "What do we do if he's not there?"

My boots clanked the cement sidewalk that sparkled as though it were made of granite. "Then, I guess we go look for the rakshasa demon. It's the only other lead we have. Unless his parents know something."

"And that's *if* they're willing to share," said the cat. "You heard what happened with Pam."

The afternoon sun was high and bright as we made the climb. The cool September wind whipped my hair around and soothed my hot face. Once we crested the hill, houses became larger but fewer, peeking from long driveways that snaked around larger lots. Estates. These were no regular houses. These were mansions.

Tyrius swore. "Damn. It pays to be part angel. Doesn't it? How much does the Legion pay you people? Only lords of the Netherworld have digs like this, and that's if they can stay on top of the souls business."

"The souls business?"

"Mortal souls are like money in the Netherworld," said the cat. "The more you have, the more powerful you are."

I frowned, unable to put the words to my mouth. My eyes darted to a red brick house with tall Roman pillars at the front. I wondered what it must have been like to grow up in a neighborhood like this. It must have been awesome.

"Which one is Jax's?" said Tyrius after a moment.

My gaze fell on the estate across from us, sprawled within rolling green fields. A two-story Tudor manor house was arranged around a central courtyard. The grounds were framed by woods overlooking a large spring-fed pond that was occupied by a flock of Canadian geese and a great blue heron.

I pointed to the Tudor house. "That one." My awe might have subdued my fear had I any room left for that emotion. I didn't.

"Are you sure this is where Jax's parents' live?" asked Tyrius, his voice holding traces of amazement and shock.

I checked my phone for Pam's text. "That's the address Pam gave me." I smiled. "Close your mouth before you swallow some flies."

Tyrius snorted and leapt off my shoulders, landing gracefully and soundlessly on the ground. "Nothing wrong with a little protein snack."

My pulse quickened as we crossed the street and made our way towards the elegant Tudor home. My boots crunched on the gravel path that separated a garden of rose bushes, lilies, and tall maple trees before leading to the main doors of the house.

No cars were parked in the driveway as I stepped up to the impressive double doors, Tyrius at my heels. I pressed my finger on the doorbell, which was in the form of a lion's head. In another time, I would have taken a few minutes to admire the gardens and the home's architecture, but tension had manifested into a pounding headache.

"Stop fidgeting. It makes you look nervous," said Tyrius, sounding like my grandmother.

I glared at him. "I'm not."

"Uh, Rowyn?"

"I'm not fidgeting!" I hissed.

The cat quirked a questioning brow as he stared at my hips. "You think it's wise to bring a death blade—the weapon that *kills* angels—to an angel-born house?"

Blood drained from my face. "Shit." Panic jerked me into motion as I flung my death blade from my weapons belt. Turning on the spot, my chest contracted as I desperately threw my gaze around to find a spot where I could hide it. *There.* I leapt to the large green ceramic pot spilling with white impatiens and red geraniums and shoved my death blade in the soil until it was covered.

"There, that should do it," I said, stepping back and putting my hands on my hips, just as the front doors swung open.

A man stepped from the threshold and I jerked to a halt. I was expecting to see Jax's mother, having mentally prepared a clever one-liner should she have attempted to slam the door in my face. But this was a male, and something told me by his dark hair and eyes as well as the harsh looks of him, he wasn't Jax's father.

The man towered over me and I needed to arch my head back to see all of him. Gray peppered his temples, staining his otherwise dull black hair, which was cut short but without style, and he held himself with confidence. His long, hawk-like nose and permanent frown were cemented to his lightly wrinkled face. He wore a pair of gray slacks with a black business shirt, which fit him perfectly. Through the collar of his shirt, I spied a P-shaped birthmark on his neck. The archangel Michael's sigil. He was from House Michael. Just like Jax.

"Yes?" said the man, his voice slightly mocking at the sight of us.

Tyrius snickered. "Is it me, over have we just stepped into an episode of *Downton Abbey*? He's a bit dingy for a butler, but who's judging."

The cigarette and lighter in his hand told me otherwise. The man lowered his brows in annoyance. Maybe a family member or a friend?

The man's eyes rolled over me, *very* slowly, his eyebrows rising with each inch. "Who are you?"

"She's the Mother of Dragons," Tyrius intoned, "and I'm—"

"My name's Rowyn, Rowyn Sinclair," I said quickly before Tyrius got the door slammed in our faces. A slight twitch in his brows told me he'd heard of me. "I'm looking for Jax. Is he here?" I raised my head trying to see past the man's large shoulders, but all I saw was wood paneling.

The man's gaze was cold and intense. His eyes were a dark brown almost black, and the more I stared back, the more I realized he wasn't blinking. *That* was creepy.

And I hated the smile that twitched on his thin lips as he said, "Rowyn Sinclair. The Hunter. I've heard a *lot* about you. And none of it paints a pretty picture. There are some pretty crazy things said about you."

"Well, I specialize in crazy." I met the man's cold gaze as Tyrius snorted. "Is Jax here? Yes or no."

He leaned against the threshold and gestured with his hand. "He's here. You can wait in the den while I fetch him."

I let go of the breath I didn't realize I was holding. "He's here? *Here...* in this house?" My pulse hammered in my chest. *Jax is alive!*

"Yes, that's what I said," replied the man, enunciating every word as though he were speaking to a small child.

Relief had my knees wobbling and I struggled to keep my emotions from showing. Jax was here. He was alive and safe. But then why hadn't he called? Why hadn't he called Pam?

I smiled down at Tyrius and made my way forward—

The man stuck out his foot. "Not the baal demon. Mrs. Spencer is allergic, and she won't have them in the house. Just you."

My temper flared as I was tempted to kick his foot out of our way. "We're a team. He goes where I go."

The man stiffened in repugnance. "Not here, it doesn't. Like I said, no *animals*."

Tyrius flashed the tall man his tiny pointed teeth. "I promise I won't shed."

The man ignored Tyrius. "You can either wait outside or come in without the demon. Your choice."

I'd made up my mind to wait outside, but Tyrius brushed up against my leg, interrupting my answer.

"It's fine," the cat said dryly and then glanced up at me. "I'll wait for you here. I think you guys need to talk privately anyway," he winked and sat on the step. "But if you need me, just give a holler and I'll hear it..." his eyes fixed the man. "This *animal* has very good hearing."

I bit the inside of my cheek to stifle the laugh that threatened to explode out of my mouth and followed the stranger in.

I gasped. The outside was remarkable, but the inside was stunning. Miles of crafted wood paneling extended in every direction, all polished and glowing. A grand, double sided staircase split the house in half. And I smiled imagining Jax sliding down the banister as a child.

The walls were decorated with paintings and warm wainscoting. All the furniture looked like a nineteenth-century design, elegant with lots of wood detail.

Following the man, I stepped into a room left of the staircase. It had a very masculine feel, with lots of brown leather sofas and chairs and dark polished wood, which stood out handsomely against the white walls. An antique Persian carpet in deep shades of wine, blue, and gold stood out against the dark wood floors.

At the end of the room was an enormous limestone fireplace, which was empty at the moment but could have been suitable for roasting a deer. Light spilled through tall windows, bathing the room in a golden glow.

Over the mantel was an enormous portrait of a light-haired beauty in a blue gown. *Mrs. Spencer?* No. Her face was round and youthful. It was a girl, around eleven or twelve, and she had the same eyes as Jax—

"Wait here," said the man, jerking my attention back to him. "And don't touch *anything*." He turned on his heels and disappeared around the corridor.

And don't touch anything. Right, because all Hunters were thieves. So, of course I had to touch everything now.

Smiling, I crossed the room to the bookcase and ran my fingers along the edges. Sighing, I grabbed a small statue type carving of a man with a sword. Not a man, but an angel. I set it back and ran my fingers over the spines of books, wondering what it must be like to own such a fine library.

My mind went to Jax. I wasn't sure whether to punch him or kick him when I saw him.

My eyes fixed on a picture frame. There was Jax, maybe ten years old and beside him a girl about the same age and wearing his face. Gillian, his twin sister. She looked just like him, but in a feminine sort of way. They were so cute together, laughing freely in the way all children do. And I felt a pang in my chest. She had died not long after the picture was taken.

My eyes darted to the walls where more pictures of Gillian looked back at me. There must have been fifty frames, and they were mostly Gillian. She was everywhere—baby pictures, when she and Jax were toddlers, birthdays and trips—but it was obviously mostly her.

"This is a shrine," I whispered under my breath, the hairs on the back of my neck rising. I felt wrong just standing in this room, like I'd stepped into someone's private memory—

"Rowyn Sinclair, what a surprise," came a woman's voice, melodic but firm.

I spun around. A beautiful woman with hair the color and texture of honey tied at the base of her head in a heavy, low knot stood in the doorway, regal and icy. She wore fitted black pants with a matching top. She was fit, the sort from working out for years in the gym, and shorter than me, even with her heels giving her two inches more height. Thin lines creased her forehead and around her large green eyes. A glass of red wine was clasped in her hands, her fingers bejeweled with every possible precious stone. Her eyes were fixed on me. Jax's eyes. The face was older, but it was the same face as in the portrait above the fireplace.

Yup. I was looking at Jax's mother, and her expression was one of pure disgust.

CHAPTER
9

I wasn't sure I liked the way she was staring at me, as though I were a rat standing on her expensive Persian rug.

"Mrs. Spencer," I said in way of greeting, my tongue feeling fat and useless in my dry mouth.

Mrs. Spencer took a sip of her wine, her eyes never leaving my face while regarding me in that same, pinched way like I was a stain in her beautiful home. "So, you're the Hunter?" She crossed the room and lowered herself into the leather armchair nearest me, no doubt in an attempt to intimidate me. She was so close I could smell her perfume and the wine on her breath.

She didn't slam the door in my face, but she might as well have. "Yes." *Jax, where the hell are you?*

I felt her furious gaze and smelled something reminiscent of cigarettes. "I met your parents once," she said, and I stiffened as she gave a little laugh. "Not much there, I'm afraid. Your father was as dull as paint and your mother wasn't much to look at. They didn't have much to offer their House or the Legion. Not that it matters now." She smiled at me, her teeth brilliantly white and perfect. *What the hell is this?*

"She was tall, just like you, but ordinary and plain." Smiling, Jax's mother took a sip of her wine, and red blotches marred her face. "You look just like her."

I wanted to slap this woman. I faced the full force of her stare and matched it with my own. Jax's mother personified the terrifying elegance that seemed bred into the wealthy founding families.

I wouldn't let her intimidate me. I didn't care how much money she had. That meant nothing to me.

Mrs. Spencer surveyed me from head to toe. Her perfectly formed mouth tightened, and I could see through her eyes she didn't like what she saw. Next to her elegance and perpetually unruffled self, I probably looked like a monkey in human clothes.

Her eyes lingered on my fingers and then a sly smile formed on her face.

The flower pot. I blushed and shoved my hands in my pockets, having forgotten to wipe the earth from them after I'd shoved my death blade in the flower pot. Crap. So much for first impressions.

The woman's perfect lips widened into a smile at the sudden embarrassment she saw on my face. She leaned forward, her smile disappearing as her eyes narrowed. "I *know* what you are, Hunter."

I swallowed. "That's nice." The woman's intense stare was unsettling. I could see real hatred there, hatred for me. I wasn't sure I liked the way she was saying *Hunter* either, like the word itself was a disgrace.

"There's demon in you, Hunter," said Mrs. Spencer, and I felt my stomach clench.

"I don't know what you're talking about," I said quickly, seething inside.

Her smile widened at my sudden discomfort, delight sparkling in her eyes. "Yes, you do. You know exactly what I mean." She leaned back in a graceful, confident gesture as though she'd just won some battle between us. "It's all over the community. Word travels fast in our world. You should know that, Hunter. Secrets never stay secrets."

My bravado did a swirl down the crapper. In the sudden silence, I could hear my heart thumping against my ribcage like a manic drumbeat. Had Jax told his parents?

It was clear the woman hated my guts. Yes, I was part demon, or something very close to it, but I was also part angel. That secret wasn't for Jax to tell, and I felt resentment spike through me.

I had thought of ways to tell the council, to tell them what the archangel had done to me and the others. But I hadn't gotten around to it yet. Seems I wouldn't have to now.

The secret was out, and it was out badly if I were to guess by the hostile expression permanently tattooed on this woman's face.

All my life I'd been shunned by the council and the other angel-born. All because I was different. Because I was Unmarked. But this was worse. Way worse. I was part of the creatures they were sworn to kill, their sworn enemies. Demon essence pounded through my veins.

Now that my secret was out, would the council hunt me?

I looked at her and bit my lip. Tears of frustration welled, but I forced them away. Angry, I gathered myself and straightened. I would not be ashamed of what I was.

I was going to embrace it.

Looking straight at Mrs. Spencer, I smiled at her defiantly. "So you know," there was no point in denying it now. "Big freaking deal."

Mrs. Spencer's pretty features twisted in what resembled a snarl. "Why are you here?" It sounded like an accusation. "Louis tells me you're looking for my son. Your contract with the council is fulfilled. There's no reason for you to come here to my house. So, what do you want from my son?"

I stiffened as Mommy Dearest silently watched, evaluating. My head hurt, and taking a slow breath, I looked up. I opened my mouth to tell her to shove it up her rich, upper-class ass just as Jax strolled into the den, followed by the man I assumed was Louis.

Jax looked at me and for a moment I forgot where I was. Damn he was *pretty*, so very pretty.

He sauntered into the room with that same fluid grace, but there was a hurried edge to his movements, as though he was uncomfortable, nervous. He was just as handsome and mesmerizing as ever, though his perfect face was pinched in worry. He wore casual jeans and a snug t-shirt, which showed off his muscled chest and arms to perfection. Even in the brightness of the room, I could see dark circles below his eyes, a stark contrast against their vibrant green. There was a darkness in his gaze that I'd never seen before, and it made him look older. Such pain lingered there—and exhaustion.

He raked a hand over his dark, golden brown tousled hair. He looked thinner than I'd remembered, and there was a tiredness to his eyes and face, as though he hadn't slept in days.

Our eyes met and my heard jumped into a gallop. All my thoughts dissolved like dew beneath the morning sun. *Damn he is beautiful.* There was no shame in thinking it.

Jax ran his eyes over me in a way that made my ears burn. "Rowyn?" he said as he closed the distance between us. I inhaled his musky scent that was just way too pleasant to be legal. "What are you doing here?"

My face heated. I raised a brow, not sure I liked his tone. "Talking antiques with your mother," I snapped. "What do you think?"

"I would like to know why a Hunter is in my home," said Mrs. Spencer, her glittering eyes fixed on mine. "Especially *this* one. She is rude, foul and repulsive. I'll have to have the carpets cleaned once she leaves."

Ouch. I clenched my jaw as my hatred for this woman thundered through me.

Jax launched into a volley of what sounded like really fast French. He kept his voice low, but there was no disguising the anger in it.

"Yes, yes," said Mrs. Spencer impatiently, waving a hand to her son. "So she saved your life? We've all heard the story, dear," she said as she and Louis shared some secret smile. "But don't forget it was her job to keep you alive. If you died, she wouldn't have gotten paid. It's all about the money for those Hunters. That's how Hunters are."

My blood pressure spiked as Jax cast a nervous glance at his mother and then turned back to me. "You shouldn't be here."

A low growl escaped me, not sure if it was directed at Mrs. Spencer or Jax, maybe both. "I came because I—Pam was worried." My temper flared like gasoline thrown on a bonfire. "You're right. I shouldn't have come here. My mistake." I hated having an audience around me when I felt and looked like a fool. "Screw this," I seethed, yanking my hands out of my pockets. "Now that I see you're alive and well, I'll be going."

Temper flared in Jax's eyes, and as I made to move, he grabbed my arm and said, "Rowyn, you don't understand."

I yanked out of his grip and placed my dirty hands on my hips, not caring that everyone would see the dirt on them. "Start explaining then. What's going on?"

"Louis," ordered Mrs. Spencer, waving her empty glass at the man who'd answered the door like he was her servant. Obligingly, Louis took her glass, moved to a small bar area and poured her another full glass of red wine.

I looked at Jax while Louis gave his mistress her wine. "Why haven't you called Pam?" I said, voice low so it wouldn't tremble. "She's freaking out, you know. She came to my apartment. She's the reason I came here looking for you." I sighed waiting for him to answer. "Well?"

Jax opened his mouth and then closed it, clearly struggling to find a way to tell me something.

I looked into his eyes. "What?"

Jax shook his head and exhaled loudly. "I can't talk about this right now."

My eyes traced his face. "You look tired. What have you been doing, Jax?" By the alarm that flashed in his face, I knew I was on to something. "You shouldn't be doing it alone."

"I know what I'm doing."

I narrowed my eyes, peeved. "We came all this way to check up on you. The least you could do is call Pam back and tell her you're all right—"

"We?" Jax titled his head.

"Me and Tyrius."

Jax looked behind me as though expecting to see Tyrius. "Where's Tyrius?"

"Outside by the door where I left him," I said, feeling a stab of guilt as I threw a glare at Louis. "Apparently, *animals* aren't allowed in this precious establishment."

His face took on a severe cast, and he leaned forward, close enough that I could see the hint of stubble caught in the light on his chin. "Rowyn, I—"

"What *I* want to know is why you've invited this... this *thing* into my house!" Spit flew from Mrs. Spencer's mouth, and wine spilled to the floor as she gripped her wine glass with a trembling hand. The wine coiled down her wrist like blood.

It was my turn for my jaw to drop. "I'm not a *thing*," I protested, shocked. But then, maybe I was?

Whatever respect I'd had for her when I walked through those doors vanished. I'd been called a lot of nasty names in my years, but a *thing*? That was just downright *wrong*. Still, I wasn't as insulted as I believed Mrs. Spencer thought I would be. Surprising even myself, I felt—nothing. I would have told her to go screw herself, but I didn't want to upset Jax. The vile woman was still his mother. Though, I didn't know why I even cared what he thought.

I met her glare, unmoved by her words, and that just pissed her off even more. *Touché.*

"That thing shouldn't exist. She shouldn't be allowed to live." Mrs. Spencer's eyes turned from her son to me and she said, "It should die."

Nice. This is just getting better and better.

"Now you're talking crazy," said Jax addressing his mother, but I could see the tension flickering over his face. "You're embarrassing yourself. You're embarrassing me."

"A thing like that killed your sister!"

Jax sighed through his nose. "Stop it, mother."

"There's demon stink everywhere!" raged Mrs. Spencer. "It's in the air, on my walls—my pictures! Her very presence is an insult to your sister. How could you do that to her? How could you do that to Gillian! What were you thinking!"

The woman was really starting to tick me off. "I think your mom's off her meds."

At that, Mrs. Spencer whirled on me, fury creasing her perfect brows. Her body shook as she raised her wine glass, and for a second I thought she was about to toss that wine into my face.

"Mind your own business, Mother," said Jax and stepped in front of his mother's glass, clearly thinking the same thing. "This has nothing to do with her."

"It has everything to do with her!" Mrs. Spencer was practically screaming, her eyes bulging.

Damn. I wish Tyrius was here. He'd love to see this.

"That's enough drama for today, Mother," said Jax, his face darkening into an angry red. "Rowyn has

100

nothing to do with Gillian's death. In fact, she *helped* me find the name of the demon responsible." He paused, collecting himself. "She's my… *friend*. How dare you treat her this way."

Friend? My heart clenched. We *were* just friends, weren't we? I could see that my startled reaction pleased his mother, her eyes glittering triumphantly.

Louis stepped forward. "Don't you speak to your mother like that, boy."

Ire rippled over Jax's shoulders as he faced Louis, and a strange smile formed on his mouth. He looked dangerous and about to strike. "Boy? I'll show you boy—"

"Stop it! Both of you." Mrs. Spencer got to her feet, dripping more wine on the carpet. I don't know why she had such a problem with me being so dirty. She was the one messing up the expensive rug. Wine is harder to get out than blood. Trust me, I know.

Louis turned to Mrs. Spencer. The look he gave her was full of admiration and something else that made me wonder where Jax's father was. "Celeste, come take a walk in the garden with me," he said as he made to take her hand. "This is my fault. I shouldn't have let her in. If I'd known how upset you'd be, I would have turned her away. I would have left her outside with her demon kin."

Demon kin?

"You don't need to be in her presence anymore," continued Louis. "Jax will show her out."

Celeste smacked his hand away and pointed a red manicured finger at me. "I see the way that thing is looking at you." Her eyes darted from me to Jax. "Tell me you didn't, Jax. Not with that."

More heat rushed to my face. Ah hell, now this was embarrassing. But I felt worse when I saw Jax's face take on another deep shade of red.

Celeste stared at her son and arched a delicate brow. "What does Ellie think about this? Does she know you've been messing around with a demon?"

Ellie? Feeling numb, I turned and stared at Jax, but he wouldn't meet my eyes. My throat tightened. Why wouldn't he look at me?

Before I could control myself, I blurted, "Who's Ellie?"

Jax raked a hand through his hair, giving away his nervousness. "Don't, Mother. This isn't helping."

Celeste gave me a winning smile, reminiscent of one of Amber's. She brushed a delicate strand of hair from her eyes, her oval face showing a surprising amount of sly amusement.

"His fiancée."

My stomach clamped. I felt like I'd been stabbed with a blade, a white-hot blade, right into my heart, slicing it into tiny pieces.

I stilled my emotions, feeling the room beginning to spin. When I faced him, his green eyes were as ruthless as the churning sea. But he didn't deny it.

Jax had a fiancée. And I was the biggest fool of the century.

"Get out of my house… *demon*." Celeste's face held nothing but that cool amusement.

The word was a slap in the face, and she'd meant it to be. I barely heard Jax's outrage for the loud pounding in my ears. I met his mother's gaze and held it.

My heart hammered and my face went cold. "With pleasure."

And with that, I stormed from the den and out the front doors.

CHAPTER
10

I'm not going to cry. I'm not going to cry. Ah, hell. I was crying.

I brushed my tears away before Tyrius saw them. Hunters didn't cry. Hunters never cried. Hunters *made* people cry.

I'd never been so humiliated in my life. And yes, I'd been through my share of crap. But for a horrible minute there, Jax's mom almost, almost made me feel ashamed of who and what I was.

Screw her.

I didn't need her. I didn't need Jax. I didn't need anyone. Well, except maybe Tyrius.

My mood fouled and the only way to remedy it was to kill something. Preferably demons, though

Celeste's face kept flickering before my eyes. Damn that woman made my blood boil.

After calling Pam to tell her Jax was alive and reasonably well at his parents' place—because I didn't trust that Jax would remember to call her—I'd gone home and packed as much salt as I could carry along with other supplies in my large leather messenger bag. Once I had gathered everything I needed for the journey, had eaten a bite, and had checked that my weapons belt was loaded, Tyrius and I went in search of my mark.

We strolled down Riverside Park, gravel crunching under my boots. Blasting trucks and roaring cars echoed all around us as we neared the stone arches of the Riverside Drive viaduct—one of the entrances to Elysium.

By the time we made it to the entrance, the sky was a deep orange, reflecting on the Hudson River like blood. A dark omen or a warning not to enter? Through the mouth of the wide tunnel, swallowing the light and leaving only darkness, was the entrance to Elysium.

I stifled a shiver. It wasn't smart going after a half-breed at night in a place I'd never been before. A place like Elysium housed abundant demons and Rifts, waiting to pull you into the Netherworld.

My gut tightened. "We should hurry. It'll be dark soon." Demons came out at night, feeding on the darkness and shadows, which gave them strength.

"It doesn't matter," said Tyrius as he sniffed a retaining wall covered in numerous layers of graffiti.

"Inside Elysium it's always nighttime. That's why it's the place of choice for most demons. The lack of light makes it a relatively easy passage into this world."

From where I was standing, I could see part of a railroad, cluttered with rubble and running deep into the hollow mouth of the tunnel in silent invitation.

"You okay?"

I looked down to see Tyrius's blue eyes bright with worry. My heart gave a little tug. "I'm fine. Don't worry," I added with a tight smile. "It's nothing a little demon killing can't fix."

Tyrius gave a small sigh. "This sucks. I kind of liked Jax, you know? He wasn't stuck up. He didn't have the god complex attitude that most angel-born share. He liked beer and guns. He was cool."

"I know." My throat closed and I sighed. I had to kill something fast or I was going to lose it.

"Now he's just a Grade-A ass."

"I think he takes after his mom." I gave Tyrius a smile and hiked my bag higher, securing it over my shoulder where it wouldn't move, as I yanked my soul blade free from my belt. A girl could never be too careful.

"Let's go." There was no point in standing there. The sooner I found this Ugul character, the sooner we could get out of there.

I'd never tracked a faerie before, and among all the foul stench of demon and human waste, it wasn't going to be easy. I moved forward, my boots crunching loudly on the gravel, and then I froze.

A feeling of being watched crept over me like icy fingers wrapped around my neck. Heart pounding, I whirled around, my soul blade thrust before me.

Tapping into both my angel-born and demon senses, I searched for the familiar cold feeling of demons, but all I perceived was the recognizable warm wave of humanity. No supernatural entities. No demons. Nothing.

Humans strolled in the park, not even giving us a glance as they went on their merry way along the walkway that edged the river. There were no demons or half-breeds that I could sense. But I *had* sensed something. I was sure of it.

Tyrius was next to me in a flash. "What is it, Rowyn? You saw something? Are you getting your Jedi vibe?"

"I thought I did, but now I'm not so sure." I couldn't help but wonder if the Greater demon Degamon still wanted a piece of me. I had killed some of its minions, but they had attacked first. The sensation had been so fast I couldn't tell if it was demon or maybe even angel. Vedriel's allies would eventually come after me. It was only a matter of time before their angel asses found mine.

I strained my eyes around the park, searching for that feeling of being watched again. But it was gone. "It's nothing," I said, shrugging. "Come on."

"If you say so," muttered the cat as he padded next to me.

A rush of excitement mixed with trepidation soared through me as we stepped through the mouth of the tunnel, my usual high of going on a hunt. It stank of mold and dust, but the air also held the smell of rotting eggs and decay. It intensified as we treaded into the tunnel—the stench of half-breeds and demons. But there was also a flicker of something else, something cold, dark and powerful. A darkness leaked from somewhere inside the tunnels, and it tugged inside my chest as a cold shudder ran through me. *Rifts*. It was the only explanation for such a strong supernatural pull—doorways to the Netherworld.

Yikes. I didn't want to think about what would happen if I accidentally stepped through one of these portals. I'd sent a lot of demons back to the Netherworld. I doubted they'd throw me a Welcome Home Party.

I picked my way along the tracks, my eyes slowly adjusting to the darkness around us. The entrance was large and dark, but with my enhanced angel and demon senses, my eyes quickly adjusted like I was seeing the world through Tyrius's eyes. He could see in the dark just like any ordinary cat.

Soon I couldn't hear the loud traffic behind us. There was only the sound of my boots echoing around me. Tyrius's soft padding was silent, as usual.

After a two-minute walk along the tracks, there was a gap on the right-side tunnel's wall, large enough to fit an SUV. Concrete rubble lay below the opening, as though a giant creature had busted through to get to the mortal world from the Netherworld.

A cold, damp breeze leaked through the crack, bringing forth the smell of sulfur, rotten flesh and the sticky, metallic odor of blood.

The pulse of darkness was stronger here. I could almost see it seeping out through the hole in the wall like a black mist. This was the true entrance to Elysium, not the viaduct. I wondered how many stupid humans wandered through the opening, never to be seen again.

"This is it," said Tyrius. "There's no going back after we cross that threshold. You sure you want to go through with this? There's no shame in refusing the contract." He stuck out his tongue. "We are talking about the fae. We HATE the fae. Remember? We can get more work from Father Thomas. Closet demons abound this time of year."

"No," I said. "I'm doing this." *I need to do this.* I needed to work. Working kept me focused. If I didn't, I'd be laughing in self-pity of how stupid I was, how I got played by Jax's pretty face. Just the thought of him sent a sharp stab of pain through my chest. *I'm an idiot. He has a freaking fiancée.* She was probably drop-dead gorgeous, a pure angel-born from an old family, and stupid rich, just like him.

Whereas I was a stain on his mother's expensive carpet.

My eyes burned, and I wanted to kick myself. *Nice going, Rowyn.*

I vowed that when I was done with this hunt, I was going to find myself a nice human and have some angry sex.

109

I looked down and my cheeks flamed. Tyrius was staring at me with a knowing expression on his face. I'd always wondered if baals could read minds.

"How hard can it be? It's just one stinking faerie," I said, trying to focus on the job, not wanting Tyrius to read too much into my emotions. Yet, my gut also told me that it wouldn't be so easy if the fae queen's Dark Arrows hadn't been able to locate their trickster faerie.

"You sure you're not doing this for the wrong reasons?" questioned my furry friend.

"Like what? Getting twenty grand for a measly faerie?" I cocked my hip. "If I don't get the rest of this money, my grandmother loses her house. There's no way I'm going to let that happen. This money—this damned faerie money—is going to help me keep her house. It sucks, really sucks, but it's my only way to help my grandmother." Frustrated, I gritted my teeth. "I hate these pointy-eared bastards, but I'm a professional. I know what I'm doing."

"Uh-huh," Tyrius said, his expression skeptical. "Fine. Then I'll go first. Watch my back."

Squaring my shoulders, I faced forward, pushing all thoughts of Jax from my mind as I followed the Siamese cat through the gap. My ears popped and I was immediately hit with the sensation of a change in pressure, like landing in an airplane.

Once through the threshold, I found myself in another tunnel. Unlike the New York City subway or Amtrak tunnel with smooth stone walls, these walls were rough and haphazard as though carved by hand. They had the musty, earth-like smell of a cave.

A breeze blew from the black depths, pushing strands of my hair past my face. A shiver ran down my spine. A mix of cobwebs and tree roots sprouted over the tunnel walls. Moisture was thick and I felt a thin film of it sticking to my face and neck as soon as we'd crossed the threshold. The tunnel was silent except for the soft trickling of water somewhere.

Suddenly the ground shook, and something cracked behind me. When I turned, my breath caught. The tunnel wall was completely smooth, the rock surface flat and intact. The entrance to Elysium had vanished.

"Tyrius," I said alarmed.

"Don't worry. The entrance is spelled, but we can still get out," said the cat as he crept next to me and stood by the wall. He bit his paw, black blood seeping from his wound, and then he pressed it against the wall. When he took his paw away, a perfect paw print was left. Then he bounded right through the wall where the entrance had been and disappeared, only to reappear the next second. "See? It wants you to go through, but then it wants to keep you inside too. Now we know which way is out."

Smart cat. "I'm glad you're here with me, Tyrius," I said, smiling.

Tyrius beamed. "Stick with me, kid, and I'll have you farting through silk."

Laughing, I followed the cat down the passageway. The ground was covered in dust and hard-packed dirt, no doubt from the throng of demons and half-breeds that wandered through along with the occasional idiot human.

After a half hour of trudging down the path, the air became hot and thin, only to be replaced by the stink of sulfur. Sweat trickled down my back and temples as it became harder to breathe, like the air was toxic and every breath was labored. *This is what the air must be like in the Netherworld.*

We plunged into a void, a wasteland of brutal blackness, choked of all sense of time or awareness of place. Tyrius kept stopping and sniffing the walls, his ears low and his face pinched like he was smelling something foul. His edginess was making me nervous, and my pulse raced, making me lightheaded.

I need air. Fresh air.

Amidst the hot stinking air, I felt the cold darkness and the faint stench of death and rot. "Damn half-breeds," I said, trying to keep breathing through my mouth. "They always pick the most charming places to hang out. How can they want to live down here? I mean, I get why demons do—they're demons—but half-breeds are part human. Don't they need some fresh air? I'd go mad if I had to stay here."

"They probably don't have a choice," said the cat. "It's either this—or death."

Prickles of sweat popped out on my forehead. "I don't know about you, but my demon radar is going into overdrive. It's hard to pinpoint a particular half-breed. Everywhere feels… feels like the flow of random demon energies."

"The Rifts are doing that," said Tyrius without looking up. "It's raw demon energy, naked and pulsing through them. They're bound to screw with our demon mojo."

I picked my way around a pile of fallen rocks and rubble. "It's going to make it that much harder to find Ugul. He could be anywhere down here."

Tyrius looked over his shoulder and said, "Just follow the stink. There's always a faerie at the end of the crapper."

I laughed, letting myself relax a little. The sound bounced over the walls, foreign and out of place in the tunnel, as though the sound of laughter itself wasn't allowed.

We'd moved another hundred feet when Tyrius halted before three equally dark and imposing tunnels that branched off from the main one.

The baal demon turned and looked up at me, his eyes wide. "I think we should keep going straight."

I examined the other two tunnels. "What's wrong with these two?"

Tyrius shrugged. "A veterinarian with a giant needle with my name on it." The Siamese shivered. "Okay, maybe not. But there's something evil brewing down there, especially the one on the right."

I wiped the sweat from my eyes. "Okay," I said, feeling useless. My hunting skills weren't as effective down here as I'd first imagined they would be. Whenever I sent out my senses, I'd get the same cold, demonic pulse back, as though it had bounced back from the wall. I'd be willing to bet the Rifts were affecting my demon *and* angel mojo.

Crap. That was *not* good.

After two hours of trudging down the same path, I began to notice a rising sense of panic as we moved. I felt overly tired, like my energy was being drained into this place. A queasy feeling tightened my chest, feeling like the tunnels were trapping us.

My heart throbbed as I tried to squelch the panic from my thoughts, only to have it bounce back tenfold.

"Damn this place," swore Tyrius and he halted.

I stalked towards to him. "What it is?"

"Our own tracks. We've been going around in circles!"

"What?"

I knelt down to focus my eyes on the baked earth at our feet and recognized size ten women's boot tracks and paw prints. Our own. *Shit.*

My throat clamped shut. We were screwed. If Tyrius couldn't find his way down here, how were we going to find our way out of this hell?

I stood up slowly, heart pounding in my throat. "We're lost."

"And you're trespassin'," said a voice in the shadows.

The hairs on the back of my neck stood on end. Tyrius's eyes snapped open in sudden, startled shock.

I hadn't felt them coming, but I'd recognize their stench anywhere—the mix of old beer, rotten fruit and a dash of skunk.

Leprechauns.

CHAPTER

11

Four leprechauns stepped from the shadows and faced us, blocking our way.

Contrary to popular belief, they were not the four-inch-tall bearded men, wearing green top hats and green clothes, nor did they hang around the ends of rainbows counting their pots of gold. Nope. These were over six feet tall, bulging with muscles like men who spent too much time in the gym. They were big. Really big. They were taller than me and twice as broad.

Dressed in only jeans with black motorcycle boots, their masculine, hairy chests were covered in a colorful array of skull, eagle, and tribal tattoos. But the assortment of weapons had me really impressed—

knives, hunting daggers, short swords, sickles, axes, and even hammers were strapped over their bodies.

The thing with leprechauns, they didn't really abide by the half-breed rules, nor did they have a court or any sense of loyalty to the Gray Council. That was probably because, as the product of vamps and faeries breeding, they were shunned from the other half-breeds.

There wasn't a written law that forbade half-breeds from mixing or from having relations with other half-breeds, but it was still frowned upon and taboo among most of the races.

The other peculiar thing with leprechauns was that they were all male—and sterile, like mules. They were more of a rare half-breed race, but they were mean and angry. Totally understandable.

Being from both vampire and faerie, leprechauns had the physical strength of vampires and some magic from the fae, but they weren't blessed with good looks or grace. Nope. More like trolls. The best I could describe leprechauns was as the half-breed mafia, paranormal gang members, the half-breed hired muscle.

"Well, well, well," mocked Tyrius. "If it isn't the *leper*-chauns," he added, laughing sourly at his own joke. "Get out of our way, lepers. We don't have time for any of your crap. We're on a job."

I never understood Tyrius's deep loathing for this race of half-breed, and he never wanted to elaborate on it either.

The only redheaded leprechaun stepped closer. He wore his hair longer in the back and short on top, and I pinned him as their leader. "This is *our* tunnel, witch-demon," he said, his voice harsh and deep, rich with an accent I couldn't place. White marred his hair and beard, and he had lines on his face, putting his age at well into maturity. His eyes were green, wild and blazing with excitement.

"You don't say?" Tyrius sat, head straight, looking regal in the dungy cave. "Because the last I checked, Elysium didn't belong to anyone, and especially not to you *leper*-chauns."

The red-haired leprechaun growled, and I was shocked at how much it sounded like a werewolf's growl. His grubby fingers twitched as they neared the sword at his waist.

Shit. I moved Tyrius back with my leg and sheathed my blade. "We don't want any trouble," I said, though I cocked my hip to show them I was willing to entertain a little trouble if it came to that. "This is Hunter business," I said, glad that my voice was even. "There's no reason this has to get ugly. Just let us through."

The red-haired leprechaun smiled, revealing a mouthful of rotten teeth. "Can't do that, sweetheart. See, this here," he said as he reached back and pulled out an axe. I couldn't help but notice that the blade was stained in black. "This is our tunnel. *Our* tunnel. *Our* rules. And the rule is you gotta pay the toll." His green eyes moved to my bag, and they brightened with greed.

I gripped my shoulder strap protectively and gave a sour laugh, "I'm not giving you shit. Forget it."

"Then you can just turn around and go back, sweetheart," commented the redhead, and he sneered at the scowl on my face. "That's *if* you can find your way out again." He laughed, and the other three exchanged knowing grins.

"I say we smoke them, Rowyn," said Tyrius, his voice carrying as he leaped to his feet. His claws dug into the dirt. "Anyone who still wears a mullet deserves to die. You take those three—shotgun on Carrot Top."

I shifted nervously. I wouldn't kill a leprechaun in cold blood, not unless it was in self-defense, and I wasn't a defenseless little female. Hell, I could probably take all four. But the tunnel, the smell, and the lack of air gave me pause. The longer I spent in the tunnels, the more energy was drained from me. Something just didn't feel right about this place. And I wasn't about to take a chance on my life or Tyrius's.

"I'm under contract to find a half-breed," I said, glad that I had the leader's full attention. "I'm a Hunter. It's my job to track down evil bastards. If you try and stop me with your weapons, I'll take it as an attack upon my person. I'll have no choice but to defend myself. I might even kill you."

The leprechaun's smile turned malevolent. "Hunter or not, everybody pays. No exceptions."

"Let's kill them, Ramis," said the largest of the leprechauns, with short black hair and skin like tree bark. "Then we split what's in the bag," he added and pointed a knife towards my messenger bag. "And we could fetch a good price for the witch-demon."

Tyrius hissed and spat. "Bite me, lepie."

Now I was pissed. "Come and try to take my bag, big boy. I dare you," I said, smiling, my hand reaching for the hilt of my soul blade.

"Have it your way then," said Ramis, his expression hard. Sweating, I watched Ramis force the visible tension from his face and stance until he was the casual, confident gang boss on the surface. The air pressure shifted, and suddenly the leprechauns crouched, ready to attack.

"Fight!" howled Tyrius, and I swear I saw a smile on his face.

The leprechauns sprang forward.

My pulse hammered, and I lowered myself. I had my soul blade at their faces before a single one of them managed to clear an axe from their belts.

I swung the blade and cut through the air as they advanced, snarling and howling like beasts. Man, they were ugly.

It was like a sea of tan, rough skin and denim coming at us in waves. The smell of rotten fruit burned my eyes. The big dumb one launched at me, his eyes on my bag—

"Wait!" Ramis wailed and the leprechaun halted before my eyes, my blade pointed at his neck. He moved back and alarm shone on his face at how quickly I would have struck him down.

I pulled my gaze back to Ramis, his eyes lingering at the death blade on my hip. *Took them long enough.* The other leprechauns froze.

"I've heard about you," said Ramis, his yellow teeth bared. "You're the Hunter, the angel-born Hunter with demon blood." He took my silence as confirmation. "You're more of a freak than we are." He laughed, and the others joined him, but he laughed the hardest.

"Oh, I have to disagree," Tyrius said snidely. "I don't think there's anything more freakish than a band of half-naked, mullet-haired, all male *leper*-chauns."

Deep hatred flashed on Ramis's face, but he turned to me and said, "I have a tender spot in my heart for freaks. Who you lookin' for?"

I kept my face from showing my surprise and pursed my lips, debating how much I should tell this leprechaun. "A faerie that goes by the name of Ugul. The faerie queen of the Dark Court sent me," I admitted, watching the leprechaun's fat fingers flex around his axe. There was no love there.

"It's why we're here… in your tunnels." I figured if these leprechauns claimed the tunnels as theirs, it meant they knew their way around Elysium. Our unlucky encounter could turn out to be very lucky indeed. I could use that.

Ramis scratched his red beard. "How much does this faerie mean to you?"

I didn't like the smile on the leprechaun's face. My grandmother's livelihood depended on me finding this damn faerie, but I wasn't about to share that with the leprechaun. "The faerie means nothing to me, but I do have a reputation. I said I'd get the job done, and I'll do everything in my power to keep my word."

Ramis crossed his arms over his large chest and axe. "I know this faerie."

My heart leapt. "You do?"

"Where is he?" demanded Tyrius. "Tell us."

Ramis's smile never flickered as he said, "I can tell you where to find him, but you still need to pay the toll. It'll cost ya double."

"Double! You scheming bastards," spat Tyrius. "Let's just waste these dicks and find him on our own."

I met Ramis's gaze. His brow lifted at the hesitation that crossed my features. "How much?"

Tyrius whirled on me. "Rowyn, no! These cronies are just like the fae—only uglier. You can't trust them. You can't believe anything out of their leper-chaun mouths."

"It's not like we have a choice, Tyrius," I told the cat. "I don't want to be down here in this stinking place longer than necessary. They say they know where he is. So, let's find out."

I waited for the leprechauns to stop whispering amongst each other. "How much," I repeated when Ramis looked at me.

Ramis was still grinning as he said, "Five hundred."

I clamped my jaw, feeling my blood pressure rising and making my head spin.

"What!" shouted Tyrius. "You're out of your freaking mind. There's no way we're going to pay that much. Tell them, Rowyn."

But Ramis kept talking as though the cat hadn't spoken. "Two fifty for the toll and another two fifty to take you to the faerie. Without us, you'll never find him. You know I'm right. I can see it in your eyes. You'll be lost in Elysium. Forever."

Crap. He was right. He knew it. I knew it.

"Fine." I reached into my bag for my wallet, feeling Tyrius's angry glare on me. I flipped through my wallet. "I don't carry that much cash on me," I said pulling out all the bills as I moved towards him. "I only have a hundred and twenty."

Ramis snatched the cash out of my hands. He counted it, seemingly satisfying that I wasn't lying, and then jammed my money in his front jean pocket. "This'll do."

I scowled, peeved that I knew he would have probably taken a lot less.

"This way," said the gang leader, his smile wider.

"Wait!" I called. "What about our way back? Once we get the faerie, how do we know which way is out?"

"Yeah," agreed Tyrius looking furious that I had actually given them all our cash.

Ramis reached inside his pocket and flipped me a coin. "Leprechaun gold," he said, as I caught it and turned the coin over in my hand. It was the size of a penny and looked more like copper than gold. I had heard of leprechaun gold before, but I'd always dismissed it as a myth. Like witches used amulets and talismans as conduits for specific magic, they said leprechauns used coins. Each coin had its own magical ability. And this one was our ticket out of this place. Rolling my fingers over it, I could feel indentations, but it was too dark to make them out. I could also feel a hole, right in the center.

"The coin'll get warmer the closer you are to the exit. Cold the further away."

"Right." I pocketed the coin, hoping he wasn't lying and hadn't just duped me with a regular penny.

With Ramis leading the way, we doubled back and followed him down the tunnel. The other three leprechauns trailed behind us, the big black-haired one still eyeing my bag whenever I turned to look behind me. Tyrius hissed and cursed with every step, but he was following. We didn't have much choice.

Then, to my surprise, Ramis began whistling, very skillfully, just as the other leprechauns joined in. My skin was riddled in goosebumps. The sound was—beautiful and mesmerizing, reminding me of meadows swaying with wildflowers. The tune was so very different and felt odd in the dark tunnels. I had no idea leprechauns were so musically gifted.

"What the hell is this?" mumbled Tyrius. "Disney's Snow White and her four leper-chauns?"

Ramis and the others never stopped whistling their tunes as they took us back the way we'd come. When we arrived back at the spot where the tunnels split into three, he took us through the tunnel on the right, the one Tyrius said he'd gotten a very bad vibe from.

We arrived at the edge of a vast chamber that rose up fifty feet above our heads. The floor before us wasn't the same compact dirt and dust, but water as cold and still as stone. In the center of the water was an island, a mountain of rock with a hole, a cave within a cave I realized. Soft golden light came from it, and I could smell the faint smoke of a fire.

But the water was a problem.

Just like real cats, baal demons hated water. It was more of a fear than an actual hate for it. I had never asked Tyrius why. I just assumed he didn't like baths. And when I looked down at the cat, my chest clamped. Tyrius had gone still, his eyes fixed on the black waters. Fear shone in his blue eyes.

"You sure this is the place?" I looked at Ramis, hoping he'd been wrong.

"He's there," answered the leprechaun pointing at the stone island. "He's been living here for the past eighty years. He's the only faerie to live down here. Never bothered to ask him why. He keeps to himself."

Slowly I exhaled. "How do I know you're not lying?"

Ramis arched a red bushy eyebrow. "You don't." He watched me for a moment. "He's there."

I looked over to the water, which was eerily still, like a black mirror. "How deep is this water?"

Ramis shrugged. "Don't know. The faerie uses a boat to get to shore."

Sure enough, when I looked again, I spotted a small rowboat tied to a tiny pier. My frustration doubled when I knew what a boat meant. A boat meant that the water was too deep to walk.

Damn. I would have to swim.

"Looks like you're gonna go for a swim," laughed the leprechaun with the silver hair and goatee, reading my mind exactly. "I hope he's worth it."

"He *better* be worth it," grumbled Tyrius, but he still hadn't moved.

Looking across the eerie water, I wondered if or how many of the fae had tried and failed to cross. Maybe they'd never made it this far. Maybe they took the wrong tunnel and got swallowed up by a Rift. Oh well.

"Don't stay too long in the water," Ramis called.

I turned around, fighting with my growing fear. "Why not?"

The leprechaun was watching the water with anxiety in his eyes. "I would hurry if I was you." He flashed me his rotten teeth. "Good luck, sweetheart. You're gonna need it."

Before I could ask him more about this water, Ramis and his fellow leprechauns turned and disappeared through the tunnel, leaving only the faint whistling as a memory that they'd actually been there until I couldn't hear it anymore.

I let out a long breath and knelt next to Tyrius. "Do you want to wait for me here? I understand if you don't want to come."

"Absolutely not!" Tyrius spun and faced me. "Are you crazy? There's no way I'm letting you go to the island alone. I just… I'll be needing a ride, thank you."

He leapt to my shoulders and draped himself around the back of my neck like a furry scarf. The heat from his body sent much needed warmth through me, a welcomed comfort in the cold, musty cave.

"Hang on," I said as I straightened and made my way to the water's edge. I made a face. "The water smells nasty. It smells like carrion and death."

"And you're about to take a bath in it," commented the cat. "Nice."

"Keep it up, kitty, and I just might slip and fall in," I said, "with you."

Tyrius clamped his mouth shut, nudging his cold nose against my neck. "I think it's about waist-deep," he said, his breath tickling my jaw. "Try and slip in as quietly as you can. We don't want to disturb whatever's in there."

"No," I exhaled. "We don't." I never liked going swimming where I couldn't see the bottom. I always imagined there was a great white shark waiting to chomp me into tiny pieces. *Note to self—stop watching* Jaws.

I stepped to the water's edge and looked down. The water felt wrong, ominous, and thick like oil, too thick to be considered normal.

I pushed my fears away. I *had* to do this. There was no other way. I had to do this for my grandmother. And not even water that looked like it belonged in hell was going to stop me.

Gripping my soul blade in my right hand, I yanked out my death blade with my left and eased myself slowly into the black, icy water.

CHAPTER
12

"**H**oly crap, it's cold!" I hissed as I lowered myself further into the cold, stinking water. Worse was the feeling of it seeping to my clothes, to my skin, like cold soup. *Euwie.* I was going to smell like a sewer after this.

Tyrius snickered. "This isn't a spa, dearest."

"Keep it up, furball and you're going in next."

I glowered as I thought of all the nasty crawlies that thrived in brackish water and clamped my mouth shut. There was no way any of that water was going into my mouth. The water was cold, but not unbearable. I hiked my bag higher on my shoulders so it wouldn't get wet. Despite my slow movements, ripples spread out from me, silver on the dark water.

My boot caught on a rock and I stumbled, making a splash.

I held my breath for a few seconds, but nothing happened, so I kept going. I moved slowly with my arms held just above the water. Tyrius had been right. The water never went higher than my waist. I had no idea how he could have known. Must be a baal thing. Or maybe it was a cat thing?

Progress was slow, but I felt some tension leave me as the water started to lower until it was knee-high. And when my boots crunched the shore, I smiled.

I stood and stretched the cramps from my tight muscles. "Well, that wasn't so hard." I looked down at what looked like sea-weed stuck to my jeans, but I knew it wasn't. "I'll need a shower, but it wasn't as bad as I thought."

"That's because the water wasn't the problem. They are."

Behind me, I felt a sudden, repugnant presence. Demons. And a crap load of them.

"I knew it was too good to be true." I rolled my shoulders as Tyrius jumped to the ground, clean and smelling of my grandmother's perfume. Whereas I smelled like the crapper. Literally.

Checking the thrust of my blades, I spun, bringing my weapons around with lightning speed. For an instant, I saw a snarl of fangs, red eyes, and wet, slippery skin with scales like a fish. Yikes. Long and thin, they looked like a cross between a dog and a fish, misshapen as though they had not finished forming. Lesser demons that had escaped the Netherworld, their red eyes gleamed with hunger for my soul. Hell no.

"Veth hounds," said Tyrius, his eyes glowing with his demon magic. "I've never seen so many all grouped together like that." The baal demon seemed to glow with an internal light, expanding until he became frayed at the edges. I knew he was about to Hulk-out and change into his alter ego—a spectacular black panther. "These uglies were bred to serve only two purposes—to guard and to kill."

"Fan freaking tastic."

When I cast my gaze around the chamber, the walls seemed to be moving. Then I realized in horror that the walls weren't moving. The veth hounds were—hundreds of them. Now I knew why the faeries had never recovered their quarry. They never got past these hounds. Swell.

A horde of them had emerged between us and the cave. If I didn't know any better, I'd say they were either blocking us or guarding the faerie inside the cave.

"And they look like they haven't been fed in a while," said Tyrius.

"We need to get past them into that cave," I said crouching low, my eyes on the glowing golden light that spilled from a small entrance.

"Yeah, and then what?" said Tyrius as his internal light grew and grew. "If we make it to the cave, they'll still be here when we want to get back out."

"Right." Shit. That was true. Damn it. Why were things always so complicated? It seemed I could never catch a break.

The sound of claws ripping stone reached me. I whirled and caught a glimpse of a malicious glare, and then my blade made solid contact. Whatever I hit was rendered unrecognizable as it disintegrated into a cloud of ash.

Tyrius nodded his head, staring at the pile of ash. "And that's what happens when demons get voted off the island."

The rest of Tyrius's words were drowned out as a burst of light, too bright to look at, consumed the tiny cat. Within a few seconds, there was no Siamese cat shape left, but a three-hundred-pound black panther. Damn. I wish I could do that.

And not a second too soon, as a wave of veth hounds attacked hard and vicious.

Howls split the cavern silence.

A flash of scales raced across my vision. It was incredibly fast. With supernatural speed, a hound hit me in the chest. My breath escaped me as I was flung backward. My back hit the hard rocky ground, and I smacked the back of my head. Black spots hit my vision, but I was up before they settled. Driven by instinct, I swung my blades as I spun, slicing the hound in the chest. Its hot, putrid breath gusted out as it burst into ash.

The back of my head throbbed, and nausea flooded me. But I couldn't stop. Stopping meant death, and I had too much weighing on me getting this faerie. I needed to get paid.

Movement caught my eye. I turned, drawing my sword as more hounds poured over and around the rock island. The air stank of rotten fish, making me choke, yet more continued to come for me. The hounds, teeth snapping, bounded up the rock in a violent onslaught.

Blood roared in my ears as I cut down the first wave and then retreated farther up the rock as more hounds came for me. I kicked out hard, sending a hound scrambling down on the rock, just as another bounded over it and flew at me.

I ducked. Whirling, I came up blades swinging and cut it down as it soared towards my throat.

And still more came.

I swung my blades, cutting through the veth hounds as they advanced, spitting and howling. It was like a sea of scales and fangs, coming for me in waves.

This was an impossible mark. The queen had sent me on a suicide mission. Damn her. Damn all the fae back to the Netherworld.

I released myself into my anger, fighting with fury as I advanced into their ranks. I couldn't fail my grandmother, not now.

The air seemed filled with yellow teeth, all coming for me. Blood from those I'd killed was everywhere. The world turned to black.

Frantically, I slashed and stabbed at them, trying to back away at the same time. Still more came. For every one I struck down, ten more would replace it.

A loud, bone-chilling roar shook the cavern. I climbed another rock, catching a glimpse of Tyrius the black panther. His yellow eyes blazed with deep hatred as he attacked a veth hound. The lesser demon's thin body was no match for the three hundred pounds of predatory muscle. His massive maw clamped around the hound's neck. There was a terrible snap, and the hound's head flopped to Tyrius's feet.

Some of the veth hounds halted, their red eyes watching the black panther with confusion and fear. But Tyrius never stopped. He hit another wave of hounds with the force of a train hitting a wall. Limbs tore, and blood flew. Veth hounds howled in fury and panic as they tried to get away from the large cat.

More howls hit my ears as another horde of veth hounds answered their kin's call and rushed to meet the black panther, pouring out through crevices like giant ants.

They hit the black panther at the same time, with a blow so strong Tyrius's head slammed into the rock. As the big cat surged to his legs, a rush of hounds leaped onto his back, thrashing wildly with their claws and fangs. Tyrius roared in pain.

The veth hounds attacked, merciless and deadly. My chest ached at the sight of Tyrius's refusal to stop, despite his limp, the cuts and the blood.

Veth hounds reeled back but then lunged, jaws snapping. Tyrius thrashed madly, trying to break free from the hounds on him, but he couldn't escape the jaws that latched on to his back and neck.

Again and again, Tyrius thrashed on the ground, but he couldn't get free.

Tuffs of black fur and skin flew in the air, Tyrius's flesh. As they buried their heads into his flesh like giant ticks, my heart stopped. Tyrius's whine was of agonizing, soul-shredding pain, the likes of which I'd never heard.

They were just too many.

"Tyrius!" I screamed, white-hot fury plaguing my mind.

Damn that Isobel. I should have never taken the job.

Letting my anger anchor me, I moved with an instinct to kill what was not from this world. I fought the hounds back, killing any that got close enough and leaving a path of dead veth hounds in my wake. It was a futile effort, I knew. There were more than Tyrius and I could hold back. If we wanted to survive, we had to reach that small cave.

I screamed and kicked, my legs barking in agony. *Tyrius. I had to save him.*

I knew it was stupid. There was no way I could defeat them all. But I would not let them take my friend. Never.

Something hit me on the side of the head, and then pain exploded on my back. Agony lashed down my spine so hard I fell to the ground, and my blades flew out of my hands. Pain spiked down the tendons in my neck as I felt hot breath and sharp teeth sink into my flesh around my neck, legs and arms.

I tried to speak, but I had no breath. I couldn't move. Tears plagued my vision. I couldn't see Tyrius.

Light flared. Not from me or Tyrius, but from the cave. So bright was this light, it lit the entire cavern as though it was daylight. Veth demons howled and hissed, and through my cracked vision I saw them retreat back into crevices and holes, away from the light.

What the hell just happened?

A small mass of tawny and black fur lay on the ground twenty feet from me. Tyrius. He'd changed back into his Siamese form. And he wasn't moving.

"Tyrius!" I felt the blood leave my face as fear gripped me. Groaning, I propped myself up on my elbows and blinked towards the source of the light.

Standing in the middle of the island, hands raised over his head, was a small man. His shape was a sharp silhouette against the light.

The man lowered his hands and the light diminished until all that remained was the same eerie yellow glow from the cave.

I could see him clearly now. The face that was staring at me didn't belong to a man, but a goblin.

CHAPTER
13

I stared at the creature, the goblin. I'd only heard of them, never actually seen one with my own eyes, but I knew it was a goblin. I was sure of it.

No more than four feet tall, his skin was brown and cracked like old leather. Wisps of white hair spotted his nearly bald head, and a white beard hung below a very large and bulbous nose. The edge of one of his pant legs was shredded while the other was tucked into tall weather-worn boots. He wore a tan linen shirt I was sure used to be white. And by the wear and tear of his clothes, he hadn't been shopping since the turn of the twentieth century.

Why did he save us? Right then, I didn't care. I was pissed. I didn't have time to make friends with goblins.

I forgot my pain as anger welled in me. There was no faerie here. The leprechauns had played us. *Bastards.* It had all been for nothing.

Ignoring the half-breed, I struggled to my feet and fetched my blades from the ground, securing them to my waist. I had no idea if the goblin was a friend or foe, but I didn't trust him. Even if he did save us, I didn't know if he had some ulterior motive. Maybe he had saved us just to have our flesh served on a platter later.

I wouldn't take any chances, not with Tyrius lying over there. He still hadn't moved. Wobbling like a drunk, I collapsed next to him.

"Tyrius?" I placed my shaking hands carefully over his body and let out a cry of relief when my palms felt a warm body. His chest rose and fell. "Tyrius?" I said again, but the cat wouldn't open his eyes. When I took my hands away, they were covered in black blood. His blood.

"Oh no. I'm so sorry, Tyrius." My lips trembled. My words were a sob, and I blinked the tears from my eyes. "We shouldn't have come here. This is all my fault." Guilt was a hot dagger stabbing into my gut. I had thought I'd done the right thing by coming here to save my grandmother's house. Looking at Tyrius now, I wasn't so sure it had been the right choice.

I'm a damn fool. I'm going to lose my only true friend.

"Yes, that's right. You shouldn't have come," barked a voice behind me, no doubt the goblin. His deep voice seemingly echoed off the stone walls. I heard a loud sigh. "Why did you come here? What do you want?" The last part was more of an order. My anger flared, and I let it.

Boots scraped the hard rock behind me. "Did you hear me? Or are the angel-born hard of hearing? I'm speaking to you!"

I all but snarled as I whipped my head around, not caring that tears spilled down my face. When I spoke I tasted salt. "Get away from him or so help me God I will cut out your groin and feed it to you."

The goblin made a small o with his mouth and then closed it. His large brown eyes studied me for a moment. I had no idea what he was thinking, and it just made me angrier.

"Your friend needs help," said the goblin, surprising me at his use of the word friend and not demon. "Take him inside," he ordered again, gesturing to the small cave with his hand. "I can help."

I leaned over Tyrius protectively and the goblin lifted an eyebrow. "Do you want him to live?"

I yanked out my soul blade. "Do *you* want to live?"

Annoyance flashed in the goblin's eyes as he pressed his hands on his hips. "Even if you made your way out of Elysium, he would not survive the journey. If you want him to live, you'll take him inside. Otherwise he will die. Don't be a fool. Come."

Fool? Yeah, maybe he was right. I watched the goblin as he walked towards the small entrance to the cave, wondering how he'd made that bright light. He wasn't carrying anything that I could see. Then, making up my mind, I sheathed my blade and scooped up Tyrius, trying not to cry and fall into pieces.

I didn't know what I'd do if Tyrius died. The thought of him dying sent my heart shattering into pieces.

My body ached as I stood, but it was nothing compared to the blows Tyrius had suffered. Cradling him ever so gently against my chest, I followed the goblin into the cave.

My first impression was that it stank of cooked cabbage. It was tight, smaller than my apartment, but cozy and surprisingly warm. The source of the heat came from a small fire pit in the middle of the chamber with a mounted grill and pot. The smoke of the fire rose and disappeared into a small opening in the cave's roof, which I suspected the goblin had created. There was a small cot in a corner, a chair that faced the fire and a wooden table with two chairs.

"Put him on the table and lay him on his left side, the wound side up." The goblin placed a black medical-looking leather bag on the table next to a towel. Then he rolled up his sleeves.

Obediently, I lowered Tyrius onto the small table but stood close enough to him, should the goblin try anything stupid. I made sure he saw my hand on the hilt of my blade.

The goblin huffed in irritation at my gesture. I didn't care. One wrong move and he'd find his head next to his feet.

"If this is a trick," I said, twisting my hand on my hilt. "If you're thinking of eating him, I'm going to—"

"Yes, yes, I heard you the first time," the goblin waved a hand at me. "You'll cut out my groin, isn't that right?" He let out a laugh. "Well, I'm a vegetarian. All right? Now, shut up so that I can save your friend."

I raised my brow. I'd never heard of vegetarian goblins, but then again, I didn't know much about them. Maybe he was lying? Maybe not.

The goblin grabbed another towel and pitched it at me. "You're bleeding at the back of your neck," he said, his eyes on Tyrius.

I pressed the towel against my neck, keeping a watchful eye as he dabbed the other towel on Tyrius's side. The towel came off smeared in blood. From the bag, the goblin pulled a needle and thread.

"What are you going to do with that?" I asked, suddenly scared.

"I'm going to stitch him up," said the goblin, as he put the thread to the needle. "Baals are very much like real felines when they're on this side of the world. When they take this form, they are every bit like a real cat, with internal organs and the like. And just like a real cat, I need to stop the bleeding. If I can do that, he's got a real chance."

My eyes burned, and since I didn't trust myself to speak, I simply nodded.

The goblin cut around a patch of wet fur, which I realized was blood, until the wound was clear of fur and had only skin around it. I nearly threw up at the sight. Tyrius's skin was mangled, and I could see teeth marks on his flesh where they'd pulled to tear it.

The goblin didn't seem to notice my alarm as his steady hand reached in, pinched the cat's skin together and began stitching. For such thick, short fingers, he was surprisingly gentle and proficient.

Unable to do anything else, I stood and watched as the goblin's expert hands stitched up my furry friend. An invisible hand seemed to wrap around my throat and squeeze each time the goblin pulled at a stitch.

Hang on, Tyrius. Please hang on.

After an intense twenty minutes, the goblin tied and cut the last stitch. "This should do it. Put him next to the fire. The warmth will help him heal faster."

"So, he's going to be okay?" I said, blinking fast. Hope kindled inside my chest as I stared at the long strip of stitches on my cat, cut through his beautiful coat. I knew when Tyrius woke up, he was going to *hate* it.

The goblin nodded. "He's still not out of the woods yet, but I think we got to him in time before he bled out."

I slipped my hands under Tyrius and lifted him up. He still hadn't opened his eyes, but the bleeding had stopped. It should have comforted me, but I felt ill.

"Are you some kind of healer?" I asked as I made my way towards the fire and gently eased the unconscious cat to the floor. My thoughts went to Pam and I was certain the woman would have had a fit at the sight of Tyrius. I had the feeling I wasn't the only one who loved him dearly. Tyrius had that effect on people, especially women.

The goblin washed his hands in a water basin and then dried them on his pants. "No. But I'm a damn good tailor."

I sighed through my nose. I wasn't in the mood for the goblin's misplaced sarcasm. I settled next to Tyrius, my back to the wall so I had a clear view of the goblin. "Why did you save us back there? You don't even know who we are. You could have let the veth hounds kill us."

The goblin placidly arched his brows. "It seemed like the right thing to do."

"No one does the right thing anymore," I said and shifted to a more comfortable position. "And no one does anything for free either. Do you want payment for this?"

The goblin tossed the bloody towel in the water basin, his face creased in anger. "Payment? Do I look like a leprechaun to you? If I hadn't stepped out, you'd be dead. Both of you."

That was true. Still, I wasn't buying the good Samaritan act. "Why do you live here in this cave with those hounds out there? Aren't you afraid that one day they might kill you?"

"No." The goblin lowered himself into the chair next to the fire, his bones cracking and popping with the effort. "They were here when I moved in. I couldn't make them leave, so I chose to live here among them."

Surprised, I stared at him, squinting in the fire light. "Why? Are you suicidal?"

His wrinkles deepened. "The hounds don't bother me. Not with my light. They are afraid of it, you see. I don't bother them, and in return they don't bother me."

I watched the tiny goblin. "That was no ordinary light, and you know it." I leaned back and crossed my arms over my chest. "If I had to guess, I'd say that was some witch light or something equally spelled. Am I right?"

Orange light from the fire flickered in the goblin's large eyes. He was silent in thought. Deep concern in his gaze, he looked at Tyrius but still he said nothing.

I could see loneliness in his eyes, or possibly something was troubling him. "How long have you lived down here?"

For the first time, the goblin looked tense. "Long enough."

My face twisted. "Why don't you leave? I'm sure you can find a better home than this creepy place. No offense."

The goblin continued to stare at the fire but never answered. I slipped my fingers through Tyrius's fur, watching as his eyelids flickered. The goblin said he would be fine, so why hadn't he woken up yet? How long did baals need to recover? I'd seen Tyrius wounded before, but never to this extent. Never this bad. Would he ever wake up?

Fear had my blood pounding in my ears so much that I thought my eardrums might burst, but the rage knocked it out of existence. This was my damn fault. If Tyrius died, it would be because of me. I might as well have stabbed him myself.

Damn those leprechauns. They sent us here to die. I should have never trusted them. Because of my stupidity, I had possibly gotten my best buddy killed, *and* my grandmother would lose her house.

My mind whirled, leaving me with the feeling that I was spiraling down into an endless black hole of self-pity. First with Jax, and now Tyrius…

I felt the meltdown-sweats trickling down my back. I couldn't have a meltdown now, damn it. Not when my life finally felt organized, and I was settled.

There was no other choice. I had to find the faerie.

Where was that stupid faerie? How was I supposed to find him now that Tyrius was out cold?

My eyes darted back to the goblin, who was still staring at the fire. Pitiful little creature. A thought occurred to me. If he'd lived in this hellhole for ages, he might know something of the faerie I was hunting.

I watched the goblin carefully. "Have you ever come across a faerie called Ugul?" I asked, praying the souls would give me a break.

The goblin turned and faced me, the nostrils of his large nose flaring. "Why?"

My anger returned. "Because I want to discuss mortgage rates with him." I glared at the goblin, feeling that I was at my wits' end. "Do you know where I can find him or not? It's a simple question?" I was running out of patience, and seeing Tyrius lying next to me looking dead, I was about to go psycho-bitch on his ass.

"I know where you can find him," said the goblin after a moment.

"You do?" I sat upright and held my breath. "Where? Where is he?"

The goblin snorted. "Right here. You found him. He's me."

My tongue felt heavy in my mouth as I narrowed my eyes, thinking this was another trick. *"You're* Ugul?" I leaned back shaking my head. "No, you're not. You can't be."

"Are you hard of hearing, angel-born? I just said that *he is me*. Unless you're looking for another faerie named Ugul, and that would be my great-grandfather, but he's been dead for three hundred years. The only Ugul in this mortal world is me."

I felt the start of a headache pound on my temples. "But Ugul is a faerie. You're a goblin."

The goblin's brown eyes gazed earnestly at me and he said, "Goblins *are* faeries. Faeries of the Light Court."

CHAPTER
14

I didn't know what else to do, so I started to laugh. "You're screwing with me. Aren't you, goblin?"

The goblin snarled at me. "What did you expect? A tall, handsome faerie with a muscled chest, small nose and dreamy eyes?"

I pursed my lips. "Something like that."

"Nah." He swiped a hand at me. "You watch too much television." The rest of his conversation was lost to me as he turned his head and mumbled to himself while looking into the fire.

"But…" Never had I ever come across any books or records that stated goblins were faeries. If I had, I think I would remember. This was nuts.

I exhaled slowly, my mind whirling. There was no way of knowing if this goblin was speaking the truth. But then again, I had never had the pleasure of meeting a faerie of the Light Court. I'd only ever encountered those foul Dark Court faeries. Maybe… maybe this goblin-faerie was telling the truth. Maybe he *was* Ugul.

It would explain why he was living out here, why he had an army of veth hounds surrounding his home, and why the faeries of the Dark Court could never reach him.

My eyes traced over his somewhat overly large head, misshapen face, ears that drooped nearly to his shoulders, flaky balding scalp, and brown skin deepened with wrinkles as he pondered over something. He would scare the daylights out of human children. And yet…

Conflicting emotions spiked through me like a shot of adrenaline. If he truly was Ugul, then my job was done. And with a simple delivery to the dark fae queen, I'd pay off my grandmother's debt and set things right again.

The thought made me smile. Still, the half-breed had saved us. Shit. I was so screwed.

"This makes no sense," I blurted out loud before I realized what I'd done.

"What doesn't make sense?"

I flinched at the familiar voice. Tyrius was sitting up, his blue eyes wide and healthy. His stitches had disappeared and white stubble spotted his belly as his fur was already starting to grow out. "What'd I miss?" said the cat.

My eyes burned as I fought to keep my tears at bay. I reached out and cupped his face into my hands, knowing he hated it but not caring. "Thank the souls. How do you feel?"

Tyrius pulled his head from my grip and looked down at himself. "Like I've been through a meat grinder. What happened? I don't remember. Must have blacked out. Did you patch me up?"

"No," I said, feeling the goblin's eyes on me as I turned and said. "He patched you up."

Tyrius looked at the goblin. "Thank you, kind sir," said the cat. "I'm in your debt. I'm Tyrius."

"Ugul," said the goblin and I watched Tyrius for a sign that the goblin was lying. My throat tightened when Tyrius didn't react the way he did at lies. He would have given me *the look*.

The cat turned his gaze on me and arched a brow, telling me with his eyes that the goblin was indeed the faerie we'd been sent to find. He sniffed the air. "You got any food in this joint? I'd kill for some pizza or a cheeseburger."

The goblin was eyeing us strangely, having seen our silent exchange. Clenching his jaw, his fingers gripped the arms of his chair as he said, "No. No meat. Just vegetables and some dried fruit."

Tyrius made a hacking noise. "You light faeries don't know what you're missing."

Faeries. It all but confirmed it. My pulse leapt, and I took a fast breath. "Here," I said, as I yanked a strip of beef jerky from my bag and gave it to Tyrius. "You knew goblins were faeries?"

"Uh—yeah," chewed the cat hungrily. "Goblins are faeries from the Light Court. I thought you knew that," he added between chews.

I moved my gaze back to the goblin. "I didn't." My heart rate was up.

"But the light and dark fae never did get along. Did they?" inquired Tyrius, as he moved next to Ugul, still chomping on his beef jerky. "Some sort of conflict between the courts, right?"

Ugul narrowed his eyes at the cat but said nothing.

Tension grew in the sudden silence, and I could see the faerie was regretting his decision to save us. I shifted my weight into the earth in case I had to move fast. A sting of cold seeped through my jeans as the leprechaun coin pulsed, reminding me there was still a way out.

Am I really going to do this?

Cool damp drifted in, and I looked out through the dark entrance of the cave to the darkness beyond. I was conflicted. That had never happened to me before on the hunt. Getting rid of demon scum was my specialty. Hell, I was damn good at it. It was the only thing in my life that brought me a sense of purpose. But this goblin-faerie gave me pause. He wasn't the demon filth I was so used to dealing with. Whatever he'd done had nothing to do with me. It wasn't my problem. Was he truly evil? He had saved us, but he had also killed the faerie queen's son.

"Why are you here?" Ugul's eyes rounded. "Who sent you?"

"Who says anyone sent us?" said the cat as he looked at me with encouragement. His eyes said *do it.*

Crap. My heart pounded so loudly I was sure Ugul could hear it.

"She sent you. Didn't she?" pressed Ugul as he pushed back his chair and stood, his resonant voice vibrating in me though he stood ten feet away. "Clever. She knew I'd keep you safe because of what you are. I should have let the veth hounds kill you." He took a step back, his eyes contemplating.

From my ear Tyrius snickered. "Awwww, he's so sweet I could fart hairballs."

I clenched my jaw, and my hands fisted. "I don't know what you're talking about." Anticipation tightened to a hard ball in the pit of my being. This wasn't good. The longer I waited, the harder it was going to be. Besides, I'd seen some of the magic he could do. I had no idea what else the faerie could pull out of his ass or just how powerful he was.

"Yes, you do," the goblin said softly, his dark expressive eyes flicking from me to Tyrius. "You came here looking for me. But you should never have come. I hate to kill the angel-born, but you're giving me no choice. I must protect myself. I must protect us all."

Tyrius laughed. "What's he been smoking?"

"Know that it gives me no pleasure, no pleasure at all. But I must kill you," Ugul said, and a shudder rippled through me as I crouched down low. "She will bring the end to everything, and I cannot allow it."

A hard expression marred Ugul's face, reminding me of just who he was and what he was capable of. He had killed the queen's son, after all. A cruel smile curved the corners of his mouth. The goblin raised his hand, his lips moving in a soundless spell as a ball of white light formed in his palms, the same white light I'd seen him use on the veth hounds.

And in a blinding fast motion, he hurled it at me.

But the goblin had no idea who he was screwing with.

I dove to the side, but not fast enough. I cried out as the ball hit my right arm. I crashed to the floor as the sphere exploded into white sparkles. Pain ripped through my body, and tension pulled my muscles tight one by one as the hot tingling started from my toes and worked its way up to my neck. A metallic stench tickled my nose and then I smelled burnt hair.

"Rowyn!" yelled Tyrius, over the ringing in my ears.

Trembling, I pushed with my knees, not entirely of my own will, and forced myself upright. When the wave of nausea stopped, I looked at Ugul's stunned face.

The goblin stared at me, frowning with frustration rippling over his face and deepening his wrinkles.

"Goddamn it. That hurt," I yelled, staring at the small remnants of his light magic like tiny electrical currents coiling over my body. It hurt like bloody hell, but I wasn't dead. By the look of utter shock on Ugul's face, I knew he'd planned to kill me with that ball of light.

But it hadn't worked.

Somehow his faerie magic hadn't done what he'd intended. My twisted angel and demon mojo had saved my ass.

A smile quirked my lips, and I aimed it at the suddenly unsure goblin. "You shouldn't have done that, dearest Ugul."

Ugul's face was murderously furious. Clearly ticked, the goblin strode to Tyrius, a strange language spilling from him. "Quiso ru setodies ipsos antgu?" he said wrathfully. Tendrils of white energy twined around his fingers, and I about lost it.

Screaming in rage I flew towards the faerie.

He turned his head at my approach, his arms up to hit me again with that light faerie magic crap. Using my momentum and with an open hand, I hit him as hard as I could on his left temple. Ugul opened his mouth to say something but then froze. His eyes rolled into the back of his head, and then he dropped to the ground, out cold.

Tyrius bounded next to me. "Rowyn, you did it! Not that I had any doubt whatsoever. You know what this means? We can save Granny's house!"

I stared down at the unconscious goblin-faerie at my feet, my stomach queasy. "Then why do I feel like an asshole."

CHAPTER
15

"He's a lot heavier than he looks," I panted as I dragged the goblin-faerie back through the tunnels by his feet. We'd used his small rowboat to get back across the water, and to my surprise and relief, the veth hounds never showed up again. He stank of cabbage and firewood. After he'd fallen unconscious I'd bound his wrist with iron cuffs—iron being a natural magic repellent—to keep him from doing any of his faerie magic and his feet with large zip ties. Not taking any chances, I'd gagged the goblin with an old scarf I'd found in his cave. I was sure, given the opportunity, he would try to conjure his magic.

The leprechaun coin was pressed against the skin of my right palm, sending waves of warmth pulsing into it. Using the coin as a guide, we were making really good time.

"Are you sure this is the right way?" questioned Tyrius as he padded ahead of me. Already the baal's fur had grown out and I couldn't even tell where he'd been stitched up. "We could be lost, you know. That coin might still be a trick."

"Why would it be?" I said, hearing my voice rasp. My heart was pounding and sweat had broken out all over my body. "The leprechauns told us where to find Ugul, and they were right. Why would they lie about this coin if they told us the truth about the faerie?"

"Because they want to mess with our heads? I don't like it," grumbled the cat.

"I know. You've told me a hundred times already. Think of it this way. Maybe this coin will bring us some luck. God knows we deserve a little."

Tyrius mumbled something but I couldn't make it out. My clothes were dry, and whatever was in that water had crusted over my jeans in thin flakes of dark green. My mood worsened with the effort of dragging the faerie, but I suspected the guilt of what I was about to do was even heavier than him.

My shoulders burned in pain. I exhaled loudly and pulled the faerie over a large rock.

"God I hope we're getting to the end of the tunnel soon," I breathed. The coin pulsed with warmth, telling me we were still on the right path. "I'm tired of hauling his faerie ass."

"We're almost there," answered the cat. "I can smell the grime from the Hudson River. Shouldn't be long now."

I raised my brows, feeling a trickle of sweat drip between my breasts. "Impressive."

Tyrius turned and looked up at me. "Have you thought about how we were going to get him to Mystic Quarter without the humans calling the cops on us with a kidnapping charge?"

"You mean faerie-napping," I offered and yanked the faerie by his feet. "I'm calling a cab once we get to the park. He's my drunk dad and we're taking him home."

Tyrius tsked. "A cab to Mystic Quarter? You sure that's wise?"

Annoyed, I glared at the cat. "As close as the cab driver's willing to drive us. I'll drag him to the bloody tower myself if I have to."

Tyrius flinched at my sour mood but said nothing as he kept walking, though a little faster now.

When we finally made it to the large cleft in the wall, the entrance to Elysium, I nearly collapsed in relief. I smiled as I spotted Tyrius's paw print on the wall and hauled the unconscious faerie through the gap. We'd made it out.

I thanked the leprechaun's coin silently as we finally arrived at the mouth of the tunnel. I didn't think Tyrius would appreciate me kissing it. Pocketing my lucky coin, I set Ugul gently on the ground and stepped out. Closing my eyes, I inhaled the fresh early morning air and then crashed into something hard yet soft.

A body. And I recognized its musky scent that had my heart pumping.

My eyes flashed open. "Jax?" I cried out, nearly tripping over Ugul. "What the hell are you doing here?"

Jax looked at me, and as our eyes met, I felt my chest contract. Damn. Why did he have that effect on me? I should be mad as hell, not tingly inside like a girl with a schoolboy crush.

Then his eyes drifted to Tyrius and finally came to rest on Ugul. A frown creased his face. "Father Thomas told me where to find you. I've been watching all the entrances not knowing when you'd show up. Who's that?"

"None of your business," I snapped, remembering that I had told the priest of my job with the faerie queen before I'd left, in case I never came back. I was suddenly aware of how close he was and how terrible I must look and smell. Heat rushed to my face. I loosened a tight breath, and I avoided looking at Jax as I felt his eyes slide to me.

I would not be hypnotized by his physical beauty, no matter how hot I thought he was. Damn he was hot. Hot. Hot. Hot.

Don't be stupid, Rowyn. He has a fiancée, I reminded myself.

"Why are you here, Jax?" I repeated. And when I looked at him, it was his turn to avoid my eyes.

Jax scratched the back of his neck. "I wanted to apologize for my mother's behavior."

"And yours too, I imagine," scolded Tyrius, staring at Jax as though he was ready to bite him. "Rowyn and I have no secrets. We're besties. I know all about the fiancée situation. Not cool, Jax."

More heat rushed to my cheeks. "Not now, Tyrius," I warned. I did not want to talk about this now. Besides, there was no way in hell I wanted Jax to know how I truly felt. It would pass, as all heartaches do. It had only been the one kiss. It *had* been just a kiss. Hadn't it?

Jax opened his mouth but then closed it, clearly not ready or willing to share whatever was on his mind. Dark spots stained his face, which only confused me even more.

"Father Thomas should have kept his mouth shut," I said and I pulled out my phone, scrolling through my directory. Where was that stupid cab number? "He had no business sharing my whereabouts. Especially when I'm on the job. As you can see, we're working here. I don't have time for idle chitchat."

"I came because I was worried." Jax ran his gaze down me and back up. Even in the darkness, I could see those thick lashes outlining his green eyes. My eyes moved to find his lips, a warm feeling starting in my middle.

I snorted. "Please."

"What possessed you to go in those tunnels alone?" Jax's tone was hard, clearly irritated. His features were tight and drawn. "You went inside Elysium? Every angel-born knows these underground passageways are traitorous and deadly. Which is why we *never* go in. Why didn't you call me?"

Peeved that he thought I needed his help, I said, "You don't return phone calls. Besides, I wasn't alone. I was with Tyrius."

"You bet, hot stuff," said the cat.

Jax exhaled slowly. "I meant to call you," he said and I nearly rolled my eyes. "Things have been tough lately."

"Why's that? Conjuring any lesser demons of late?" I was showing too much emotion again. "You don't owe me anything," I expressed, reeling in my feelings. "We worked on one job together. That doesn't make us married."

Jax sighed through his nose and I almost smiled at how peeved he looked now. "My mother needed me to stay with her at the house while my father was out on council business overseas," he said. "She can get pretty harsh when she's in one of her moods."

"You don't say?" I said pleasantly, and Tyrius snickered. I didn't care that she was his mother. I'd lost all respect for that woman.

"I know what you must think of her," Jax continued. "She said some pretty awful things."

"She's a pretty awful woman."

A muscle twitched in Jax's jaw. "She wasn't always like that." He hesitated. "Things at home have been very different since Gillian's death. My mother can't get past it."

"I never said that she should," I said, knowing that deep, excruciating pain from my own parents' deaths, "and I can't imagine the pain of losing a child, but she didn't have to shit all over me either. I shouldn't have gone to your house—a mistake I won't repeat."

An entrancing smile curved over his clean-shaven features. "You were worried about me." He gave me a goofy smile, the sort men gave when they thought the girl was smitten with them. He moved closer and lowered his voice. "I knew you liked me."

Damn him. Damn me.

"You should leave." I scrolled through my phone again, the names blurring as I swiped the screen. The last thing I needed was to be near Jax. "As you can see, we're good."

A groan rippled from Ugul and my breath caught. Crap.

Tyrius leapt next to the faerie. "We should hurry with the cab. He's waking up. Unless you want to hit him again?"

"No." I wouldn't hit him again. It wasn't my style. I wasn't about to knock him out whenever he came to. I wasn't a sadist.

"Who is he?" Jax knelt next to Ugul. "A goblin, by the looks of him. He's an ugly bastard. Isn't he?" he laughed. "Is he dangerous? Is that why you tied him up? Why does he smell like cabbage?"

"What he is, is not of your concern." *Go away, Jax.*

Jax gave me a wry smile. "I love an angry woman. Just shows how she likes to be in control."

My heart slammed against my chest and I scowled at him. What was wrong with this picture? "He's going to the faerie queen of the Dark Court. After that, he's not my problem anymore."

"I'll take you," offered Jax as he jumped to his feet. "My car's just over there on the street."

"No." There was no way in hell I was getting into a car with Jax. I wanted him to go away so I could hear myself think.

"Thank you. We'll take the ride," said Tyrius, and my mouth fell open.

I glared at Tyrius. "No, thank you. I'm calling a cab."

"Don't be stupid, Rowyn," mewed the cat. "Take Jax's offer. A cab will only call attention to ourselves in Mystic Quarter, not to mention that the driver might not even take us with your drunk *dad*."

Tyrius had a point. But I was stubborn. And right now, I didn't care how offended Jax looked. He had a freaking fiancée.

"I'll take my chances with the cab," I said, my voice flat. "There. I found the number. I'm calling it."

"Rowyn, let me take you," started Jax. "You'll need help dragging him to the queen. He looks heavy."

"I can manage," I snapped. Tyrius was looking at me like I was being an idiot. Okay, so maybe I was. I could accept it. What I couldn't accept was being around Jax. I didn't like the way he made me feel, like I was losing control. It wasn't a good feeling.

At that moment, my magic coin sent a cold pulse, making the skin under my jean pocket tingle. Maybe it was warning me to stay away from Jax. *Smart coin.*

A voice came on the other line. "Hi," I said and watched as Jax turned around looking upset. "I'd like a cab on the corner of Riverside Drive and—"

My hand cramped and I dropped the phone. It hit the pavement with a clang and a shriek of tearing plastic.

"Rowyn? What's wrong?" asked Tyrius, his eyes wide with terror.

My mouth was dry, and I felt like I couldn't get enough air in my lungs. "I don't know. I feel… strange." My gut cramped up, stopping my words. I blinked. I was getting dizzy. Maybe Ugul's magic had finally caught up with me.

A firm hand gripped me. Jax. "You're probably dehydrated. I have water in the car. When was the last time you had something to eat?"

"It's not dehydration," said the cat. "Something's not right. I can feel it too. There's a darkness in the air, and it smells of death and corruption."

My eyes fell on Tyrius and I blinked again, trying to focus. "I think it's gone now—"

Hot pain assaulted me from nowhere, and I cried out, staggering. My heart leapt, and I gasped. Fire seared across my skin and my rasping scream ripped through the air. I collapsed to my knees, shaking. My insides were on fire. I was burning from the inside out. I couldn't breathe. It hurt that much.

Voices were shouting. Jax and Tyrius. But I couldn't hear them over my pulse firing madly. Every beat pushed the fire through my pores. I managed a harsh gasp, and then I saw her.

An old woman with long wisps of white and gray hair stood in front of me. Her small eyes were lost in the heavy wrinkles, but I could make out one, milky white eye staring at me. I'd have recognized that face anywhere—the dark witch I'd stolen the grimoire from.

Evanora Crow smiled like…well, the devil, and then a heavy blackness finally smothered me.

CHAPTER
16

There was a faint scent of ash and candle mixed with the reek of mold, and I heard the distant murmur of an incantation. Closer, the sounds of voices speaking in Latin tickled my memory, winding gradually through my brain until they found a conscious thought.

I bolted upright, eyes wide and adrenaline slamming through me as fear jerked me from my drugged haze.

I was in a basement. Fake pine paneling decorated the walls, the ceiling was low, and a dirty plywood floor ran the length of the room. At the far end under the high basement windows, a platform took up the entire end of the room.

I was in the middle of the room, sitting in the center of a pentagram inside a large circle. Candles marked the corners below demonic symbols that I didn't recognize. Horror shot through me as I realized someone had used blood to draw the circle, not salt.

Crap. This had dark magic written all over it.

I felt eyes on me and looked up. Through the cluster of my damp bangs, I made out a group of black-robed figures standing outside the circle. The scent of earth and vinegar was almost a slap. Dark witches.

I knew stealing the dark witch grimoire would eventually come back to bite me in the ass. Apparently, the time was now.

The same cold throb in my pocket sent my skin tingling. The magic coin hadn't warned me about Jax. It had tried to warn me about the dark witches.

"Rowyn?" Panicked, I turned to the sound of Jax's voice. He sat with his back against the wall, his hands and feet bound with rope. His perfect features were pinched and angry, but there was also some underlining fear—fear for me. Blood trickled down his lips and I saw a nasty bruise on his forehead. Next to him was a brown lump, which I knew was Ugul, eyes closed, seemingly still out cold. Shit.

I'd had my share of misfortunes, but I'd always had them alone. Now I'd gotten Jax involved in my mess. He should have stayed home with mommy-dearest. I didn't want to have his death on my conscience.

Guilt hit hard. I'd gotten us all killed.

Fear pounded through me. "Where's Tyrius?" Maybe the clever cat had escaped and gone for help. But my drop of hope evaporated as I followed Jax's eyes to a cage next to him. I could see tan and black fur. Tyrius. He was in a freaking cage!

"Tyrius! Tyrius!" Rage flared through my being as I struggled to stand, still dizzy from the dark magic.

The cat's eyes met mine, and the sadness in them broke my heart. "She put a collar on me, Rowyn. A goddamn collar."

"Yes, well, we don't want you to use your magic, now do we?" Evanora Crow stepped from the cluster of witches. Bent with age, her shapeless linen forest-green gown dragged behind her as she shuffled forward, her fingers gnarled with severe arthritis. She was even uglier up close. Her one milky white eye seemed to roll around in its socket until it focused on me.

I was going to kill that witch bitch. Nobody put *my* Tyrius in a cage.

Steadying myself, I straightened and then shot forward. When I made it to the edge of the pentagram, I smacked my head on what seemed like an invisible wall—one that burned and hurt like hell.

I fell back on my ass. The shield that contained me hissed and burned, and I held my head in my hands as the pain only increased my sense of fury and desperation.

"Let me out!" I shouted. Twisting, I got a view of my weapons belt. My blades were gone. I was trapped inside the circle with nothing to defend myself. The smile on the witch's face only confirmed it.

The hag had me trapped in her blood circle. "Let me out, now! Or so help me God I will butcher you! I'm going to kill you!" I said again, giving in and smacking the shield with my hands.

The Greater demon Degamon's face flashed in my mind's eye. I could totally understand now why it'd been so pissed, being trapped in a circle, bound to the summoner. It explained why demons wanted to kill those who'd summoned them. It was a violation.

But I hadn't been summoned. I'd been spelled. I was trapped, bound to the circle as though it held me down with invisible chains. I was a prisoner in a jail made from the dark witch's circle. My eyes darted to the blood-stained dressing wrapped around Evanora's left hand. She'd used her own blood to make the circle. Great.

My eyes met Tyrius's in panic. "Don't worry, Tyrius. I'm going to get you out of there. I promise."

"Evanora Crow thanks you for her new familiar," said the old witch. "She has not had the pleasure of having one so powerful. Yes," said Evanora as she poked a knotted finger through the cage. Tyrius hissed and spat at her. She leaned back, a cruel smile playing on her thin lips. "Yes. He will do just fine. Evanora is glad of this gift."

Gritting my teeth, I glared at the witch. "Do you realize how creepy it is to refer yourself in the third person? You freaking sicko."

I was helpless. For all my skills of being both angel and demon-born, I was completely helpless.

I moved my gaze around the coven. Two males looked to be in their late forties, and a young blonde could have been the girl next door. Another's face was hidden in the shadows of his cowl. I knew he was male by the mere shape of his shoulders, and there was a small mousy-looking female witch with large eyes and a small mouth.

"What do you want?" I narrowed my eyes at the old hag. "You going to curse me or something? Go ahead. Give it your best shot." I knew some of the curses wouldn't work, thanks to my super-duper demon blood. But then again, she had trapped me in here. Maybe I was out of demon mojo.

Evanora shifted forward and stopped at the edge of the blood-circle. "What did you expect? That you could steal from Evanora Crow and not suffer the consequences? That there'd be no repercussions for what you did?"

"Maybe." I raised my chin. "You had so many other books lying around… I didn't think you'd miss it."

"Where is it?" Evanora tilted her head in a way that made her white eye the dominant one.

"I lost it. Sorry." I gave her my most innocent smile.

Evanora leaned forward, so close the reek of vinegar made my eyes water. There was also the unmistakable stench of an unwashed body. Gross.

"You're lying. You took it and now she wants it back. It does not belong to you. Where. Is. It."

"Like I said, the book is gone." I shrugged and added, "Even if I knew where it was, I wouldn't tell you." I grinned. "Plus, you didn't say the magic word." I knew the moment I told her where it was, we were all toast.

The witch's face went savage, her lips moving fast in some spell I knew was coming. I was very resistant to pain and illness, and I healed incredibly fast—but I wasn't immortal.

Evanora's spell hit me sharp and low, just beneath my heart, as though someone had shoved a blade through me. I fell back hard on the ground, and searing pain shot through my right hip as I hit the floor. The pain was getting worse as chills soaked in and I started to shiver. I needed time to think of a plan of escape. My mind raced, and I struggled to put together a plan. But it was hard to think about anything while my brain felt like it was melting and seeping out my ears.

"Tell Evanora where the grimoire is," said the witch, "and she can make the pain stop."

Yeah right. Like I was going to believe that. No way. I wasn't telling her.

When the worst of the spell was over, I pulled myself up. My mind remained muddled with the effects of the spell, but I could think clearly again. I'd read that damn grimoire more times than I could remember. Was there a chapter on how to break a magic circle? There had to be a way out. I knew sometimes demons had escaped their summoner's circle, only to kill the summoner. So there was a way. I just had to keep her talking until I figured it out.

Pain was tight around my throat, making me struggle to speak the words. "You stink," I said, my voice sounding old and tired. "Maybe you should have a dip in your cauldron."

Evanora frowned, and the other witches hissed their outrage. But the young blonde one giggled, not like a cheerleader's innocent giggle, but the laugh of a mad woman. Yikes.

Evanora's good eye was a very pale gray, and right now it was wide and calculating. I wanted to throw her off so she'd make a mistake, or make her angry enough that she'd step over the circle and break the connection. Then the bitch was mine.

I raised a brow at her hesitance. "No? Don't like soap, eh? Like to linger in your own stench?" The old witch was watching me, but I hadn't pissed her off yet. I dragged myself to the middle of the pentagram. "What happened to your eye? How did you lose it?"

"Rowyn, what are you doing?" came Jax's voice.

Evanora's face twisted in sudden fury, her mass of wrinkles nearly swallowing up her eyes.

"Don't have enough of your own magic so you have to borrow it, right?" I smiled at her visible anger. "Did you give it up in exchange for a demon's borrowed power? Did Evanora Crow dabble in a little too much of the dark magic? Could she not handle it?"

The witch's face slowly flushed scarlet, sweeping up from the white skin of her collarbones and throat over her chin and cheeks and up into her scalp.

"Oh…" I mocked, eyes wide. "The demon took it. You never wanted it to, but it was the price you had to pay for your powers. I'm right. Aren't I? You stupid dark witches. Never know when to give up. Never know when to stop. Don't have any powers of your own, so you have to borrow it from demons."

Evanora snarled, and with a swipe of her hand, something caught around my throat, choking me. I felt my breath cut off.

"You. Are. Weak," I managed. Her face darkened as she took a step closer to squeeze the life from me. I writhed under her spell, struggling to breathe as stars swam in front of my eyes.

When my vision cleared for a few seconds, I could see the tips of her shoes bordering the circle. *Just one more step. Come on, you old hag. Just one more step.*

Evanora watched my face, and then she looked at her feet. Her hard expression shifted and I saw the realization dawn on her at what I'd just attempted. Shit.

It was her turn to smile at me. "Nice try." Evanora drew back. Air flew into my lungs as I collapsed on the pentagram.

"Rowyn, just tell her where the damn book is," yelled Jax. "It's not worth your life."

Evanora's milky white eye rolled towards Jax. A small whimper escaped me, but I knew it was too late.

"If you hurt any of my friends," I screamed, thrashing madly, "the Gray Council will hunt every single last one of your stupid coven asses, and they'll burn you. You hear me! And I'll be dancing around the fire. Naked." I threw myself at the invisible shield, again and again. But it was no use. I couldn't break it.

I looked across at Jax. His face was pale and his eyes were wide. He was bracing himself for the pain that was coming. *Not Jax. Please not him.*

The witch spat a word or two, and then Evanora raised her open palm, flickering sparkles of black energy from her fingertips.

A hurtling black sphere struck Jax in the left shoulder and exploded into shards of black ice. He let out a short, harsh grunt of pain and sank to the floor, trembling as the effects of the dark magic coursed through him.

The blonde witch clapped her hands and jumped in the air, her eyes wide with amusement. "Do it again, Evanora! Cut his pretty flesh. Oh, so pretty, pretty, pretty. Where are your mighty angels now, eh? Angel-born," taunted the witch, looking mad with her large eyes and matted hair as though she'd never brushed it once in her life. She walked slowly around Jax and stopped on his right, pleasure dancing in her eyes at his pain.

I shivered to see Jax in such pain. I knew how he felt. When I saw the blood trickling from his ears, I let out a cry as my eyes filled with tears.

A guttural growl escaped me, deep and vicious. I didn't know where the sound came from—my inner beast, I guess. Maybe it was from my demon heritage or maybe it was my angel blood, but I was pissed. I wanted to kill this witch. No doubt she knew as soon as I was free, her ass was mine.

"If I tell you where it is," I said, swallowing, "will you promise to let me and my friends go?" It was a long shot. The hag had me by the balls, but it was worth a try. Who knew, maybe she could keep her word. "They had nothing to do with this. I stole your damn book, not them."

Bones cracked as Evanora turned her attention back to me. "Tell Evanora where the book is or he dies."

The blonde witch laughed and I glowered at her. *You're next*, I told her with my eyes, but she just smiled at me.

The problem was, I'd hidden the grimoire at my grandmother's for safekeeping now that Degamon had seen it. I couldn't risk leaving it at my apartment. But there was no way in hell I was going to give these dark witches my grandmother's address. They would kill her. Torture her, then kill her. I would never let that happen.

"It's at St. Joseph's church," I lied, hoping that Father Thomas could handle a few witches. "Hidden in the archives in the basement. It's hallowed ground. You can't get through," I lied again, knowing full well that dark witches could easily access the church being part human. Seeing Evanora's smile, she knew it too.

The old witch's grin was both terrifying and revolting. "Evanora will get her book back."

"Okay," I said, shaking inside. "A deal's a deal. You know where your damn book is, now let us go." I doubted she was going to let Tyrius go without a fight, but I would definitely smack that white eye out of her head to get him back. I raised my fists. "Let me out."

Evanora hobbled to the back of the room towards the long table. When she turned around she had a golden cup in her left hand and a dagger in her right.

"Evanora is going to bleed you," said the witch, as she shambled towards me, "bleed you to your very last drop."

Suddenly, the entire coven went to the table and when they moved away from it, they all had similar cups in their hands.

A sliver of fear ran up my spine. "I gave you the book," I said, my voice shaking. I couldn't help it. "We had a deal." I looked at Jax and he slowly pushed himself against the wall, the traces of pain staining his face.

The old witch crossed the room until she stood next to the circle. "Evanora will not abide by those restrictions anymore. You are the exception to every rule, every law." Her lips thinned from a past anger, and she pointed the dagger at me. "Evanora wanted her book back, but she also wanted you. Your blood. Your blood is a gift to the coven. It holds more power than you know. It will make Evanora more powerful than any dark or light witch combined.

Shadow and light flows in your veins and Evanora wants it. All of it."

Bile rose up in the back of my throat. "You're sick. You're a seriously twisted bitch."

The old witch thought if she drank my blood, it would give her power. Was that even possible? Was the source of my power in my blood? Evanora seemed to think so. Maybe she was right.

My heart sped up at the greed and desire for power in her small eyes. Evanora's triumphant, toothy smile made my blood turn to ice.

Whatever I was, the other witches all stared at me with starving, feverish eyes like I was some juicy steak.

But they weren't going to eat me. They were going to drink me to death.

CHAPTER
17

"**M**y blood is poison," I said, hating the hunger in her smile. "It's toxic. The archangel told me just before I killed him." Crap, I shouldn't have said that. "Just one drop and it will kill you. You'll die a very painful death. Slow, I imagine."

Evanora chuckled. Lips moving, she raised her daggered hand and I was thrown on my back as a weight held me down, my arms and legs splayed out. I was paralyzed. Fear pounded through me, but I couldn't move.

I hated dark witches. And now I think I hated them even more than faeries.

"Rowyn!" This time Tyrius's frightened voice shattered my soul. I had failed him. I should have never stolen that stupid book. Look what it had brought me. He would be her slave now. She would use him and drain him. Maybe even kill him.

I couldn't even see him. When I tried to move my head, it was as though it was cemented to the ground.

The sound of metal rattling reached me mixed with a heartfelt growl. I knew Tyrius was beating on his cage. He was trying to get out. Trying to save me.

Hot tears spilled from the corners of my eyes into my hair. My lips trembled, and I couldn't stop them as an ache throbbed from my chest to my throat. This wasn't how I'd imagined my death. I always thought I'd die in battle, standing up with dignity. A badass. Not lying down, helpless like a chicken ready to be slaughtered.

"Evanora Crow will be the most powerful witch that ever was," said the old witch as she knelt next to my right wrist. "Eternal power," her milky white eye was spinning. "Immortal."

"Screw you," I seethed, unable to spit in her face—because I would have if I could move my head. "I'm going to come back as a ghost and haunt your ass, witch."

Evanora laughed, and then she sliced the blade across my wrist.

I hissed at the initial pain, but it was nothing compared to the disgust I felt as she caught my blood with her cup, licking her lips, careful not to damage the circle.

Bile rose up in the back of my throat again and it took some effort to push it back down. If I vomited now, I might choke on it. A lame way to die.

The hairs on my arms rose at the sound of sudden loud chanting. The chanting took on an edge of vicious, spiteful satisfaction and continued to rise in pitch until it sounded almost like shouting.

To my horror, the hooded witch removed his cowl and knelt to my left. I could only see half of his face in my paralysis. Candle light reflected off his dark bald head, his skin nearly as dark as his black robes.

And then something hard slashed across my left wrist and I felt the cold metal of another cup press against my skin.

"Bastards!" I shouted as loudly as I could over the thunderous chanting, blinking back my blurred vision. "You'll pay for this! I swear it on the souls. I'll kill you! I'll freaking kill you all!"

The last part came out more in a sob as my throat closed up.

This is really happening. I am really going to die this time—

There was a loud bang, followed by the sound of footsteps hurtling down to the basement.

"You!" I heard Evanora cry out, sounding both surprised and outraged. Grimacing, she pushed herself straight, cradling the cup with some of my blood protectively against her chest. "How dare you interrupt Evanora!" Her shock transformed into snarling anger in a heartbeat, and spit flew out of her mouth.

179

From the corner of my eye, I saw the black witch dart forward, black energy spheres in his hands as he screamed words of some incantation.

What the hell was happening? Dark figures ran around my line of sight, but I couldn't make out anything. My stupid eyes were on the ceiling. Cries and incantations sounded all around me, followed by the horrid sound of flesh being torn and the fast, thrashing sound of fists pounding on soft flesh. Again. And again. And again.

The witches were fighting. But fighting who?

My skin tingled and I felt a release, like a sudden unleash of a tight rope that had bound my limbs to the floor.

I was free. I could move again.

I rolled to my side and my eyes found him. Shirtless and barefoot, the goth-rockstar-finger-licking-good-drop-dead-gorgeous-brooding vampire snapped the neck of the black witch and tossed him easily to the floor.

Danto.

And what a sight for sore eyes he was. Even if he was a vamp, I could have kissed him. And he had brought two of his posse—a female vamp with black pigtails with purple tips wearing sunglasses and a thin lanky male vamp with fair hair and skin. I almost smiled.

A dark figure ran forward towards Danto, dagger in hand. From the shadow of the wall, the witch sprang at the vampire. With impossible speed, Danto ducked to the side and sank his teeth into the witch's neck. The witch's eyes went wide, and I recognized the horror in them.

"Payback's a bitch," I snarled and watched as Danto bit down with such force I heard the snap of bone, and then the witch collapsed to the floor.

I pulled myself to my knees and inspected my wrists. Crap. They were in bad shape. The cuts were deep and my blood trickled down my arm. The wounds would heal, but I needed to stop the bleeding fast. Ripping the edge of my shirt, I made two makeshift bandages and wrapped them tightly around my wrists. Then, gathering up what energy I had left, I stood. Head spinning, I ignored the sudden nausea and straightened. Jax was sitting on the ground, sawing at his bonds with something sharp. He looked up and our eyes met. His mouth dropped open at something behind me, and his eyes widened in sudden fear.

"Rowyn! Behind you!"

I spun and faced the blonde witch. She had a black dagger in her hand, its black mist coiling around her wrist. My death blade.

"That's mine," I said. "Didn't your parents teach you that it's not polite to play with other people's toys?"

The witch giggled and wiped her bloody nose. "Doesn't matter. I'm going to kill you with it. And I'm going to take your blood."

She moved forward and I backed away. My back hit something solid and I hissed as the invisible shield of the circle burned my skin. Damn. I was still trapped in the stupid witch circle.

"Why should Evanora be more powerful than the others?" said the witch. "She's old. Her time's up. It should be me. *I* should have the power." She had the crazy eyes all people have before they do something crazy, and she stepped over the blood outline and into my circle. "It's my turn. Give it to me!" she shouted and sprang.

A large cup smashed against the back of her head. With a small cry, the witch fell to the ground, splayed over the pentagram. Blood poured from a large gash on her scalp, a fatal one.

Ugul stood where the blonde witch had been, his bound hands still holding the cup he'd smashed her head with. There was blood on it. I didn't understand the expression on his face as he dropped the cup. He hobbled forward and dragged his foot through the edge of the blood circle making a five-inch gap. The circle was broken.

Twice he had saved my life. Twice he didn't look happy about it.

And I was the asshole who would bring him in.

I didn't have time to dwell on my guilt. Freed, I sprang into action, grabbed my death blade and hurled myself towards Tyrius's cage. Using the hilt of my weapon, I smashed it against the lock. It fell to the ground with a loud clang and I swung open the cage's door.

I reached in and pulled out my cat, my friend, my Tyrius.

A delicate, silver collar was wrapped around his neck. "I knew you'd save me," said the cat through heavily lidded eyes. His voice was low and weak, as though that freaking collar was draining him.

I had just one thing left to do. Slipping my hands around his neck, I grabbed that goddamn collar, and putting all of my rage in it—ripped it in half.

Tyrius sprang up and stretched, yawning. "Thanks, Rowyn."

I smiled and tossed the collar. "You bet." Tyrius's fur was dull and he swayed on his feet as though drunk. Not wanting to take any more chances with him, I picked him up and draped him around my shoulders, his favorite spot. Once I knew he was secure and safe, I spun around, dagger in hand. I was going to kill that old hag for what she had done to Tyrius and what she had planned to do to him.

I darted back into the fight, my eyes flitting around the basement looking for Evanora. Only then did I realize the sounds of battle were gone. There was just the sound of my blood hammering wildly in my ears. The fight was over.

Five witches were dead on the basement floor, some with their necks torn and bloodied. But there was no sign of the old witch.

Danto crossed the room towards me with a predatory grace that only he could pull off barefoot. He wiped the blood from the corner of his mouth. "You okay, Rowyn? Tyrius?"

"We're good." I sheathed my death blade, just noticing that my wrists had stopped bleeding. I felt my skin prickle and tighten as it was already starting to heal. Where was my soul blade? "I don't know how you found us, but we owe you." I sighed loudly, not even knowing where Evanora had taken us. The last time I'd seen the vamp, he'd been really pissed. He was the last person or half-breed I would have expected for a rescue mission. But here he was. Interesting.

I smiled at the vamp. "Thank you." A feeling of nausea rose at the thought of the witches drinking my blood.

Danto's expression was unreadable, but his eyes were hard. "Do you even know where you are?"

"No," I said glancing around. "Should I? I don't recognize this place."

A frustrated sigh slipped from me, catching as my gaze fell upon Jax. He stood in the shadows of the basement, rubbing his wrists. There was an odd expression on his face as he kept his distance from the vampires. I looked away before he caught me staring at him.

Ugul sat next to the bloody circle, his hands and feet still bound. He gave me a hard look. I would deal with him later.

"You're in Mystic Quarter," said Danto, and I spied his two vamp friends exchanging words. "My friends saw the witches drag three bodies into their shop. When I heard that they might be angel-born, I had a feeling it might be you. You do have a talent for attracting trouble."

"Thanks." My face warmed. "This is a witch's shop?" Figures it's where they'd assemble and do their dark magic crap.

"The Rusty Cauldron," said Danto. "I believe the owner is the young witch with a cracked skull."

My gaze swept the room. The metallic smell of blood was mixed with the scent of candles and incense. This had been self-defense, but still, I didn't know how we were going to explain five dead witches. The bite marks would definitely alarm the Witch Courts. They would take this as a vampire attack. How could I explain that the witches were about to sacrifice me for my blood and the vampires had come to rescue me? And from what I'd heard Isobel say about Danto, he wasn't favored among the courts. I didn't want to cause him more hardship for saving my ass.

There was also Ugul to think of. The Gray Council would take him into their custody and bring him to Isobel instead, and I would lose my money.

"I see you've found your faerie," said Danto, following my gaze. His brows creased in a frown. "His name sounds familiar. I thought so the first time I heard Isobel mention it. I'll have to do some more digging, but," he said turning his gray eyes back on me, "are you sure you want to take him to the fae queen? There's something she's not telling us about him."

I knew Danto and the queen shared some history, but I wasn't about to give away my chance at saving my grandmother's home just because the vamp hated the fae queen. Hell, I hated her too, but I was going to see this through. I had no choice.

"How do we dispose of the bodies?" I asked, wishing to change the subject.

A knowing smile curved over him as his eyes fastened on me. "We'll take care of them."

"Good man, uh, vampire," muttered Tyrius, his voice heavy with sleep. I felt him purring against my neck.

I couldn't believe our luck, but something told me I wasn't finished with the old witch. A feeling of unease pulled at my chest tightly.

Evanora Crow was gone. And she had a cup of my blood.

CHAPTER
18

I sat on the dirty floor, my back against the wall as I watched the vampires haul the bodies up the basement stairs. I marveled at their strength. Even the female vamp, whose name I heard was Vicky, was as strong as an ox, and she was shorter and more delicate that I was. But that was just an illusion. She could probably kick my ass.

I especially enjoyed watching how Danto's chest muscles bulged as he dragged the dead black witch. He seemed to have found a purpose, making his features even more pleasant to admire. What could I say? There was no law that said I couldn't look. I was single, and the rule was, single gals were *allowed* to look. Besides, I had almost died, might as well enjoy the view.

I didn't ask and didn't care what they did with the bodies. I just didn't want to see or think about them or how they'd wanted to bleed me dry and then drink my blood. Those witches had almost killed me.

Tyrius had left about forty minutes ago to scout out the streets of Mystic Quarter for any more dark witches or anything else that looked suspicious and out of place, which could be anything really in this quarter. But he was so adamant on going, I let him, knowing he felt guilty about what almost happened to me, to us. But that was in no way his fault. The fault was mine. All mine.

Danto had thought it best to camp out here for the rest of the day and get some much-needed rest before we showed our faces in Mystic Quarter. Faeries slept during the day, and the dark faerie queen would not open the tower until sunset. Once the sun was down, we'd bring Ugul to the faerie queen.

Staying in the basement for a little while longer seemed like a smart idea. I was also hoping to catch Evanora Crow. I had a feeling the old bag would return. But after an hour of waiting, I realized she probably wasn't coming back. Ever.

Ugul sat next to the basement stairs across from me, looking foul and angry that he was still tied and gagged. I tried not to look at him too much. Otherwise my guilt might make me do something stupid.

I looked up at the sound of hard-soled boots on plywood to see Jax lowering himself next to me.

"Here," he said and handed me a dagger, which I recognized as my soul blade, and my leather messenger bag. "Found it with the rest of our stuff."

"Thanks," I said, feeling myself warm at his nearness. His thigh brushed against mine as he settled next to me, and the faint smell of soap and musk rose up around me. The scent was pleasant, too pleasant. *Why does he have to be so damn close?*

"I wanted to talk to you," said Jax as he folded his hands on his lap.

Shit. Here it comes. My heart leapt and then settled back into its usual pace. I wasn't ready for a *talk*, talk. A shiver lifted through me, and I blinked as his eyes fixed on me from under his lowered brow. Just freaking great.

I sighed focusing my attention on Keith, the pale vampire, as he examined the fingers from the young blonde witch. Then, with a quick jerk of his hand, ripped off one of the dead witch's fingernails and pocketed them. Creepy.

"Please don't," I breathed. "I know what you're about to say, and frankly, I don't care." My voice came out hard, and I was fine with it. He had no business kissing me when he had a poor woman waiting for him somewhere. I would never take another woman's man. Ever.

Jax rested his head against the fake wood paneling, our shoulders touching, but I wouldn't move away. Instead, I felt myself easing against him. I shifted back. *What the hell am I doing?*

"When I first met you," he began, his voice rumbling pleasantly, "I was impressed with your skills, your abilities—just the way you moved like a deadly shadow. I thought you were the hottest thing on two legs."

I frowned at the smile on his face. "Don't patronize me," I growled. "I'm too tired for this crap."

"I'd heard many things about Rowyn Sinclair, the Hunter," continued Jax, ignoring my outburst, with the same sly grin on his face. "Imagine my surprise when they all turned out to be true. You're fierce and beautiful and downright scary at times."

"Damn straight," I muttered, satisfied. *Did he just call me beautiful?*

"You're tough and have more balls than most of the guys I know." He laughed, showing off his pearly whites. "And you can take a serious ass whooping—"

"What are you getting at, Jax?" I met his green eyes, my heart thumping madly in my chest.

He pulled his eyes down. "I kissed you. I shouldn't have done that."

Was that an apology? Didn't really sound like one.

Danto turned around and my face flamed as he met my eyes, a curious expression playing on his features. Damn that keen vampire hearing. I couldn't even have a private conversation. No doubt, Vicky and Keith were also listening in. Great.

"It was just a kiss. I'll live," I said, making sure my voice didn't betray me. *If we had slept together, I would have kicked your pretty ass. Okay, maybe I would have slapped it playfully a few times—then, I would have kicked it!* "It was a spur of the moment thing. We don't have to talk about it anymore. Okay? Are we good?"

Jax didn't say anything for a while, and the uncomfortable silence was sending my pounding heart into overdrive. "The thing is," he said, "it wasn't. Not for me."

Crap. My pulse pounded, and I hated how he could do this to me. How his just sitting here turned me into a hot mess idiot. I reeled in my feelings before they had me found out.

"I care about Ellie," he said in a very business-like tone, as though he were commenting on the weather. "She's kind. Funny. Smart. You'd like her, you know. She's a good person. She's not as badass as you are, but she can hold her own in a fight."

I fumed. "I don't care." *Liar. Liar. Liar.*

"We dated for a while," said Jax. "And when I brought Ellie to meet my parents..." he took a labored breath, "I saw a change in my mother, a happiness I hadn't seen since Gillian was alive." He paused for a heartbeat. "At the time, I thought I was doing the right thing. I knew if I married Ellie, it would make my mother happy."

My breath caught and my eyebrows rose. "You would marry someone just for the sake of your *mother?*" I didn't care how harsh my voice sounded. I hated the woman. She was vile, a drunk, and overly medicated. "This isn't seventeenth-century Europe. You do have a choice." Not that I cared...

Jax's face held traces of a deep sadness, something I recognized in myself. "Since my sister's death, my mother's never been the same," he said, his voice melancholy. "She's in some perpetual depression, her own hell. I barely see my own father because of it. He can't stand her when she's like this."

"I can relate," I mumbled. That woman could get under anyone's skin.

"That's why I've been so persistent in trying to find my sister's killer," said Jax, his voice low and controlled. "I thought if I did, she would change somehow. Knowing that I killed it, and knowing it would never hurt another child."

My head jerked. "You found the demon?"

Jax's voice was strained. "No. But I'm close. I've been tracking it for the past six months. There's a pattern with the way it chooses its victims. I finally figured it out. And it's how I'm going to kill it."

"Jax, a rakshasa demon is deadly. You shouldn't be hunting it on your own. It's too dangerous." I cringed as I realized I almost offered to go hunting with him. The last thing I needed was to be stuck alone with Jax, hours on end, in crappy motels searching for a demon. It would be way too easy to get into trouble with him, looking the way he did, the way his green eyes lit up when he looked at me...

"Right." The smile he gave me never reached his eyes. "And what you've been doing is any different?

Face it. We're both hardheaded and we'll do whatever it takes to kill demons."

"Maybe." I twirled my soul blade with my fingers. I had to admit he was right about that.

Jax let out a long sigh. "I love my mother. It kills me to see how much she's suffering. Is it so wrong for a son to want his mother to be happy again?"

No. I guess not.

And in the silence that followed, I could easily visualize Jax and some mystery, gorgeous blonde walking down the aisle with his mother wiping away false tears alongside the echo of his father.

"Everything was fine," said Jax, "until I met you." The sudden heat in his voice pulled my skin tight. "Now things are… complicated."

"Complicated?" I raised my brow at him, not liking how he had said the word, like I had somehow screwed up his perfect little life. That somehow this, this thing, whatever this was, was *my* fault. Hell, I never asked for this.

He pressed his hand against mine, and his warm skin sent a flame through my body.

"Are you going to go through with it?" I asked, my voice low, surprised that I even went there. Sweat trickled down my back, and my pulse thrashed like I'd just run around the block.

Jax clenched his jaw. "I have to. You don't understand—"

My breath shook as I exhaled. I pulled my hand away. "Whatever. It's your life. Just leave me out of it." I noticed a flicker of movement and then saw Tyrius clambering down the steps.

"Rowyn, I'm sorry. I didn't want to hurt—"

"What? My feelings?" I laughed, but my face flamed. "Please, I barely know you. Don't presume to think that you know me either because you don't. You don't know anything about me." Now I was pissed.

Jax raked his fingers through his hair. "I still want us to be friends."

"Sure," I said with a false brightness. I felt sick. I was going to puke. My stomach cramping, I jumped to my feet. I turned to face him, keeping my face void of emotion. "Let me give you a tip, Jax. Just so you know. Men with fiancées don't go around kissing other women. That's on you. You should remember that." I turned around before he could see the moisture in my eyes.

Damn him. Why did he have to tell me all this? Did he think it would help or was it his plan just to confuse me more?

He was being his noble self, a white knight, hoping to cure his mother's grief, and I was being a selfish ass.

I should have kept my feelings in check. Jax and me, that was never going to happen. It was a fact.

I needed to get away from Jax, and he needed to stay the hell away from me.

CHAPTER
19

By the time we left the basement of The Rusty Cauldron, my mood had soured to the point where I could actually feel the anger seeping out of my pores, like stinky sweat. I was *that* ticked off.

The streets of Mystic Quarter were unusually empty for this time of night, the gathering darkness rushing in quickly to fill the spaces left by the broken streetlights like a black fog. I spotted a few vampires watching us from their balconies and windows, but the two faeries that had been sitting quietly in the quarter's park hurried in the opposite direction as soon as they heard our arrival.

Tension and adrenaline raced through me. Something was not right. And by the cut off conversations of the others, I knew they felt it too. Taken all together, it had the feel of a brewing thunderstorm, and we were it.

I was tired and hungry. My emotions were spinning out of control, and I was angry at myself for letting them get this far. I needed to focus. I needed to forget about me and focus on the real issue. My grandmother was about to lose everything. She was my only family left. Helping her was more important than my selfish desire to have a relationship, to get more kisses from Jax, and maybe something more.

I wasn't weak, and I wasn't in dire need of affection. I didn't need a man to feel complete, to give my life value, or to function. And I wasn't one of those women who would wait around in the hopes that their man would eventually come around. Hell no. Life was too short to wait around for something that might never happen.

Were soul mates real? I had no idea. Still, I was never one to believe in the "happily ever after." Things just didn't happen. You had to work at relationships. You had to make your own happily ever after, your own destiny. That's what I believed in.

If I did happen to meet a great guy, well, that would be wonderful. But if I didn't, if it never happened for me, I wouldn't feel sorry for myself. I would keep on going.

I was blessed, or cursed, with being special. With having the best of two worlds—of shadow and light—and I was going to use it.

I might be screwed up when it came to relationships, but Jax's situation was worse. That was a nightmare I had no desire to be a part of. Knowing myself, the best way to deal with this sort of situation was to put as much distance as I could between Jax and me. I would eventually forget his hot ass.

But the fool had decided to come. I didn't want to make a scene, so I'd kept my mouth shut. I didn't want Jax knowing how much his little *talk* had left me feeling worse. Much worse.

But it would pass. It always did.

"Uh, Rowyn, you okay?" Tyrius padded next to me. The worry in his voice pulled my eyes down to him.

"I'm fine," I lied. "Let's just get this over with. And by this, I mean him," I said and pulled Ugul forcefully next to me. Danto and Vicky had sneaked ahead of us while Keith kept watch at the back with Jax.

"You do know why he's coming. Don't you?"

I kept my eyes on the street. "To be a pain in my ass?" I said finally.

Tyrius snorted. "The douchebag likes you."

"He's engaged."

"Engagements are broken all the time," said the cat, his voice light and airy.

"Yeah, well, I don't think this one will. His mother thinks I'm a demon," I said. *Maybe I am.*

"Nothing wrong with that," mewed the cat. "Seriously. Demons are awesome. We lie, cheat, steal,

197

and drink just like regular folk. Angels have a celestial stick up their asses. They're boring."

"There's no future there." I stole a glance behind me. Jax had gone back to fetch his car, which explained the dangerous looking double barrel shotgun draped over his shoulder. He had a swagger in his step like he was anxious to kill something.

My legs grew heavier with every step. I felt drained, like I needed to sleep for a week.

Tyrius titled his head as he walked, trying to get a look at Ugul. "Your faerie looks a little off."

"He's an old goblin," I snapped. "Of course he looks off."

"No, I mean he looks sick." Tyrius's voice had turned serious. "Rowyn, I think he's sick or something."

Remembering how the goblin tried to kill me with his faerie magic, anger welled inside my chest and I dragged him harder. "He's just trying to trick us into thinking that. I'm surprised you would get suckered into his act."

"Rowyn, stop!" shouted Tyrius and I whirled around. "Look at him. He can't breathe. Take it off!"

Still frowning, I looked at the goblin and I cringed. The skin around his face had darkened, looking almost black, and he was sweating, so much so that he looked like he'd just stepped out of the shower. This didn't look like an act. If it was, he deserved an Oscar.

This wasn't me. I wasn't this cruel. I knew if I kept handling him like this, he'd end up dead before we even reached the tower.

With my chest tight, I hooked my arm under the goblin's and lowered him so he could sit on the sidewalk. Ugul let out a sigh through his nose, his lids fluttering like he was about to pass out from the lack of air.

Making up my mind, I removed the makeshift gag around his mouth. He took a deep breath, then another, then another, all of them sounding wheezy. Man. I *was* cruel. What was wrong with me?

I pulled out a water bottle from my bag and put it to his lips. The goblin drank long and deep, finishing the entire bottle in four big gulps. He closed his eyes, seeming to enjoy the moment.

As I let myself fall next to the goblin, a little motion to the left caught my eye. I spotted half-breeds stepping out from the shadows. Their faces were covered in darkness, but I could still read the curious expressions. Two witches watched us next to a lamppost like silent wraiths, and a collection of faeries stepped out from a neighboring shop. Tyrius's sudden cry had been like an alarm in this place, and now they all came out. No doubt, in a few minutes the entire quarter would know we were here. Queen Isobel would know.

Jax, Danto and the other two vampires all gathered around us, seemingly to make a protective circle.

Tyrius leapt onto my lap. "You did good, Rowyn. I didn't think he was going to make it past the next block."

Shame hit me hard as I looked at the goblin sitting there, hunched over, his breathing strained and looking ill. I wished things were different. As a Hunter, I killed demons. I didn't know how to feel about bringing in some poor old goblin to a queen I hated. I wasn't supposed to feel guilt. I was supposed to get paid and move on. But this sucked.

Ugul, with his eyes still closed said, "Thank you."

My eyes went to his wrists. The cuffs I'd tied them with were stained in blood. "Why did you save my life, back there? You could have let the witch kill me. Then you'd be free."

Ugul's eyes snapped open and he looked at me. "Are you still going to bring me to the faerie queen of the Dark Court?"

I swallowed. "I have to—"

"Then it doesn't matter now, does it?" Ugul let his head fall to his chest, and I could still smell the cabbage rolling off of him.

Tyrius looked up at me, his eyes sad, which only made me feel worse. Great. Now Tyrius thought I was evil.

"Is it true what she said you did?" I asked, gazing at the sidewalk and hearing the guilt in my voice. "Did you kill her son?"

His voice cold, Ugul enunciated clearly, "If I told you he'd tried to kill me first, and I was only trying to protect myself, would you believe me? Would you let me go?"

"I don't know." I was belligerent because I was afraid and confused. My throat closed, and I sighed. I hated feeling this way. I was not accustomed to it. A moment of clarity would be better than all this confusion. And awkwardness. And misery. *Souls help me, what do I do?*

"Your baal knows I speak the truth."

A brief look of pain passed over Tyrius's features. "It's true. There are no lies in his words."

My eyes widened. "Then why would she go all this way and hire me to find you if you're innocent? It doesn't make sense."

"She wants something from me," said Ugul, his voice strained. "I have something she wants. But she can't have it. She must *never* have it."

"Like what?" My gaze rolled over the goblin's clothing. "We searched all your pockets. There's nothing on you."

"Maybe it's back in his cave?" said Tyrius, and he looked up at the goblin. "Is it in the cave?"

Ugul's slow shake of his head sent a tug on my heart. "You cannot bring me to her," he said, his face scrunching up in fear. "Please. She will bring only darkness to this world, a mighty darkness that will devour and corrupt everything. Please believe me. You mustn't take me to her. You must let me go."

We were almost there. I could see the silhouette of Sylph Tower in all its ugliness through a clearing of buildings.

I met his large brown eyes, reading a sad understanding there.

"Rowyn?" came Tyrius's voice, his eyes both worried and defiant. "What do you want to do?" I could tell he wanted me to let the goblin go. Tyrius believed him. And so did I. Maybe I always had.

Making up my mind, I yanked a key from my bag and unlocked the iron cuffs at Ugul's wrist. Before the cuffs fell to his feet, I had cut the bounds at his ankles with my soul blade.

Ugul looked up at me, surprise flashing in his big round eyes.

"I can't do this," I said, my throat dry and closing in. "It's wrong. I won't. I won't do it." I took a steadying breath because of the wrath I knew would come from my decision. "You're free to go, Ugul."

Tyrius jumped to the ground as I lurched to my feet and pulled Ugul up with me. I gripped his elbows and steadied him until he stopped teetering.

Ugul's eyes filled with tears, and I let him go. I turned my head and looked away, blinking fast. Who knew an old goblin almost had me crying like a baby.

"You have a kind soul, Rowyn," said the goblin. "Don't let anyone tell you otherwise."

"Yeah, well, I'm not perfect." I turned to see the goblin rubbing his wrists. The flesh around them was raw and oozing.

"Perfection is boring," said the goblin, making me laugh.

A scuffing in the street brought my eyes up from the goblin. I caught a glimpse of the faeries hurrying away and leaving the street deserted. Jax was staring at me like I'd lost my mind, but Danto was smiling, a beautiful dazzling smile, clearly pleased that in the end I wasn't going to bring the goblin in.

"You know what this means. Don't you?" said Tyrius, a gleam in his eye. "Cheese cake and beer."

I laughed long and hard, breaking through the sullen silence of Mystic Quarter. "You're one crazy cat. You know that?"

Tyrius sat and curled his tail around his paws. "Don't forget charming. You've never set your eyes on a more charming feline than this, baby."

I lost my smile when I looked back at the goblin's face. Tiredness and worry pulled his shoulders down, and he looked older as though this ordeal had aged him fifty years. "Where will you go?" I asked softly. "Back to Elysium?"

"No," said Ugul. "It's time for a new home." His thin lips curved into a smile. "Maybe someplace warm."

"I hear Mexico is great this time of year," said Tyrius. "Lots of caves near the Pacific shoreline."

An image of a beautiful golden beach and aqua-colored water flared in my mind's eye. A vacation sounded great. But without any money…

I knew letting Ugul go would be a devastating blow to my grandmother. I went cold at the thought of the look on her face when I told her. When I told her I failed.

Something rough grazed my skin and I looked up, startled that Ugul was holding my hand in his. His skin was harsh and calloused like rock scratching my skin.

Ugul looked at me, his face bright. "You do know *what* you are. Don't you?"

I shifted on my feet, awkward at his closeness and that he was still holding my hand. "That I'm both demon and angel? Yeah, I got the memo about six months ago."

"I wasn't sure at first," said the goblin, a thin smile on his wrinkled face. His eyes were tired and weary. "Yes," he said as he put more pressure on my hand. "I can feel it. There can be no mistaking it."

"What? Is there something else I should know?" I leaned forward, having no idea what he was talking about. In my line of sight, I saw Tyrius moving closer until he nudged my leg.

Ugul blinked and then smiled. "Shadow and light are two opposing and separate things. And yet you can hold them both inside you. It's remarkable, really. It's what makes you so special."

My eyes darted to Tyrius who looked up at me and shrugged. I pulled my eyes away from the cat and watched the smile disappear on the goblin's face. "Why do I get the feeling you're about to tell me something bad?"

Ugul's expression turned serious. "Have they approached you yet?"

I frowned. "You mean the Legion? Yeah," I said, thinking he meant the archangel Vedriel, though I didn't know how he'd known that, seeing as he was stuck in a cave and hidden from the rest of the paranormal world. "Yeah they approached me all right. They tried to kill me."

The goblin narrowed his eyes. "No. Not the Legion," he said, the worry in his brown eyes running right to my core.

I felt a stab of fear. "Who then?"

The goblin let go of my hand. "Rowyn, there's something you should know—"

Ugul was thrown forward and crashed into me. His legs buckled as he fought to rise. Grabbing his shoulders, I pulled him back as he gasped, blood pouring out of his mouth.

And then I saw the bloodied head of an arrow sticking out of his chest.

Tyrius swore as I felt the sting of darkness mixed with the scent of candy and rotten eggs. Faeries.

Rage pounded through me as I turned around, slowly, still holding Ugul as he spat up more blood. Damn, the arrow hit a lung.

Across the street, their dark eyes determined and full of hatred, was a band of Dark Arrows.

CHAPTER

20

The warrior fae all wore the same long, black coat, matching shirts and pants along with an assortment of curved daggers sheathed along their baldrics. Fae symbols were tattooed over most of their skin, making them appear to have a darker completion and look more dangerous.

Tyrius growled low and vicious. "Where's a lightsaber when you need one?"

Shifting sideways, I lowered Ugul as gently as I could to the ground behind a parked gray BMW sedan, never looking away from the Dark Arrows.

"Try not to move," I told the goblin. "It'll only make it worse. Just stay put until I get back."

I straightened and moved away from the car, seeing Jax come over and stand next to me. His face darkened as he aimed his shotgun at the Dark Arrows, looking every bit the part of a warrior. Danto, Vicky and Keith moved forward, forming a protective line.

"What do you want to do?" Jax turned his head and looked at me, tension rolling off his features, but the quirk on his face told me he was looking for a fight.

"I'm not handing Ugul to the queen," I said, my voice trembling with anger.

"So we fight?" asked Jax, a gleam in his eye.

"We fight."

I scanned the Dark Arrows' faces as they leered. They were savage, cocky, and looking for blood. Our blood. And they all had arrows pointed at our faces.

Daegal stepped from the band of faerie warriors, his bow on his hip and his dark eyes pinned on me.

"Do my eyes deceive me," said the commander of the Dark Arrows, "or were you about to free the faerie you were paid to retrieve? Letting the faerie go was not part of the contract. That wasn't the deal. My queen will be very disappointed in you, Rowyn Sinclair."

I smiled at him. "Disappointing a faerie is like having an orgasm. It feels *so* damn good."

Jax let out a loud laugh and smacked his thigh for added dramatic effect. It worked.

"You think this is a joke?" Daegal snarled, the words near guttural. His pointed features were twisted in a scowl, giving him more the appearance of an animal. He was the only one not pointing an arrow at us, but it didn't mean he was any less dangerous.

"Give us the faerie," he growled, "and maybe we'll let you live."

I showed my teeth in a Colgate smile. "How about I give you the finger," I said and made a rude gesture with my hand, "and then maybe I'll let *you* live."

"Good one, Rowyn," snickered Tyrius.

Grinning at the baal, I drew both blades and then faced the faeries.

Daegal's dark eyes held mine for a brief moment. "I won't say it again. This is your last warning, Hunter. Give him to us, or the last thing you'll see is my arrow sticking into your chest."

Pissed, I shifted my weight and lowered my body. "And I thought I told you to go screw yourself."

"Have it your way." Unthinkably swift, Daegal reached back, drew his bow and nocked an arrow. "I hear the Netherworld is crawling with demons dying for a piece of your soul. They'll be thanking me for sending you off early."

I frowned. *He thinks when I die I'm going to the Netherworld?*

My thoughts died at the sound of strings going taut and arrows being nocked.

"Get cover!" I shouted.

Heart pounding in my throat, I spun into action.

Arrows, dark and fast shot for me, and I plunged down and away. But another one, and another kept coming. Arrows whistled past me, biting the side of my face like icy wind, and I hurled myself sideways to avoid getting an arrow through my face. They ripped through my hair like the brutal claws of a beast. Shit. I'd be a Rowyn shish kabob if I didn't find cover soon.

Adrenaline coursed through my limbs as I pitched forward and rolled on the ground next to a gleaming black Infinity sedan. Arrows hitting the roof and side of the car pinged like a machine gun. It had been a very nice car.

Arrows shot through the air like black hail, deadly black hail. I'd never seen anything like it. The only way to stop the volley of arrows was to kill the Dark Arrows. Somehow, I had to get to them.

Panting, I rocked forward on my flat boots. Feeling the stir of adrenaline, I lowered myself behind the car's trunk. I risked a glance and I saw someone running. Jax.

I watched in horror as he hurled himself forward, pumping and shooting into the band of Dark Arrows like target practice.

Jax's shotgun went off, louder than a clap of thunder. The bullets soared and exploded in a burst of blood and flying chips of bone. The faerie sailed back and was driven flat onto his back by the sheer force of the bullets slamming into him. He didn't have time to jerk, much less scream. He just dropped like a rock. There was a bloody, pulpy mess where the shot had ripped open the faerie's chest.

The sudden sharp smell of burnt powder told me this time Jax had put in real bullets and not the salt-filled ones.

Our eyes met and he grinned. But then his smile vanished at the sudden shower of arrows that flew at him. Jax cursed and leaped behind a lamppost.

"You idiot! Are you trying to get yourself killed!" I shouted. He poked around the lamppost to give me a thumbs up and then lowered his shotgun and started firing again. I shook my head. Crazy SOB.

Faster than the wind, faster than death, Danto shot forward, fist rammed into the faerie's face and rocking his head back. There was an ugly sounding crunch, and the half-breed crumpled. He flew at another fae, knocking his bow from his grip and with a quick succession, tore a hole in the faerie's neck the size of his fist. Blood sprayed out of the wound and into Danto's face. Arrows flew at the vampire, but pulling up the dead faerie's body as a shield, he spun and drove through the showers of arrows.

Vicky was a blur, moving too fast to readily follow. She grabbed the wrist of a faerie. There was a crack, the snap of bone clear in the night air. The faerie's scream died in his throat as she sliced his jugular with a slash of her claws. Keith followed it up with a savage kick at one of the faerie's knees. The faerie's eyes widened, but he had no time for anything else. Before the faerie collapsed, Keith had snapped his neck and slipped around to stalk the nearest Dark Arrow.

Impressive. It took some serious mastery of hand-to-hand combat to know where to hit, and they were making it look as easy as breathing. I mean, say what you will about the vampires, but they killed with serious style.

I had always envied the vamps' supernatural speed. They moved like The Flash. They were badass, and I was glad this time they were on *my* side.

A high-pitched girly sounding scream hit me and I whirled to see a cat clawing out the eyes of one of the Dark Arrows. The fae's face was covered in blood as he thrashed around, trying to dislodge the cat, but Tyrius wouldn't let go. I knew Tyrius was still recuperating, so he couldn't Hulk-out. But his tiny form was a ploy. He was perfectly capable of gouging the eyes out of his opponent with his razor-sharp claws. He also had a mean bite, his tiny teeth like white-hot needles clamping down into soft flesh and severing arteries. He was awesome.

"Attaboy, Tyrius," I mumbled, my chest swelling with pride. My gaze shifted and fell on Daegal. *Bingo.*

Grinning, I leaped around the car and charged at the skinny faerie. His attention was focused on Jax, trying to hit him with his arrows as he moved around the lamppost. I tasted rage in the back of my throat. He hadn't seen me.

He was mine. I had him.

Holding my soul blade by the sharp edge, I whipped it. The silver of the blade winked in the light of the moon as it flew, spinning straight and true while gathering speed. And just when the blade was

211

going to hit its mark, Daegal shifted his bow at the last second and met my blade with an arrow. There was a clang of metal and my blade hit the pavement along with the arrow.

My jaw dropped. So did my smile. Crap. How did he do that?

The bastard sneered at me, but before he could nock another arrow, I was running again. Death blade in hand, I was going to gut the bastard once and for all.

Something sleek and dark came at me. Too fast. I dove forward onto the pavement, but not fast enough. Slamming hard onto the ground, pain exploded on my left thigh.

Shit. I'd been hit.

Whirling, I clenched my teeth as a wave of pain hit me. An arrow had gone through my thigh and out the other side. Great. I was freaking skewered. My leg was meat on a stick. There was no way in hell I could fight with that thing in me, let alone try to run. It had severed muscle, but not my femoral artery as far as I could tell. Cursing, I reached down to pull the arrow out—

I screamed as another arrow shot through my hand, pinning it to my thigh right next to the other arrow.

Now I was really, really pissed.

A shadow moved into my line of sight. I didn't have to look up to know it was Daegal. Of course he would come over to gloat and relish in my pain.

Daegal tsked. "Hunter. You should have given up the faerie when you had the chance. Now I'm going to waste you with my arrows. Then, I'm going to gut you like the pig angel that you are."

I felt a small, sharp, throbbing pain in my thigh and hand. I looked down and found a trickle of yellow seepage coming from the wounds. A slow burning sensation began to spread from the wound in my thigh to my hand. I felt hot and cold all at once, and a cold shiver slipped down my spine. Then a burning sensation became a greater presence with each heartbeat.

The arrowheads were poisoned.

The faerie's mouth spread into a wide, smug grin. "Faebane. Our deadliest poison."

Fear squeezed my throat as I thought of Jax. If he were hit with one of those arrows, he wouldn't survive. I knew faebane. It was the faerie's version of a death blade's poison. Especially deadly to non-fae, other half-breeds and us angel-born.

But I was different.

Sweat trickled into my eyes, burning them. My death blade was a welcome weight in my hand, meaning I wasn't defenseless.

Blinking, I snarled at him. "Bite me, you pointy-eared bastard."

Daegal raised his brows and said in a sultry voice, "In another lifetime, perhaps."

Yikes. "I don't do faeries," I said, hearing the disgust in my voice. "There's something about faerie dust ending up in places it just shouldn't be."

The Dark Arrow snickered as he nocked another arrow. "You should have taken the deal, Hunter. Now your grandmother will lose her house."

"What?" I jerked, only to feel the ripping of my muscles as I pulled on the arrows. "How did you know about that? Answer me!"

Daegal gave me a shark's smile. "Was the faerie's life really worth your grandmother's demise? You are a very selfish, brat of an angel-born. Now your grandmother will be reduced to poverty because of you. What will she think of her only granddaughter when she finds out you could have saved her home but decided she wasn't worth it?"

I felt myself go rigid. "You knew," I said, my face going cold. "Now it makes sense. Why she sent you that night. The money you offered was the *exact* amount I needed. Smart. I'll admit. I never saw that coming. She knew I couldn't say no. She played me well."

Damn. Danto had been right. The queen had laid her trap and caught me. I was a damn fool.

The Dark Arrows were stirring and shifting amidst shouts and weeps. My blood roared in my ears.

"She's going to kill him. Isn't she?" I shifted and hissed as the arrows pulled at my skin. I needed to get them out.

Daegal laughed, playing with the end of his arrow. "Of course she will. He killed her only son. No mother should go through the horrors of losing her only child."

"In self-defense," I said. "This was never a hunt. This was an excuse for murder. She lied to me. She tricked me. This isn't justice. It's an execution." I shook with rage. I'd been tricked, deceived and blinded by my own desperate need to find some cash.

"Yes, it is that." Daegal pulled his lips into a cunning smile. "And you were the perfect pawn. You played right into her game. The queen has lived for over seven hundred years. You're no match for her."

"Maybe not." I pursed my lips. "But she's still a bitch."

The fae's eyes darkened. Daegal drew his bowstring back and shot in the same instant as I yanked my hand free from the arrow in my thigh and shifted.

Ow. That. Hurt.

Spinning, I kept close to Daegal, knowing the closer I was to his body, the more difficult it would be for him to draw his bow and shoot. I relished the angry grunts that came from him. Killing me would never be that easy.

Daegal's mouth was spread in a wide, manic grin. "The poison will kill you, even if the arrow doesn't."

I could already feel the effects of the poison diminishing. "I don't think so." Kicking out, I caught him just below the knee. The bone snapped under my foot. He screamed and I caught a glimpse of his snarl. Spinning out of his reach, my left thigh was stiff, making my movements jerky and stilted. My progress was slow with the arrows still sticking out of my thigh. I tried to move without touching them, but it was impossible.

Every time I brushed the arrow shafts with my movements, pain flared as though I was being sliced from the inside of my leg. I was in no shape to keep fighting like this.

There was just one thing to do.

Just as Daegal swung at me with his bow and missed, I ducked, rolling away. Gritting my jaw, I wrapped my injured hand around the first arrow and snapped it. I did the same with the other. There was no time to try and pull them out without further damaging my thigh. The buried arrow shafts would have to stay, for the time being.

A laugh escaped me at the surprised look on Daegal's face. I couldn't help it.

"Guess your precious faebane doesn't work on me, huh?"

I swung my blade in a rush as the faerie lunged. He came up swinging, a curved dagger in his right hand. Whirling, I let my anger surge and guide me. The tip of my blade sliced a gash across his smooth, pink stomach. Daegal stumbled back, stunned. I watched, not knowing the full effects a death blade's poison would have on a half-breed. Perhaps nothing.

"I'll kill you for this, angel whore," he swore.

I grinned. "Bring it on, Tinker Bell."

He shot forward. I caught his feint left, but when I dove right, he moved so swiftly that despite my superior abilities and years of training, I crashed into a parked car. The clatter of flesh, bone, and metal colliding echoed through the too-quiet street as I landed face first on the car's hood, my jaw singing.

"Like I said," Daegal sneered at me as I whirled around and slipped down the car. "I'm going to kill you, angel bitch."

My lip already aching and swollen, I tasted the blood in my mouth. "I'm going to break all those pointy, little teeth in that foul mouth of yours."

Faster than I could sense, faster than my failing body could react, he came at me, and his fist made contact with my face. I shifted enough to keep my nose from shattering but took the blow on my jaw. Spinning, I hit the ground and tasted blood. Again. Damn him.

He drew back to strike again. But with equally unnerving swiftness, I halted his second blow before it fractured my jaw and snarled in his face, low and vicious.

My breathing turned ragged as I purred, "Is that all you got?"

Hateful eyes peered at me as the faerie came at me again in a rush of daggers and bows. I twisted, bringing up a fist to smash into his face, but I hit nothing but air. Then his foot hooked behind mine in an efficient maneuver that sent me staggering.

I caught myself, but not fast enough. Daegal slammed his bow across my head, and stars exploded behind my eyes. Before I could recover, he kicked me in the gut and I slammed onto the pavement. My breath escaped me. I hit the pavement hard, rolled, and was up on my feet. I turned around, my dagger in my hand, ready to throw myself at him. But Daegal was gone.

I snapped my gaze around the street, and relief pooled inside my chest at the sight of Tyrius poised in a crouch atop the body of a Dark Arrow, looking smug and content.

Danto and Vicky were walking in a circle around the bodies of the Dark Arrows, waiting for any to twitch so they could finish them off. I spotted Keith crouched next to the body of a dead fae, picking what was valuable off of it, and putting it into his pockets.

That was one strange vampire.

With his shotgun on his shoulder, Jax sauntered towards me, his face creasing as he took in the blood on my thigh.

"Jesus, Rowyn, are those arrows sticking out of your thigh?"

"Parts of arrows. It's nothing." I pulled my shirt down, but it did nothing to hide the yellow and pink oozing from the two wounds. "I'll get Pam to remove them once we get Ugul to safety."

"Uh, Rowyn, where's Ugul?" said Jax.

Fear slid through me at the worry in his voice. I spun, my gaze darting towards the spot where I'd left the goblin.

Ugul was gone.

CHAPTER
21

I hurtled down the street, my injured thigh burning as I pushed it harder and harder. The arrow parts were still stuck in my leg and tore at the flesh like the fangs of some great beast. My left leg was drenched, soaked with my own blood.

And still I ran.

I didn't stop. I couldn't stop. The queen would kill Ugul if I didn't get there in time. An innocent was going to die because of me. I couldn't let that happen. Not on my watch.

"Rowyn! Slow down!" came Jax's voice. "You can't just barge in there."

"That's exactly what I plan to do." My eyes on Sylph Tower, I used my hate to propel me faster and faster, until I felt like my feet were barely touching the ground as I sailed down the street. I was soaring like freaking Wonder Woman.

"Are you crazy!" came Tyrius's voice behind me.

"Yes." I wasn't going to let Ugul die at the hands of the queen. I needed to know what he was going to tell me.

"Rowyn," shouted Tyrius, "you've got two bloody arrows in your leg! Think about that. You're hurt. And I won't be able to Hulk-out either. I won't be able to protect you. Let's just sit down a minute and think about this."

"Ugul doesn't have a minute," I panted, my thighs burning as I pushed them harder. He'd already suffered an arrow in the chest. How long could he survive without medical help?

"Do you know how many faeries are in there?" yelled the cat. "Try hundreds. Maybe thousands. I'm sorry, Rowyn, but you did your best. You freed him. That's something. Now stop this craziness!"

"I freed him?" I laughed. "I didn't free him. I killed him. I won't let him die. I won't." Heart racing, I could see the outline of the door. I was almost there.

I heard Tyrius yell something as I threw myself against the door. It didn't even budge.

"Damn you!" Using my weight, I hurtled my right shoulder at the door, again and again. And still the door didn't even a crack open a centimeter.

Something grabbed my shoulder and I flinched. Danto pivoted me towards him. "Rowyn, the baal is right. I think the entire clan of Dark Court faeries are in there. We can't fight that many."

My heart throbbed in my throat. "I have to try. I have to."

"If we break through this door," said the vampire, his voice surprisingly cool, "they'll see it as an attack."

"They attacked us first," I growled.

The vampire's hair lifted as he shook his head. "It doesn't matter." A shimmer of distress crinkled the corners of his eyes. "We storm in there demanding the queen give the faerie back, and she'll peel the skin off of our bones." His gray eyes traced my face as he added softly, "We'll never get him back. You must see this. It's over. I'm sorry, Rowyn, but this is a fight we can't win."

"Like hell it is." I wiggled out of his grasp and hit my blade against the door. "I'll carve my way in if I have to. But I'm getting through this damn door." My pulse was racing, and fear and tension pulled my muscles tight. "The longer we wait, the harder it'll be to save him."

"Rowyn, just listen for a second." Tyrius was next to the door.

"He's innocent," I yelled. "Innocent. He killed the queen's son in self-defense and she wants revenge. It was always about her getting her revenge. And I'm the idiot who brought him to her. This is *my* fault. I'll never be able to live with myself knowing I played a part in his death. Don't you get it?" I stopped jabbing the door and looked down at Tyrius.

"If he dies…" I swallowed, feeling the prick of tears but not able to get my mouth to work to say the rest of the words.

"Okay, so how do we do it?" asked the cat. "Do you even have a plan?"

"Yes," I lied. "We go in and get Ugul. Possibly kill a few faeries on the way." The simplest plans were the best. But this was a suicide mission. I knew it. Tyrius knew it. They all knew it.

"Okay, Sherlock," said Tyrius, clearly annoyed that I wouldn't let this go. "How do you plan on getting inside? The tower door won't open to non-faeries unless we have an invitation." He made a face. "Do you have an invitation? Uh—no. You don't."

"I've got your invitation. Rowyn, move," ordered Jax suddenly. "I got this."

Turning, I saw Jax standing, legs splayed with the shotgun pointed at me, well, at the door.

"Right." Nodding, I reached down and grabbed Tyrius before he could argue and moved out of the way.

Jax's expression turned positively devilish, in a very sexy sort of way. He pumped the shotgun and fired.

Once, twice, and the last shot blasted a hole through the door large enough to fit a person.

"So much for sneaking in," mewed Tyrius. "We've just sounded the alarm."

Not waiting for the others to try and convince me how mad this was, I dropped Tyrius and pulled my way through the opening.

Tyrius was right. The noise Jax made by blowing a hole through the door would send the faeries at us.

Ignoring the throbbing in my injured left thigh, I barreled down the cave-like corridor as fast as my legs would go. The same sconces with jade demon fire lit the tight spaces in hues of greens. The sound of my breathing was loud in my ears, and my boots hit the hard-packed dirt at a gallop. The Dark Arrows should have been upon us by now, and a cold unsettling feeling rushed in my gut that they hadn't. This was bad, but it was too late to back down.

I could hear the distant murmur of voices and the unmistakable sound of laughter.

Fury filled my mind like a fever. I reached the two ancient and enormous stone doors within seconds and, using my momentum, threw my shoulder against them.

The doors were flung open with a crash. I waited for the cries and shouts, waited to see a horde of faeries lash out at us, but the faeries just stared at me, their pinched faces especially intent.

The voices stopped. I blinked at the sudden brighter light and slowed my pace as I entered the vast, circular chamber and moved past the vine-twirled pillars, the crabapple trees, and the wild flowers, where I'd accepted the job to begin this nightmare.

Unlike the first time I'd been in the tower, there were no drum beats, no music, no happy chatting, just the sounds of our heavy breathing and our boots clunking in the chamber.

I cursed just as I cleared the trees and halted. There weren't a hundred faeries gathered in the hall. I'd guess I was staring at about a thousand. Damn. Of course they'd all turned at the sound of our explosive entrance, a sea of posh clothing over gaunt bodies. Their thin faces were amused and showing pointed teeth, their black eyes expectant.

The assembled faeries watched me for another heartbeat, and then they all turned their attention to the dais. Heart racing, I followed their gaze and my knees buckled.

Ugul was on his knees, the arrow in his chest still clearly visible. His head was pulled back, and behind him Daegal had a knife at his throat. The goblin did not look up.

About fifty Dark Arrows stood in formation before the dais, bows with arrows nocked and ready.

The dark faerie queen stood on the platform. Her single middle part of raven hair spilled down over a flowing white gown that pooled to the floor and around her feet. The white gown played against her snow-white skin, making it seem as though the gown had no beginning and no end. She was even more terrifying than I'd remembered—the perfect bride from hell.

Isobel's black, bottomless eyes fixed on me and her face pulled tightly into a smile, baring her sharp features and giving her the cold unnatural beauty of the fae.

The queen tilted her head as if to show off her crown of human teeth and convey just how evil she truly was.

"How delightful to see you again, Hunter," purred the faerie queen of the Dark Court. "You're just in time to witness the beginning of my rule."

Now why did that sound really, really bad?

CHAPTER
22

The gathered faeries laughed, and there was something terrifying in it, as though they'd already won some secret battle, and we'd arrived late at the party.

Tyrius bumped into my leg. "Rowyn, don't do anything stupid," he whispered.

I kept my eyes on the queen. "Who says I'm going to?" *Okay, so my plan of barging in seemed a little stupid now.*

"I do." Tyrius sighed loudly. "This is bad. This is really, really bad. Let's just turn around and leave. Maybe they didn't see us."

I set my jaw. "I'm not leaving without Ugul."

Jax, Vicky and Keith pooled around me. When I heard Danto's growl, I snuck a glance at him. He'd vamped out. Dark blood seeped between the fingers of his shaking fists, and his black eyes were fixed on something across from us. I followed his gaze. Below the platform stood a cluster of twelve males and females, secluded from the main crowd. From their cold, beautiful faces, from that echo of power still about them, I knew they were vampires.

A stirring of unease ruined my adrenaline buzz with unsettling speed. One stood apart. He was huge. His shoulders looked as wide as I was tall, and he showed off his physic in an elegant, three-piece suit. But his eyes were sharp, revealing a quick intelligence, and he moved his muscular bulk with the sexy grace all vampires shared. Even worse, they all had the collected, confident pride of vampires.

It was clear they'd been invited to watch Ugul's execution. But why? Faeries rarely mixed with vampires. What did the vampires gain by watching the death of a fae?

My eyes settled on Danto, and unless that big vampire didn't spontaneously combust from Danto's glare, it could only mean I was looking at the vampire Stefan. The dark faerie queen's choice for Head vampire in the New York City Court.

As though hearing my thoughts, Stefan's eyes met mine, his face impassive if not slightly bored. But then his eyes darted to Danto and he smiled to show his teeth.

Fur brushed my neck as Tyrius leapt to my shoulders. "I'd like to know why there are vampires here," he said as he settled himself.

"I was just thinking the same thing," I mused. "Why would they want to be part of this? It doesn't make sense."

Tyrius swiveled to face me. "I'm willing to bet the fur on my tail they want a piece of whatever's happening, that's what."

The air shifted next to me, and I felt Jax's breath on the other side of my cheek. "You know I love a fight, especially with these skinny bastards, but I'm running low on ammo. Any bright ideas on how we're going to get him back?"

"By asking nicely?"

Tyrius snorted as I exhaled long and slow. I pulled my eyes from the vampires and met the queen's defiant stare. She had never looked away from me, I realized with a chill.

My blood pounded in my veins, but I kept my chin high as I said, "Let him go." I winced, hearing the slight shake in my voice.

The queen licked her lips, and a dark delight flashed in her eye. "Or what?" she taunted.

I squared my shoulders. "Or I'll kill you." Okay, so that sounded really lame.

Before I'd even finished my sentence, the band of Dark Arrows, all fifty of them, shifted and came forward like a wall of soldiers. The other faeries parted, giving the Dark Arrows a clean line of sight.

Swell. The fae warriors stopped twenty feet from us and pulled back their bowstrings.

Shit. There was no outrunning that.

I don't know why but my gaze flicked to the group of vampires, and my blood pressure rose at their laughter. Stefan caught me staring and blew me a kiss. Bastard.

"Stop!" Isobel commanded, and as one the Dark Arrows lowered their bows. "Not yet. I want them to watch." She waved her hand dismissively. "You can kill them afterwards. I honestly don't care." Her eyes found Danto and her delight intensified. "Danto. I'm very pleased to see you here."

"I'm not," growled the vampire, and Isobel's smile widened when she saw him glance at Stefan.

"Oh, don't look so miserable, Danto," said the queen and gave him a small, horrible smile. "Trust me. You are going to enjoy this." She raised her voice and spoke to the crowd. "Tonight I will give you a gift worthy of my hall," she went on. "Tonight will change every night from this day forward. Change is upon us, my children. To all half-breeds, as promised, our time has come."

"Am I the only one lost here?" said Tyrius, his voice low. "Please raise your hand if you're following any of this."

Isobel made a telling face. Daegal smiled wickedly and gave a sharp tug on Ugul's hair, making his head snap back.

"Don't. Please," the goblin moaned, his eyes closed, and I began to shake.

I gritted my teeth and took a gasping breath. "If you kill him," I said, my voice ringing through the hall, "the Gray Council will come down on you hard. I promise you that. He's innocent. He killed your son in self-defense. If you kill him now, that's murder. You'll be ruined. You'll lose your tooth-crown. You'll be nothing."

The queen never stopped smiling as though I was giving her the greatest of compliments. "Oh, no. I don't think so."

"Don't you want to hear what he has to say? Don't you care about the truth?" Of course not, and I knew I was pushing my luck. But I hoped she'd care if I put enough doubt in the minds of the other faeries.

And when my gaze rolled around the gathered faeries, I couldn't help the disquiet that wrapped around my middle. They weren't even paying any attention to me. Their eyes were fixated on Ugul. But it wasn't just *that* they were staring at him, it was the *way* they were staring, with a desperate feverish hunger. Every single faerie in the hall wanted him to die, were anxious for him to die. But why? It couldn't be just because of the queen's son's death. Something else was going on here. I just didn't know *what*.

My pulse throbbed in my thigh and I shifted my weight to my other leg. "This is wrong," I continued, feeling a trickle of sweat dripping in between my breasts. "Killing him won't bring your son back."

"You broke our contract," the queen shook her head. She seemed taller now standing on the dais than

I remembered, taller and much skinnier than me. "And *that* will cost *you*."

"What?" I said defiantly. "You're going to kill me too?"

"The thought did cross my mind." The queen sighed as she stepped around the platform, moving with crisp, precise motions.

"I'd like to see you try. How about a one-on-one good old fashion cat fight?" I prompted. "Just you. Winner takes Ugul. Yes?"

The queen threw back her head and howled, the sound terrifying almost like the cry of a banshee. No one else in the hall made a sound. That was creepy.

Isobel closed her eyes and breathed deeply, as though she was trying to suck in my energy and fear like a drug. "I like you, Rowyn. I really do. A real pity when someone with such talent dies so young. I could have used someone like you in my court." The queen flashed her teeth. "But you're no match for me, darling. You're just a child." She laughed, as if I was a simpleton. "Barely a woman. I would end your miserable life with a snap of my finger," she added with a wave of her hand.

"Maybe," I said and shifted with my anger. "Or maybe I'll make you eat that butt-ugly crown of yours and you'll be shitting teeth for the rest of your life?"

"Rowyn," warned Tyrius. "I like where you're going with this—but—and this is a big but—this is pointless. She'll never give him up. Look at her. She's bleeping mad."

I nodded. "I don't doubt that," I whispered. "That's why we can't abandon Ugul."

The queen's face twitched. "He killed my only son. Do you know what that feels like?" her black eyes rolled over me as she moved towards the edge of the dais, and I felt my skin tingle, like she was trying to see past my skin, into my soul. Her eyebrows lifted. "No. You've never been a mother. I can see that. You cannot understand what it is to lose a child when you, yourself, are still just a child."

"I'm sorry you lost your son." *No, I'm not.* "But Ugul had no other choice but to use lethal force to defend himself from your son. Why? Why was your son even there? Why was he trying to kill him?" My throat tightened at the pain I saw on the goblin's face. The entire front of his shirt was soaked in blood.

"You sent your son after Ugul. Didn't you?" I added, remembering the goblin had told me the queen wanted something from him. "Because he has something you want, right?"

The queen regarded me steadily and said, "Yes, I sent my son after the faerie, but I never ordered him to kill him. That was a mistake."

"Sure it was."

Isobel's face twisted into a feral smile. "My son died trying to get something for me. But I must thank you, Rowyn. Where he failed, you succeeded." She pressed her hands against her hips. "You know, I've had my eye on you for quite a while."

I gave her a bitter smile. "You're not my type."

The queen's brows rose playfully, and the smile she gave me was truly serpentine. "When I heard of your grandmother's misfortune, I knew you'd be persuaded to do anything to help her. And just like the good granddaughter you are, you did. You brought me the faerie. You made this all possible, Rowyn Sinclair. His death is your gift to me."

My face heated and I made to move forward a step, only to be stopped by Jax.

"Don't," he hissed. His fingers gripped my elbow so hard it hurt. "She's just trying to get a rise out of you."

"It's working," I seethed, yanking out of his grip, but I stayed where I was.

"Don't be stupid, Rowyn," said Jax, and I felt my anger rise.

Guilt assailed me, sending my heart pounding against my temples and giving me a headache. She was right about one thing. This was my fault.

"I never gave him over to you. You took him," I challenged. "He was free to go. I wasn't going to give him up. I was *never* going to hand him over to you."

I looked at Ugul, and my breath caught at how pale his skin was. Damn. If I didn't get him out now, he wasn't going to make it.

Isobel glared at me, but when her gaze fell upon Ugul, she smiled broadly, sweetly. "Any last words before you die?" The queen moved to stand before the goblin.

"If you do this!" I yelled, aware that the Dark Arrows had nocked their arrows and were all pointing

KIM RICHARDSON

at my head. "If you do this," I repeated, my pulse pounding, "there'll be hell to pay. You hear me, Queen! I'll kill you!"

The queen's black eyes met mine for a moment, and she smiled. "No, you won't."

"Ugul!" My scream echoed against the high ceilings. "Ugul!" The goblin's eyes were still closed, but his face was scrunched up in pain.

I'm sorry.

I writhed as agony sang through me. Every nerve ending pulsed into a burn. A guttural sound escaped me—pain and determination. Fear cascaded over me in a giant cold wave. If I moved, I was dead. My friends would die. I couldn't do anything. All I could do was watch as an innocent faerie was murdered. Because of me.

Isobel leaned to put her face inches from Ugul's, watching him with a twisted sense of delight. Under her impassivity was a growing excitement.

Daegal jerked Ugul straighter, and blood trickled below the knife at his throat.

"No!" I screamed, expecting to see the commander of the Dark Arrows slash Ugul's throat.

But Daegal never moved.

In a flash, the queen slashed at the goblin's chest with her nails, gutting him as though she'd used a sword. Nausea hit me as the goblin's moan of pain was the only sound in the hall.

"What in the hell?" cried Tyrius, clearly shocked and appalled.

234

Bile rose in the back of my throat as the queen plunged her hand inside the goblin's chest until her hand was completely submerged by the goblin's guts.

After a moment, the queen yanked back looking both triumphant and slightly off her rocker.

And in her hand was a brilliant white stone.

CHAPTER
23

A new energy spilled into the hall, cold and fast. It hummed and cracked like an electrical storm, and my body tingled, from my center to my fingertips. I'd never felt anything like it before, and it scared the hell out of me.

The queen's face shone with dazzling white light, making her skin sparkle and amplifying her features until she looked like an ice queen.

My breath caught. I'd seen that light before. It was the same light Ugul had used on the veth hounds and on me. Crap.

Tyrius swore. "Rowyn. We need to leave. Like right freaking now."

I stood frozen as Isobel's victorious smile lit her face. She turned to the gathered crowd and raised her fist.

Daegal discarded Ugul's body like he was throwing away something disgusting that had soiled his fingers. The goblin hit the platform with an echoing thud, his lifeless eyes staring right at me, accusing me for his fate. *This is my fault.*

I watched, unable to move as Daegal clapped his hands once. A door swung open to the left of the platform and two male faeries emerged, dragging a human female between them. Strands of her brown hair stuck to her wet face, and her eyes were red and wide. She looked about my age, mid-twenties, but shorter. And the terror on her face stilled my heart.

Fear hit me in a cold wave as my knees shook. My mouth opened and closed. "What's going on?" My words were barely audible for the clattering of my teeth.

"Nothing good," came Tyrius's voice as he leapt off my shoulders and landed next to me on the ground.

The faeries shoved the woman to her knees at the foot of the dais facing the queen.

I glanced at the assembled faeries. "They can't just kill her. They know the rules. They touch a hair on her head and there'll be hell to pay."

"Seems like they don't give a shit," said Jax and I pulled my eyes away from him to look at the platform.

"This isn't right. We can't let them kill another innocent person. We have to do something."

I started forward. Jax caught my arm and yanked me back hard against his chest. "Don't." His hot breath on my neck and the side of my face sent a warm pulse through my middle. "It's what she wants. The queen wants you to screw up so she can tear you apart. I'm not letting that happen."

I let him tug me closer and felt the heat from his chest seep through my clothes. "She's going to kill her," I seethed, but I stayed where I was. The comforting feeling of another body against mine seemed to pin me to the spot—*or the bastard had spelled me.* It was a reminder of how lonely I was. I breathed in the scent of soap, aftershave, and his natural musk. God, he smelled nice.

"Maybe not," said Jax, his lips brushing against my jaw, soft and warm. "Maybe she just wants to scare her. I don't know. Just wait." I felt his other hand slip around my waist, sending tiny shivers of pleasure down into my core, wild and burning.

My entire world constricted to the touch of his hands on me. My pulse accelerated, and I could barely breathe.

God help me.

"And if she kills her?" I asked, aware that I was panting. My face flamed as my cheek brushed up against his.

"Then we're witnesses to the murder," said Jax. His voice rumbled, making me shudder. "Hers and

Ugul's. It's enough to alert the Gray Council. She's going to pay for this. Trust me."

I wish I could believe him, but there was something utterly disturbing about the stillness of the room and the manic expression on the queen's face.

"Your new life awaits you," Isobel drawled, gesturing to the kneeling woman. "Of course, if you ask me, I'd say it's a tremendous improvement. Though, given your human history with murdering our kind, I do believe I'm offering you a gift. You should consider yourself... very lucky."

"Please don't kill me," cried to woman. "I don't want to die. Please. Please don't kill me," she sobbed.

I stiffened, and Jax's arm tightened around me. Still I let him hold me like that, so close, so unyielding.

Isobel's smile was like something from a wraith. "Kill you?" she laughed and the two fae males laughed harder. The queen clicked her tongue. "I'm not going to kill you, silly human."

I tilted my head and shared a look with Jax.

"I'm offering you a gift," continued the queen. "A gift so special, so precious, that no other human has ever had." She looked down at the woman. "You, little human, are the first. The first of many."

The woman shook. "I—I don't want your gift," she stammered. "I just want to go home. Please, just let me go home."

The queen never lost her smile. "This is your new home now. Get used to it." She lifted her hand, and the white stone shone like a thousand flashlights into one. The assembled fae and vampires all waited, and I heard the intake of their collective breath as the queen reached out to the woman with her free hand.

"Don't," the woman begged. "*Please* don't!"

Someone in the crowd wept. But it wasn't the sad lamentation you'd hear before an execution. This was an elated cry, a sick and blissful weeping. They wept of joy.

The queen was grinning with wild, triumphant glee as she gently touched the woman's cheek.

At first nothing happened, and I almost sighed in relief. But when the queen withdrew her hand, the human woman cried out and collapsed to the ground. Her screams echoed in the hall as she thrashed violently on the floor while the gathered faeries' eyes were pinned on her.

This was sick. I was going to vomit.

The queen took a strained breath, her face creased with effort and her complexion blotchy, but she recovered quickly and straightened as she watched the writhing woman with a delighted, victorious expression.

It had been fast, but I had seen it.

The woman stopped thrashing and was still. For a horrible second I thought she'd died. My pulse quickened as I watched the human woman pull her knees towards her chest. Then she picked herself up slowly, standing up on shaky legs. She drew herself to her full height. She was as tall as the queen now.

My lips parted. "What the in hell—?"

The woman seemed to have heard me. She turned around and met my gaze, and I cursed. The eyes that watched me were nothing of the wide, terrified woman's eyes a moment ago, but dark and alight and eager. Her features were more pronounced, sharper, her narrow chin high and her eyes glinting. Her stance was domineering and predatorial. She brushed a strand of hair back with her long, thin fingers behind her pointed ears.

The woman wasn't human anymore. She was a faerie.

"Damn it all to the Netherworld." I felt my bowels go watery at the look of confusion on the new faerie's face as she stared down at her longer self. But she wasn't frightened anymore. Hell, she looked happy.

Jax swore deep and low. "What kind of dark magic is this?"

Daegal moved to stand next to his queen, his face twisting, and with sly delight he bellowed, "Behold Isobel, Queen of the Dark Court. For she has given us this gift. Darkness is no darkness, for the night is as clear as day. Kneel before your queen!" he shouted.

The sudden noise of a thousand bodies moving was an assault after the eerie silence. As one, all the faeries in the hall kneeled—to my surprise even the vampires and the Dark Arrows, their attention fixed on the queen with admiration.

My heart throbbed as if trying to find a way to burst out of my chest, but my muscles had gone slack. I was having a panic attack.

"What the hell was that?" I found myself saying, not even realizing that I had spoken the words out loud as I wiggled myself out of Jax's tight grip.

"The sign we've been waiting for to get our asses the hell out of here," commented Tyrius.

"I know what that is."

I turned to the sound of concern in Danto's voice. Vicky and Keith both sported the same terrified expression, their faces ashen.

The vampire met my gaze. "It's called The White Grace."

"I've heard of The White Grace," said Tyrius up between me and Danto. "It's a magic stone, and a *very* powerful one at that."

I kept my eyes on the vampire as Jax leaned in next to me.

"It's why the name Ugul sounded so familiar to me," the vampire said quickly, leaning his body towards the exit, getting ready to run. "I heard Isobel mention his name once when she didn't know I was listening. Now I know why. She must have found out he was its protector."

I felt numb. "Never heard of it," I said, my eyes on the dais, on the white stone carefully clutched in the queen's hand. How could it be in Ugul's chest? Had he swallowed it?

"It's been gone for thousands of years, disappeared," rushed Danto. "Its powerful. You've just seen what it can do."

I moved my eyes back to the queen. "But why does the queen want to turn humans into faeries?"

"There hasn't been a half-breed child of any kind in over a millennium. Procreating is nearly impossible. Our numbers have diminished greatly over the years. But with this, with The White Grace…"

"Holy hell," I said as it all fit into place. I, for one, had never seen a half-breed child, and I was shocked that I had never given it much thought. "No wonder he was hiding in that cave. He had been protecting it… and I gave it to her." The last part came out of me in a desperate whisper. I was a fool.

I looked into Danto's eyes expecting to see the I-told-you-so look, but there was only misery and fear. There was no blame in the vampire's expression.

"And now the crazy-ass Tooth Faerie has it," said Tyrius. "You know what that means?"

Danto's face tightened. "Isobel can create her own army, thousands of new faeries just with that stone. And she's going to use humans."

I moved my gaze back to the dais. The faerie queen still held the stone in her hand. With her features bathed in the light of The White Grace, for a moment she almost looked beautiful. But her eyes were steady and hard as she cast them over the bowed fae and vampires.

"If there was a better time to get the hell out of here," urged Tyrius, "it's now, while the faerie-freakshow is still happening."

My hand shook as I gripped my death blade. "This isn't over." I was going to get that stone back.

"Fine," said Jax. "But right now we need to leave!" He gripped my arm hard again as if to shake me out of my misery. "He's gone. Come on. Let's get the hell out of here before we end up like him!"

Jax pulled me with him into a run. Danto, Vicky and Keith slipped past us with their vampire speed and hurtled towards the exit. My legs were numb and stiff as I ran across the hall, past the double doors, and down through the corridor, Tyrius galloping like a miniature cheetah next to me. My vision was plagued with tears, so the vampires were just a moving blur ahead of us.

Together, we slipped through the gap in the door and ran into the night.

CHAPTER
24

Tyrius sat on the edge of the bed, his blue eyes flashing. "That's going to leave a scar."

I jerked and tried not to curse as Pam expertly clipped the arrowhead from the second arrow in my thigh and carefully dropped it in a glass jar. "Scars are just reminders of what I do. I'm a Hunter. I like scars. It just makes me more badass."

"Or that you're a lousy Hunter." Tyrius winked and laughed at his own joke.

He seemed in much better spirits with Pam around, with her expert hands carefully examining and caressing him at the same time. She'd just stopped fussing with him moments ago to look at my leg.

Not that I minded. Pam had been very concerned when we told her of Tyrius's attack in the cave. She'd been particularly troubled when he mentioned that he hadn't been able to use some of his demon mojo—specifically that he hadn't been able to Hulk-out since the attack, which had me also worried. But when she'd plopped a fresh slice of steaming pizza onto a plate for Tyrius, he was in baal Heaven and barely said a word for fifteen minutes. A baal record.

Pam had to cut through my jeans, high up my thigh to get to the arrows. Jax didn't seem abashed about staring at my exposed flesh as I sat on the edge of the bed. After our swift escape from Sylph Tower, he'd driven us to here to Parks Hollow, to Pam's ALL SOULS REPAIR clinic for the angel-born in need of fixing. Me. And I was grateful for it. So I'd kept my mouth shut.

We'd agreed to meet up with Danto later around ten o'clock tonight at Father Thomas's church. And yes, vampires, being part human, could trespass in a church without bursting into flames, though it still wasn't a place they liked to frequent.

I needed to speak to the priest about what I'd learned and get his insight on how we were going to approach the subject with the Gray Council, mainly about the Tooth Faerie and The White Grace.

Danto would speak to his coven of vampires, and I hoped he'd bring us some good news, maybe a way to kill the queen before she had a chance to do anything stupid.

Only the leaders of the courts or heads of houses could address the Gray Council, so having Danto as part of this was crucial. Father Thomas's reputation was well liked within the Gray Council as well. That was good enough for me.

Jax shuffled nervously, looking on edge with his arms crossed over his chest as he stood next to Pam. I tried not to think about how handsome he was when he was nervous. It was almost as though he cared about me. I don't know why... he should be putting his feelings towards his fiancée.

Pam kicked off with her rolling office chair over to a metal side table and picked up what looked like a pair of pliers before rolling back to my side. Although it was cool inside the clinic, droplets of sweat formed on her brow.

We'd woken Pam up at 5 a.m. by Jax banging on her door. The surprised look on her face at the sight of Jax that turned to a deep, menacing scowl was priceless. She'd been giving Jax the cold shoulder since we'd shuffled in, and it was awesome.

"Why are you smiling?" asked Tyrius, his brows furrowed as he looked up at me. "Did I miss something? Doesn't pulling arrows out of one's legs hurt? Pam... did you give her a sedative? Did she pop some valiums?"

"No," I answered for Pam, setting my expression bland. "I didn't get a sedative. I don't like the way they make me feel—all screwy."

"You might change your mind after this." Pam's large blue eyes met mine and her face became serious.

"I'm sorry, Rowyn. This is going to hurt. A lot," she said as she angled the plier-like instrument towards my thigh.

I stiffened, not liking the idea of having Jax witness this. "Do it." Pam leaned forward and pinched the broken end of the arrow. I winced at the sudden pressure on my wound.

"Wait," interrupted Jax, his eyes narrowing as he looked at Pam. "You sure you know what you're doing?"

Pam's raised brows were the only indication she'd heard him. Then with a powerful thrust, she yanked the first arrow out of my thigh.

Holy. Hell. And all that is holy. That hurt.

I bit down on my tongue to keep from screaming and tasted blood. "Damn," I breathed, feeling the spams of adrenaline hit me. I was horrified that Jax was witnessing all of this. "That felt worse than I thought it would. Is my thigh still in one piece?" Yellow pus and blood oozed out of a fleshy, inch gap in my thigh. It was disgusting. And it smelled worse. But I knew now my body could heal with the arrow out. One more to go…

Tyrius leaned forward, sniffed and then jerked back. "Well, that definitely doesn't smell like honey and roses, more like spoiled hamburger meat and sour milk. You smell like a corpse, Rowyn."

"Jeez, thanks, Tyrius," I snapped, my pulse thundering in my thigh. "You know… I still have Evanora's collar in my pocket. Silver is your color, right?"

Tyrius's eyes widened at my false threat. "I'll pretend that's the fever talking." He turned and wrinkled his nose. "What kind of poison am I smelling? Nightshade?"

I shook my head as the pain lessened a little and I took in a breath. "No. The faerie called it faebane."

"Faebane?" Tyrius looked up, his whiskers twitching. "Never heard of it. Must be new on the Night Market. But it's a lethal one. The poison was intended to kill the ones it infected."

"Can it…" Jax uncrossed his arms looking pale and distraught. Worry filled his eyes as they flicked from me to Tyrius to Pam. "Will it…"

"Kill me?" I answered for him, and I saw real fear in his eyes, fear for me. "I don't think so," I added, turning away before my emotions betrayed me. "I'd be dead by now if the poison had any effect on me. I know Daegal was hoping it would. Guess I'm immune to that too."

"Like that vampire bite," said Pam, nodding like she'd answered her own question. "You're probably resistant to a great deal of other poisons and demon viruses."

With my hands splayed on either side of me, I gripped fistfuls of the bed linen. "Right."

Pam dropped the arrow shaft on a medical-like steel table and dabbed the wound with a clean cloth. "Here. Hold this. There's one more left. After that, it's just a couple of stitches and you'll be as good as new."

My hand shook but I did what she ordered and pressed down on the cloth, holding it over my wound.

"So," said Pam as she wheeled herself closer to the remaining arrow stuck in my thigh and pushed her glasses up her nose with a white latex glove. "Tell me more about this stone, The White Grace," she added, and I couldn't help but think she was trying to distract me by talking while she yanked the last arrow out of my flesh. "How can a stone change a person into a faerie?"

"It's spelled." Tyrius lay next to my left hip snugly, his body heat very comforting like a heating pad. "The stone's power can remove a person's humanity to replace it with demon essence, changing them into half-breeds."

Pam straightened, her face twisted quizzically. "Anyone? Young or old? Sick or healthy?"

Tyrius nodded. "Anyone."

Pam's eyes widened. "But what if you don't want to be turned? Can she still turn you into a faerie?"

"Yes," said the cat, solemnly, and I shuddered when I remembered that poor young woman's struggle and cries. Even with my eyes closed, I could still picture her and hear her.

"Whoever holds the stone holds the power to turn any human to a half-breed," said Tyrius, his voice full of a venomous hatred that he'd probably kept to himself since Isobel first changed the human into a faerie.

"Souls help us," breathed Pam. Her flushed face paled. But then she looked up at me, her expression both serious and scared. "You need to get that stone back."

"Tell me about it," I said, the shame striking me hard. I didn't want to curl up and die. I wanted to get even. I wanted revenge. I wanted to get the stone back and bitch-slap that fae queen.

And then a terrifying thought occurred to me. "She's probably going to steal a human baby first," I said, remembering the look of misery in her hateful black eyes when she spoke of losing a child. "She's going to get herself a new son."

"Or a dozen babies," said Tyrius, his voice full of hatred and spite. "Why stop at one? Go big or go home, right? I pity those human parents when they discover their empty cribs. It's not right."

I felt a wave of nausea well inside me, and I strained to push it away.

"Can it change a half-breed into another type of half-breed?" asked Jax, shifting from foot to foot as he ran a hand over his jaw.

My mouth opened slightly at his question. "That idea scares the hell out of me." I looked down at Tyrius, fear tingling up my spine that had nothing to do with Pam's twitchy fingers and obvious eagerness to pull out the last arrow.

"Can it?" I asked the cat. The thought that the faerie queen of the Dark Court might be able to turn vampires into faeries or vice versa made me feel ill. Not only did she now have the power to turn thousands or even millions of humans into half-breeds, maybe she could morph an army of werewolves or vampires all into faeries.

Faeries to dominate over all other half-breeds. A shiver of fear took me, shocking me still.

Tyrius gave a tiny shrug. "I honestly don't know. I'd never seen it before and all I know is rumors that have been passed on from the mouths of witches and demons, which are not the most trustworthy sources. Who knows what's actually fact or fiction."

Suddenly I was a lot more nervous. I sighed through my nose, staring at the pliers that were an inch away from the last arrow. "That's why I want to speak to Father Thomas. I want to know if the church's ever heard of this stone. The priest has an incredible private collection of books on demonology. There's stuff in his library that would make the council salivate. Maybe we can find something there."

"And all this time it was hidden inside a goblin's stomach." Pam's eyebrows were high on her head, and she had that manic look in her eye, like she would have loved to cut open the goblin just to see how he could have carried a magical stone in his belly.

"It was a good place to hide it," I said, my voice low, and I couldn't escape the hurt that went out with my words.

"Until the queen sliced him open like he was a bag of rice and plucked it out," pointed out Tyrius.

Shame hit me again and my gut clenched. I was angry at myself for letting Ugul down, for letting him die like that, a spectacle in a show. I hated that fae queen. I wanted her dead.

"He must have had a hell of a time swallowing that thing." Tyrius shifted his body. "Must have been spelled to stay there, and not, you know… come out of his ass."

Jax snorted, which only gave Tyrius more ammunition, and he looked smug.

Annoyed that these two would find this funny, my voice rose as I said, "What I'd like to know is, who created this stone and why? Why create something so dangerous and then hide it?"

Tyrius slumped back a little at my tone. "I don't know."

"Something must have happened," I argued. "Ugul volunteered or he was forced to hide it— Christ! That hurt!"

"Sorry." Pam wheeled away with the last arrow clamped tightly with the pliers in her hand. "All done."

I frowned. "Why do I get the feeling you enjoyed that?" Pam didn't answer, but I swear I caught a glimpse of a smile on her face before she turned around. It didn't take long before she wheeled back over with a needle and thread.

Pam looked up and said, "The worst part is over. This won't take long, I promise."

I gritted my teeth as the needle first punctured my skin. Pam pulled on the thread and made the tiny first suture.

I felt a hand brush mine and turned to find Jax leaning next to me with his hand wrapped around mine. How did that happen? He was so close his breath moved my hair. His touch was soothing and sent a jolt of desire right to my core. Before I knew what I was doing, I intertwined my fingers around his, finding comfort in his touch.

Heart pounding, I looked up and our eyes met. Jax's face was creased, his elegant features marred by sorrow. His feelings were unguarded, open. The caring he felt for me was somehow beautiful on his face. But his beautiful, caring face didn't belong to me. It belonged to another...

Flustered, I pulled my hand away in a rush, peeved he thought I needed someone to hold my hand while I was being stitched up.

Jax took a breath to say something but then stopped, shifting his weight as he changed his mind.

An awkward silence followed. I could see Pam's face had darkened another shade of red and Tyrius kept shifting next to me, as though he couldn't find a comfortable position. Okay, so I'd pulled my hand away with a little too much force and emotion. Sue me. I didn't want Jax touching any part of me, not when it sent that damn tingling all over my skin and made my heart race in my chest.

Besides, I didn't need rescuing. A couple of arrows in my leg were nothing compared to what had happened to Ugul.

"He must have been really lonely," I muttered, thinking about all the years in that dark cave with no one to share his life with but those veth hounds. "Knowing the disasters that would follow should he lose The White Grace, no wonder he lived in that hell hole of a cave. Poor Ugul. He didn't deserve what happened to him."

"No, he didn't," said Tyrius. "And stop blaming yourself for what happened. I know you're doing it. I can feel it in your aura. You didn't force him to guard that stone. It's not your fault, Rowyn."

"It is my fault," I said flatly. "I dragged his ass to her front door. Well. Almost."

"You didn't know about The White Grace," said Jax, but I refused to meet his eyes. "You let him go, remember? You can't blame yourself. If you want to blame someone, blame that faerie queen."

I clenched my jaw. "I do blame her. How'd she find out where it was, anyway? If it was Ugul's job to hide it, someone betrayed him and got him killed."

"My guess would be another goblin," said Tyrius. "If the faeries from the Light Court were hiding it, then one of them betrayed him. One that's in bed with our favorite queen."

I frowned at him. "Why?"

"For the simple reasons why people turn on each other in the first place," answered the cat as he shifted next to me. "Power. Greed. Stupidity."

Frustrated, I rubbed my temples. "This is nuts. I can't believe this is happening," I said. "Especially if there's a magic stone out there that can turn humans into half-breeds or half-breeds into different half-breeds." I swallowed hard. "A queen needs an army, right? That's what she'll do. And she's not going to ask nicely. I don't think a lot of humans are going to be thrilled to be changed into faeries, creatures they thought were make-believe. She's going to round them up like cattle and turn them." And I wasn't going to stop it by sitting here and complaining. I had to act. I had to act fast.

Shaking inside, I stood up. "Tyrius, you were right."

The cat beamed. "Like I'm ever wrong."

I flashed him my teeth. "I do smell like death and worse. I need a shower, a change of clothes and food. Lots and lots of food."

"Here! Here!" Tyrius leapt to the floor and looked up. "Can we order some Tandoori Chicken and some naan? God, I love me some naan."

"Sure." I turned to Pam as she tied the last stitch. "Thanks, Pam. I owe you big time for this. If there's anything I can do to repay you, just let me know, okay? Anything."

Pam stood up from her chair smiling, but it didn't reach her eyes. "I don't want anything. I was glad to help. And you're welcome, Rowyn." Her eyes grew worried and moist. "Be careful, okay?"

My chest tightened at the concern in her tone. "Promise." I looked away quickly and slipped from the edge of the bed. Pam had done an incredible job with the sutures, and I knew the scarring would be minimal.

"Here." Pam's face reddened as she handed me a pair of pink yoga pants covered in rhinestones.

"They're probably ten sizes too big, but they're clean and comfy. You can change in the bathroom down the hall."

"Thank you." I smiled at her. I hadn't owned anything pink since I was five. "I'll bring them back."

"No need." Pam's eyes darted to Tyrius. "And what about you? You sure you're okay?"

Tyrius grinned the way only a cat could. "Better than okay. I'm awesome."

"Hmmm." Pam didn't look convinced. "I have a small sweater that belongs to my nephew that I think could fit you. I can cut out some extra holes for your legs—"

"Baals don't wear articles of clothing!" cried Tyrius, clearly affronted. "Who do you think I am? Puss in Boots?"

Pam only smiled at the cat. "It was only a suggestion."

Tyrius stood with his ears perked, tail in the air and said, "I prefer to go commando, thank you very much."

I rolled my eyes and tried hard not to laugh. If it wasn't for Tyrius, my life would be seriously depressing.

"I'll take you home," Jax offered and I stiffened. With my emotions running high on shame and fear, I feared that letting Jax drive me home might end up with Jax in my bed.

That was a very bad idea.

I didn't meet his eyes. "Thanks, but Tyrius and I are fine taking the bus." *Why does he have to be so nice?*

Why can't he be an ass like most men his age? "It's not that far anyway. Besides," I said, exhaling loudly and grabbing my bag. "I need to check on my gran first."

"And give her the bad news," offered Tyrius.

And give her the bad news. Cringing inside I added, "And you said you wanted to speak to Pam. Now's your chance." He hadn't said it, but he wasn't going to get away with not calling her. The woman had been in a fit. She didn't deserve that.

When I finally met Jax's eyes, I smiled at the visible discomfort and guilt I saw creasing his oh-so-pretty features.

I exchanged a knowing look with Pam and saw the amusement in her eyes as I walked past her and out the door, just before I saw her grab those pliers.

"Jax is going to get it. Isn't he?" whispered Tyrius as we headed down the hall.

A smile curled up the edges of my lips. "Yeah," I said, beaming. "Oh, he's *so* going to get it."

CHAPTER
25

After a hot shower, a lot of Indian food and a little two-hour nap, Tyrius and I had gone over to my grandmother's and finally convinced her to come with me to the bank to argue her case. Of course, Tyrius couldn't miss the excursion and had hidden in my grandmother's large, nineteen sixties vintage Coach bag, his head poking out from the top. No surprise, the bank employees all marveled at the beautiful and exotic Siamese cat and how the tan-colored leather bag brought out his eyes. *Please.*

Naturally, Tyrius had to put on one of his vocal shows for his paparazzi. He had a reputation to uphold, after all.

And although I despised banks for my own reasons (mainly because of the overpriced service charges and the fact that as a freelancer, they didn't want to loan me some money for a car), I'd put on my best fake smile and attitude for my gran. Anything for my gran.

When we'd first arrived and met with the loan officer, he didn't sound very optimistic about our offer of paying ten thousand now and giving us some time to come up with the rest. He'd pulled up my grandmother's file on his screen, and his face pinched as though he was about to give us the bad news. But suddenly, the lights had flickered. The screen on his monitor had flashed, and the faint scent of sulfur had hovered in the air in the tight office. I suspected the man's computer had suffered a little baal hocus pocus.

The loan officer had frowned and punched his fingers on his keyboard. Then he informed us, with the same puzzled look, that the bank would accept our offer of ten thousand and gave us an extra six months to pay off the remaining outstanding debt. Well what do you know?

Before we left the bank, my grandmother had wept. I winked at the bank officer, making him blush. And Tyrius—had coughed up a furball the size of an apple right on the man's clean desk.

Now if only the rest of my life could fix itself with a little demon hocus pocus. *Yeah right.*

It was almost ten at night when we arrived at St. Joseph's church, Father Thomas's assigned parish church. It was Thornville's oldest catholic church, dating back to the seventeenth century, and it was a thing of beauty.

The sharp-cornered, tidily mortared stones rose up as high as perhaps an eight-story building to look massive and permanent compared to the low shops that surrounded it. The church sat tightly against the curb on two sides, shading the street. There were tall oak trees on the church grounds, and golden light spilled from expansive stained-glass windows that lined the front and sides of the building. I blinked through the light of the lamppost, taking it all in. Perched high atop the towers were ornamental stone statues, stoic, mythical monsters and hybrid stone beasts peering over Thornville's landscape. Gargoyles.

Some had their horrid features carved in perpetual boredom while others seem to spit or grimace. What would they say if they could talk?

My eyes shifted to the parking lot and I spotted a gleaming black Audi A5. My heart leapt. Jax was already inside. So much for my plan of keeping my distance from him. It seemed we'd be stuck together again, at least for a little while longer.

With my boots clanking on the paved walkway, I stepped to the right and made for the side entrance under an arched oak door framed by lilac trees and then halted.

I sighed and reached inside my jacket to pull out the charmed pendant I'd made for Tyrius six months ago. I'd come across it while reading the dark witch grimoire, which was now with me inside my messenger bag. The book had brought me a lot of pain and had nearly cost me my life, but it also had its uses.

"Okay, Tyrius, you know the drill," I said and dangled a small crystal tied to a pink ribbon. "Hallowed ground and all." I'd invoked the dark spell into the crystal, a concealment spell that disguised Tyrius's demon energy from the church, making him appear as a regular cat. It was like a glamour in a way, hiding his true form.

Tyrius lowered his ears. "I hate that part," grumbled the cat. "Sucks demon balls."

"I know you do," I said as I slipped the charm pendant over his head. "Sucks demon balls and all—but you can't enter the church without it." I straightened. "Don't give me that look. It's not a collar. It's a charm pendant." I pressed my hands to my hips. "You don't want it? Then you can stay out here with the gargoyles."

Tyrius sat and curled his tail around his feet. "I think not." The Siamese cat made a face. "Why, for demon's sake, did you have to make it pink? I'm not a girl baal. I'm a boy. Boys like blue and cars and beer."

I raised a brow. "Not all boys. I'm sorry, Tyrius. I had to improvise. It was all I had at the time. Don't be such a baby. Pink looks good on you."

"*Don't be such a baby,*" mocked Tyrius, his ears still flat on his head. He lowered his chin close to the ground as though the charm was a heavy metal chain.

"You know I love you, Tyrius, but sometimes you can be a giant pain in my ass."

I waited for his tantrum to settle and then moved towards the side entrance, raising my hand.

"Any idea who the goblin meant by 'have *they* approached you yet?'" blurted Tyrius.

Shit. I halted, my pulse hammering in my ears. "I don't know. I'm not sure I fully understand what he meant. I mean, no one else has tried to kill me apart from the archangel Vedriel. Who else could he mean?"

"But he said it wasn't the Legion. This is something else," said the cat, his blue eyes glistening in the soft light spilling from the inside of the church windows.

I suddenly felt a little ill, as though the Tandoori chicken wanted to come back up through my nose. "What do you mean?"

Tyrius looked at the door. "I don't want to scare you, Rowyn."

"Too late. What?"

The baal sighed. "I think, and I could be wrong, this is just a working theory—"

"Spit it out, Tyrius!" I cried and then lowered my voice when I realized I was shouting. "Just tell me. Okay? You're freaking me out."

"The key is in the words he used," said the cat. "He said, 'have they *approached* you yet.' Not tried to kill you, but approach you. Like there's something 'they' want to discuss with you or maybe even take from you. I'm not sure."

I rubbed my temples. "I must be really tired because you're not making any sense right now." Two hours wasn't enough sleep, and I could tell my body and mind were starting to feel the effects.

"Ugul said 'there's something you should know' just before he died. I got the feeling he was talking about your essences. Your blood. The only reason the Legion is after you is because of how different you are. It's only logical to assume there'll be others."

"Others?" I said, feeling numb.

"Yes, others," said Tyrius. He waited for the information to sink in. "The Legion tried to keep what they did to you and the other Unmarked a secret."

I shrugged and said, "Yeah by trying to kill me."

"Exactly," said the cat. "But you're alive. And their secret is out. You."

"Fantastic."

"Others will be interested in what you are because of what's inside you." Tyrius looked at my blank expression and added, "And I don't think it's a good thing."

A cold shiver licked up my spine, making me shake. I didn't like the sound of that. "What?" I said. "That I'm both angel and demon-born?"

"No, that there are others *interested* in you. We don't know what kind of interests they might have."

"It's not like I can hide now," I said, my stomach turning. "Everyone knows what I am."

"Like I said, it's just a working theory." Tyrius frowned at that for a moment. "I think I'm right. But don't you worry. We'll figure this out."

I slid a hand down my face. "Evanora knew. It's why she wanted to kill me and drink my blood." The memory of being trapped in that blood circle still made me shiver.

"She probably did hear about you having both demon and angel blood," answered the baal. "That in itself is unusual. And powerful to a witch who dabbles in blood magic, which she clearly does."

"Great." I raised my wrists and looked at the thin white scars that crossed them both, just a memory now of what had almost happened. "And she has a cup of my blood."

"Thank God it isn't a liter," commented the cat. "Don't worry. A cup is nothing. I've seen my share of blood magic. The old crow needed a lot more of your blood to make whatever dark spell she was planning on."

I yanked the strap of my messenger bag higher on my shoulder. The weight of the dark witch grimoire seemed to have doubled in the mere minutes of just standing here.

I knew dark witches dabbled in dark magic, black magic and blood magic. I had the feeling Evanora Crow knew exactly what she was doing with me. With my blood.

Blood was the key word here. If my blood, my two mixed essences were a hot commodity, then I wanted to know more about them. And I had a feeling the grimoire would show me how. If there was a book out there that was dark enough, filled with the evilest spells and curses and that dealt with blood magic, the dark witch grimoire was the one.

Maybe my blood was the answer. And maybe it was just what I needed to kick the fae queen's ass.

With a heightened sense of determination, I raised my fist and knocked.

CHAPTER
26

I heard the muffled sounds of voices followed by the sound of a bolt being undone before the door opened. Father Thomas opened the door, and I blinked at the sudden light. He wore his black finest, the white square of his clerical collar standing out around his neck like a choker.

"Rowyn." Father Thomas gave me a tight smile, and from the worried look in his eye I knew Jax had already given the priest all the details.

"Hi, Father," I said. "You look just about how I feel."

"Come in," said the priest as he held the door open for us. "Jax and Danto are already in my office.

They've had lots to say in the past ten minutes, some very disturbing things."

I moved past the priest into a small lobby with wood paneling and antique rugs. "I'll bet."

Father Thomas looked down at Tyrius. "I see you're wearing your collar."

The cat wrinkled his face. "I see you're wearing yours."

Oh. Hell. Here we go.

"Come on, Tyrius," I said and ushered him in. "This is going to be a long night."

We followed Father Thomas down a long hallway. The air smelled of wood, musty carpets and sins, and distant murmurs of voices drifted out. The bursts in sudden pitch told me it was a heated argument, but I couldn't make out what the voices said. The priest led us deeper into the church and up a flight of stairs to a room, his private office. A long, carved wooden desk sat below a window framed with heavy burgundy drapes. An assortment of swords and daggers hung on the wall below a small bar area. I smiled. I'd always admired his swords. They weren't soul blades, the blades given to us by the archangels, but these were all made of silver, and sharp, perfect to gut any old demon.

A laptop sat on top of the desk, looking modern and out of place among the mismatched eighteenth-century style furnishings. A pair of table lamps lit the room in soft gold. Bookcases stood against each wall, cramped with neatly aligned tomes, the spines showing a dizzying variety of languages.

Jax and Danto sat in the leather armchairs facing the desk. At the sound of our entrance, they both looked angry, like we'd just interrupted an argument. Jax's face was flushed and Danto's gray eyes were darker than usual. Curious. I wondered what that had been about?

There was an extra chair next Jax, and I had a feeling he had put it there.

"Can I offer you a drink? Coffee?" Father Thomas moved to the small bar area and poured himself a drink.

"No thank you. We're fine," I said, glaring at Tyrius before he opened his mouth. Now was not the time to have a baal high on coffee.

I sat in the empty chair, aware of Jax's eyes on me. Heat rose from my neck to my face and I wanted to kick myself for not having better control over my emotions. Once Tyrius was settled on my lap, I stilled my expression and met Jax's gaze.

"What did I miss?" I was hoping to get a glimpse into their argument. I moved my eyes over to Danto, but the vampire was busy rolling around the gold liquid contents of his drink.

"Not much." Jax leaned back into his chair, his empty glass in his hands. "We only got here a few minutes ago. We'd been telling the Father all about The White Grace and the fae queen."

Father Thomas grabbed his drink and sat in his chair facing the four of us. A large leather-bound book lay open on his desk that I hadn't noticed before. It was old from the musty smell that rolled off of it, probably from the church's reserved collection. The pages were made of thick paper, yellowed with age, and the edges were worn and torn. Interesting.

The priest wrapped his fingers around his glass. "If what they've told me is true, then God help us."

"Amen," mewed the cat. "'Cause it's the truth, Padre."

I leaned forward in my chair to get a better look at the book. "Have you ever heard of it? The White Grace?"

Father Thomas's brow furrowed deeply. "Not until I read about it here." He reached over and turned the book so that I could read it. A black tattoo peeked from the right sleeve of his shirt, a symbol of a sword within a circle. Now that was interesting. I made a mental note to ask him about it later.

"This is Father Albertus Magnus's journal," said Father Thomas. "He was a great thinker and scholar in the middle ages, and a Knight of Heaven until he died in 1280. In this entry, he mentions a book that came to the church's possession, a book written by the Greater Demon Astaroth." Now I was really curious. "With his studies of the demon languages," continued the priest, "Father Albertus was able to decipher parts of it. He says the book talks of demon armies and their wars, but near the bottom of the page, he writes about a white stone with immense power. A stone that was created by a race of the first demons. He called them The Faceless Ones. But that's all there is. I can't find any records of the stone having the power to transform humans into half-breeds."

"You don't have to," I said and pulled the book closer to me. "We've seen it with our own eyes."

The priest took a deep breath and then nodded. "So I've been told. You think it's the same stone?"

"Sounds like it. I just wish there was more."

"Well," said Tyrius as he crossed his front paws. "Being from that side of the tracks, I can tell you that you don't have it in your precious book because the demons didn't *want* you to find out. Something that powerful, they'd keep it secret and hidden. That's for damn sure."

My eyes scanned quickly over the Latin texts. "So we've got nothing." I pushed the book away. I didn't care to hide my disappointment. I thought we'd find something about The White Grace in Father Thomas's private collection.

"What about Hallow Hall?" I looked at Jax. "Maybe we can check the archives. There's got to be something about The White Grace in there."

"I've already checked," said Jax. "I had Daniel do a thorough search in all the old texts and even in the Deus Septem, the books given to us by the archangels. There's no mention of a white stone with incredible power. Nothing." Glancing at the bookshelves, Jax tapped his fingers against his glass. "I was hoping to find something to help us destroy it."

Father Thomas opened his mouth to speak, but Danto cut him off. "Should we? Should we destroy something we can use? That can help us?"

Incredulous, I stared at the vampire. "You're kidding, right?"

"Doesn't that strike you as monumentally stupid?" commented Tyrius. "I thought vampires were blessed with high intelligence, not cursed with a bag of dumbass."

"There's a reason why Ugul had it hidden in his freaking belly," I told the vampire. "He knew how dangerous the stone was and how it could be used to do evil. He was protecting that stone but he was also protecting everyone *from* it. Don't you get it?"

"But it holds the power to do good as well," pressed Danto, his eyes glittering with a fevered intensity. "Think about it."

"I don't have to," I said. "That stone is bad. Pure and simple. I don't care if it's white and it has a really cute name—no way."

Jax clenched his jaw. "That thing needs to be destroyed. It's unnatural. If it's not the faerie queen of the Dark Court, it would have been someone else. Maybe someone worse."

"Souls help us," I breathed, having a hard time thinking of a worse hag than Isobel.

"Like I said before," said Jax, anger creeping over his face. "If half-breeds can't have any more children, that's life. You need to accept it. Maybe that's just the way your species will die out. But you can't go around making more of you with this thing."

I raised my brows. So that's what the fight had been about.

Danto's eyes went black. Shit. He was vamping out. "My species isn't the only one dying out, angel-born. Last I checked, you lot had barely a few thousand left all over the world. The archangels won't make any more of you and as time goes by, more of your females are becoming barren. You can breed with humans, but your angel-essence will diminish until there's nothing angel left in your angel-born. You'll become humans." Danto lifted his chin. "What if it can create more angel-born? An army of angel-born that can defeat more demons."

Jax's knuckles were white, but I could tell he was thinking it over. Hell, even I was.

"If anyone's dying out," Jax said after a moment, "your kind will be first."

"Enough with the pissing contest, boys," I said, my temper flaring at their stupidity. "This isn't helping. We are all in danger. All of us. Angel-born, half-breeds, and humans. We need to work together."

"Tyrius," said Father Thomas suddenly. He'd been watching the exchange silently. "You've been around much longer than most of us here." His eyes glanced at Danto. "In your time with witches, you must have encountered other magic stones. What do you make of this one? What can you tell us about them?"

Tyrius straightened proudly, his tail flicking behind him. "I can tell you that most magic stones do have a weakness. Nothing has infinite power. Not magic. Not anything. The power of the stone will run out eventually, but it could take years, maybe even centuries before we see a difference."

"Unless the queen uses it up all at once." I remembered the strain on the queen's features. The stone had drained her somewhat. Good. That was a start.

"It's a possibility," answered the Siamese cat. "But I've seen some witches go mad with magic stones. Once they get a taste of that power, it's almost impossible for them to let it go. To stop using it. I've also known one that died, but not before she became a creature, a wraith. She forgot to eat and sleep, and eventually her mortal body shut down. Magic stones are dangerous. I don't know how Ugul resisted that stone inside his chest, but he must have been a strong SOB."

My stomach clenched with guilt as I tried to rid my mind's eye of Ugul's lifeless eyes on me. "You know her better than any of us, Danto," I said. "You think she'll create a giant army right away?"

Danto was silent for a while, his drink still untouched. "She'll create an army large enough to put pressure on the other half-breed clans. One that won't alert the human police right away. She'll use the poor, the homeless, prostitutes, those who won't be missed." The vampire hesitated. "Then, when she's ready, she'll destroy all the other half-breeds who won't swear fealty to her. She wants to rule over all of them. Isobel has always wanted to be the *only* queen of the half-breeds, fae or not."

"I've got to hand it to her," I said. "She's freakishly ambitious. Crazy. But fiercely determined."

Danto leaned forward. His black eyes and held mine, and I shivered. He had an absolutely perfect mouth, and his skin was flawless. "What's going to happen is the other leaders of the half-breed clans will join her," continued the vampire. "Either from fear or because they want to be on the winning side."

"Winning side?" I scowled. "You're talking as though she's already won."

"She will, if we don't stop her."

I resisted looking away from his penetrating stare. "And how do we do that? If, like you say, she's already created what? A thousand new faeries? How do we stop an army of that size?"

Frowning, the vampire studied me a long moment while I listened to my heart pound in my chest and felt sweat break out on my forehead.

"The only way will be to join forces," answered the vampire, his voice strained. "We can't beat the faerie queen on our own. We're going to need help. Lots of it. We need to take this to the Gray Council. Half-breeds and angel-born, at least the half-breeds that will not have joined her by then."

I shifted in my seat, my frustration switching to fear. I prayed to the souls that we weren't already too late.

Danto looked at me for a second and then said, "And after she's convinced or destroyed all the half-breeds, she'll turn on the humans next."

I cringed. "Duh. Of course she will. There are even more to rule."

Danto shook his head with no expression. "Humans are weak in her mind. To her, they're at the bottom of the food chain. She doesn't want to rule the humans—"

"She wants to eat them," said Tyrius and I stared at him, my eyes wide. "Move over filet de Tyrius. Hello Homo sapiens bourguignon."

Yikes. I'd seen the human teeth crown on her head. I had no doubt she'd sink her teeth into human flesh.

Danto looked at the priest. "I don't believe she wants to turn the entire world into half-breeds. I believe she wants to turn just enough to rid the world of humans. Her hatred for humans goes back before my time. She was tortured by humans. Raped. Defiled. Atrocities were done to her, all in the name of one god or another. It changed her."

I swore. "She's crazy."

"Ya think?" said Tyrius.

"Can the stone give her that much power?" The thought terrified me and I couldn't help but feel responsible. "If only I hadn't taken that damned job, none of this would be happening."

"I seriously doubt that." Tyrius turned around and faced me. "If it wasn't you, it would have been someone else. Eventually the queen-bitch would have gotten her hands on that stone. It's not your fault she's psychotic. She just is."

"But, I must caution you." Danto's cool calmness cracked as he took a breath. It was subtle, but there it was. "There'll be those who'll want to join her," said the vampire, "and those who'll want the stone for themselves."

Jax swore. "This isn't going to end well." He stood up and went to pour himself another drink.

I jerked in my seat and hissed as Tyrius's nails broke my skin in his effort to hang on. "You mean like other half-breeds?"

"And possibly those who sit on the Gray Council." Danto's face was grim. "Once we bring it up with the Gray Council," continued the vampire, "I can promise you that some of the council members and even just other common half-breeds will want the stone. Because the one who holds the stone holds that power. The White Grace will be the number one commodity in our world. Every half-breed around the world will want it for their own."

"Including the angel-born," I found myself saying. I was positive the Heads of houses or even the Sensitive council would want their hands on that power. Fantastic.

"This is bad, Rowyn," said Tyrius. I met his blue eyes and I knew he felt the same as I did.

We needed to destroy the stone.

I leaned back against my chair, my blood pressure rising. "Then, you don't think we should go to the Gray Council?"

"As Head of the New York City vampires," said the vampire, "I'm obliged to report to them on matters that could affect our livelihood. I have to tell them, but I know it won't come without consequences."

"So, basically we're screwed. Fantastic." Numb, I stared at the bottles of gin, rum and whiskey next to Jax at the bar. Maybe I should have a drink, a very big one.

Danto leaned forward and placed his untouched drink on the priest's desk. "I'll make arrangements to speak to the Gray Council tonight," said Danto. "After they hear what I have to say, they'll want to hear from us shortly, so don't make any plans until I get in touch with you."

"I'm an outcast," I said shrugging. "There's no way they'll want to speak to me."

"No," said Father Thomas, his dark eyes concerned. "But the two of you might be called in as a witnesses."

A warm flutter of appreciation slipped through me at Father Thomas's inclusion of Tyrius as one of us. The cat, clearly pleased, purred and I reached out and scratched under his chin.

"They'll believe me," said Father Thomas. "But first, I need to speak to the bishop. The Church will want to know about this. If there's a chance of thousands of new half-breeds being created overnight, we'll need the Church's help."

My ears popped as I squished the yawn that threatened to expose how tired I was. I needed to sleep. I didn't want any of them to think, to see, how truly exhausted I was. And I was still hungry.

"All right then," I said as I stood up, looking forward to my bed. Tyrius landed elegantly on the floor next to me. "Guess I'll go home and wait for your call." I doubted I could sleep with the spike in my blood pressure, but maybe I could just relax for an hour or two.

I gave the priest a tight smile. "Thank you, Father Thomas. I'll see you later," I added quickly, not wanting Jax to offer us another ride home.

My pulse throbbed when I saw Jax coming towards me, those damn green eyes trying to hypnotize me again. My eyes moved to his full, kissable mouth and I flushed.

"I know what you're going to say," said Jax, lifting his hands in surrender, "but I still want to take you home. It's late. And we're all tired."

"It's fine. I'm ten minutes away on foot. I want to walk and clear my head—"

The sound of a car alarm blared through the walls of the church.

Jax frowned as he turned his head towards the door. "That's my car alarm." He set his drink down and was out the door before I closed my mouth with the rest of my Jax-shutdown on my tongue.

When I turned back around, Danto was leaning over the old journal, flipping through the pages with a mildly interested expression on his face.

Father Thomas stood up and came around to stand next to me. "I was really glad to hear that your grandmother can keep her home," he said, smiling.

"You have a big heart, Rowyn. That was very kind of you."

Embarrassed, I looked at my boots. "Yeah, well, it's nothing. I'm just happy she's happy," I answered and felt a tug on my awareness.

A thread of apprehension unrolled as I took a deep breath and felt the pulse of darkness, the shift of demon energies. Ah. Crap.

The wrinkles at the corners of the priest's eyes deepened. "What is it, Rowyn? You look like you want to say something."

"Demons," growled Tyrius. "Outside. And by the buckets of that rotten stench that are attacking my delicate nose, I'd say a shit load of them."

My eyes widened. "Jax."

The priest shot to the back of the room and grabbed one of his swords from the wall, brandishing it expertly, like a seasoned warrior.

"Jax!" I cried. My hair lifted off my face as a flash of black clothes and hair whipped past me. Danto was out the door before I even blinked. I shot through the doorway after him and bounded down the hall.

Shit. Shit. Shit.

"Jax! Wait!" I shouted just as I cleared the side entrance. My legs pounded with adrenaline, and my hand was perched on my soul blade as I rocketed through the door and out into the night air. My boots hit the walkway just as the two parking lot lamppost lights exploded and went out.

I halted, nearly crashing into Danto.

The vampire stood still, his body crouched slightly with his clawed hands splayed out. His black eyes were fixed on something before him.

I followed his gaze over to the parking lot.

My breath seemed to freeze in my throat.

A thin, humanoid demon, standing over eight feet tall with decomposing, seeping skin as red as blood and a mismatch of black fur along its back, arms and legs stood in the Church's parking lot.

And hanging in its grasp by the neck was Jax.

CHAPTER
27

The Greater demon Degamon's black eyes focused on me and it smiled, revealing an excessively large mouth with an excessive number of sharp, yellow teeth.

The parking lot was slowly misting in a black, rolling fog, plunging it into darkness as wraiths—creatures layered with scales, fur and muscle—stepped from the shadows. Their rat-like tails thrashed behind them with black eyes glaring from beneath their flat skulls. Their nostrils flared out, taking in our scent, with drool dribbling from their elongated maws.

Igura demons. Lesser demons. Stupid, but deadly. I counted about twenty, but only half of them carried death blades. Good.

"Hello, angel brat," sneered the Greater demon, his low voice making me shudder. "I'm here to collect my end of our bargain. Little Jaxie Spencie."

Jax's eyes met mine, and the whites of his eyes shone in the light of the moon. His face was turning a disturbing shade of purple. The red demon had him by the neck, his feet dangling four inches above the ground.

"Don't look so surprised," chortled the demon. "A deal's a deal. I gave you want you wanted, and now I'm here to collect what's owed to me. Him."

Six months ago, I had stood and watched as Jax had given his name to the Greater demon in exchange for the name of the demon responsible for his sister's death. I knew what that meant. From what I'd read and learned over the years, referred to in many demonology books as the Law of Names, knowledge of a true name allows one to affect another person or being magically. In this case, demon magic.

With Jax's true name, which he had given freely to the demon, Jax was bound to it. Forever maybe. That part I wasn't sure about. But I knew it gave the demon power over Jax. The demon could control his mind and body, maybe even possess him. Degamon could use him against us, and Jax would have no choice but to do as it commanded.

In our haste to find the killer of the Unmarked, we hadn't specified the details. We hadn't gone down to the nitty-gritty of the contract. The loopholes are in the fine print of any contract. Big mistake. Degamon's claim on Jax would end, most probably, when Jax was dead.

I shook with rage at my own stupidity. I should have done something. Found a charm or a spell to counter the demon's claim on Jax, if there was such a thing. I had no idea.

My head pounded and I felt as though my eyes were about to burst out of their sockets.

Damn you, Vedriel.

But then in that moment when Jax's eyes met mine, I didn't see fear in them, but fury—cold and practical, the kind when a plan didn't unfold the way you'd wanted. And that's when I realized what Jax had been doing for the past six months, what had him looking thinner and tired. He'd been looking for a way to get out of his deal.

Sure Jax had been searching for his sister's killer, but he'd been searching for a way to get out of the deal with Degamon too.

"Degamon, I thought it was you." Tyrius's voice echoed loudly in the night air as he halted at my feet. "I'd recognize that low-grade demon stink anywhere." The scent of aftershave told me Father Thomas was behind me, to my right.

Danto looked over at me, his jaw clenching. "What do you want to do?" His black eyes were strained, and he and I both knew that with any sudden movement, Degamon would snap Jax's neck.

Fear hit my stomach like a stone dropping into a stream. "I'll trade you for him," I said hastily. "I'm more valuable than just a regular angel-born. You know it, and I know it." I stepped forward, my eyes darting from the iguras to Degamon. "Let's trade."

Degamon lifted his head, seemingly interested.

"Rowyn, don't," Jax forced out. "Don't... be... stupid." His last words warbled as he shook, and I was seriously wondering how much longer he could live without air in his lungs.

"Yeah, Rowyn, what the *hell* are you doing?" hissed Tyrius. Then he added quickly at the priest's raised eyebrow, "No offense, Padre."

Father Thomas's eyes shone with a deep loathing at Degamon. "None taken, baal." The priest looked badass with his long sword gleaming in the moonlight. We shared the same tastes in swords apparently, and in our hatred for demons.

I flicked my eyes back to Degamon and lowered my voice to the cat, "I'm trying to save his life." My thighs were stiff and throbbing from refraining from attacking Degamon.

Its eyes twinkled with amusement. It was enjoying us squirm, afraid to move. *I'm going to kill that SOB.*

Tyrius shifted nervously on his feet. "By sacrificing yours? Jax wouldn't want that."

"Maybe," I said, feeling my palm wet with my own blood, as the hilt of my blade cut through my skin from holding it too hard. "But you want to leave him to die in the hands of that demon?"

"I don't want that either," said the cat, "but what you're doing is suicide. Don't be stupid. Think!"

Jax was going to die if I didn't do something. "I'm out of options. Stupid is the only thing I've got."

A well of fury ripped open inside of me, vast and unyielding and horrible. A guttural growl rolled in my throat at the sight of Jax's tears falling down his cheeks. A rage boiled up in me so blistering it was an effort to keep from lunging to stab Degamon with my soul blade. But even before I could reach them, the demon would kill Jax.

"Rowyn, Rowyn, Rowyn," mocked the demon. "Yes. I know who you are. But don't worry, I'm not here for you. This little runt is mine," said Degamon, black and red mist coiling off its body. "He was mine the second he opened his mouth and sealed the deal," the demon snarled, bringing Jax close to his face. "The things we are going to do together makes me all tingly inside."

Jax's face twisted and then he spat in the demon's face.

Degamon yanked Jax back, his black eyes narrowing. "A year in the Netherworld will teach you some manners."

"No!" Cold and hot spiked through me. I was going to be sick. "No," I faltered, my voice barely above a whisper. "No, you can't." Hot rage boiled inside me. *This can't be happening. Not now.*

Degamon chuckled, the sound sending waves of fear through me. "Of course I can. This little fellow,"

Degamon shook Jax, "gave me his name. He's mine until I decide that he isn't… or when he's dead."

"You bastard!" I shouted when I heard Jax make a choking sound. "You can't do this! You hurt him and I'll kill you. I'll freaking kill you."

"I'm honored," Degamon said, tension in its voice and posture. "Jaxie Spencie is mine. You will not touch him." The demon laughed. "As if you have a say in the matter."

I do. I bent my body forward. I was going to rip off its head. The air moved and from the corners of my eyes I saw Danto and Father Thomas do the same.

A shadow of grief and horror flashed in Jax's eyes. I couldn't take my eyes away, and my pulse hammered. He was a pain in my ass, he had a freaking fiancée, but I still cared for the fool. I cared a lot, apparently.

"Come on, Degamon," I hissed. "I'm a much better catch. I'll make it worth your while. You're a business man—business demon—whatever. You know what I mean. I'm worth ten of him."

For a moment, Degamon watched me. Its expression was unreadable but the pressure on Jax's neck seemed to lessen.

"You would sacrifice your life for him?" Degamon asked, shifting its clawed fingers around Jax's throat. "Why? Why would you do this?"

"Because he's my friend. And that's what friends do."

"Just a friend?" inquired the demon, its eyes rolling over Jax and then flicking back to me. It fell back and laughed. "Oh… I think not. He's too pretty for anything platonic. Looks at those lips. Humans pay a lot of money for lips like those."

My face warmed and I shifted on my feet. "So, do we agree? Me for him?" My pulse leapt at its sudden interest. Maybe it was enough to completely pay off Jax's debt. "Interested?" I taunted. "Clear his debt to you, and in exchange you can have me. Deal?"

"Rowyn, don't be an idiot!" snapped Tyrius. "He'll kill you. We'll figure this out. There's got to be another way."

"I agree with Tyrius," said Father Thomas suddenly. "Perhaps the Legion can help. They could find a way to get him back."

"Screw the Legion," I spat, thinking of Vedriel and what they'd done to me. "They're worse than demons."

I heard the intake of breath from the priest at my slight for the Legion. Okay, so I'd gone a little too far with that last remark. But I was pissed and scared and out of my mind with fear for Jax. I couldn't let this happen to him. I couldn't. I wouldn't.

I shook my head, clenching my jaw. "There is no other way. I have to do this," I said, my voice low. "If we don't stop him now, he'll take Jax to the Netherworld. You know what that's like. You think Jax will survive?"

Tyrius cursed. "Even if the toxic air doesn't kill him straight away, we'll never see him again."

"I've got demon blood," I whispered, my stomach clenching. "If anyone can survive the Netherworld, it's me. I can find my way back." *I hope...*

"It's not that simple." I looked down at the strain in Tyrius's voice. "The Netherworld isn't like this world. You can't just jump on a plane and go to another country. The Rifts that allow you to pass are rare and dangerous, and you'll be a prisoner. It's not like you'll be able to roam freely," he said. "Don't forget the Netherworld is a prison to all demons. They'll hate you for what you are. They'll torture you and do other things to you for their own sick pleasures. You might never find a way out. You might die there. Alone, Rowyn."

"I don't care," I lied, feeling as though this might not be such a good idea. My bravado died at the snarl of pleasure coming from the Greater demon.

But it was too late. I'd already given my word.

"So?" My voice echoed in the air and my ears, my heart pounding. "What'll it be?"

Degamon had been watching us with a slight interest. "I'm tempted. You would bring me a very large sum. However, I will not break my deal with Jaxie Spencie," said Degamon. "I already have a few buyers interested in him, who are willing to pay a large sum to play with him." The demon reached out with its other hand and grabbed Jax's crotch suggestively. Its black eyes focused on me. "But I'll be back for you later."

"Bastard!"

I shot forward, pushing off with my legs as a surge of adrenaline spiked through my core. The air shifted and was mixed with black mist, and then a mass of igura demons rushed towards me.

Crap.

Danto was already moving for the nearby iguras that had leapt forward at the same time.

Drawing my death blade in my other hand, I spun and sliced, slashing across the throat of the nearest igura demon. I twisted and shoved the dying demon into the demon closest to it as I plunged my other blade deep into the gut of a third.

In my line of sight, I caught a glimpse of the priest yanking his sword from the belly of a groaning demon and spun to slice the head off another. Impressive.

I couldn't see Tyrius, but I knew he wasn't far behind me.

Calming my senses, I moved on instinct, letting my training and supernatural abilities flow through me and guide me. The air moved with the smell of rot. An igura demon stabbed the air with its own death blade, a direct attack to my chest. Cursing, I parried the thrust aside with one dagger, spinning into its exposed torso. Hot, reeking black blood shot onto my hand as I shoved my other death blade into its eye. A cloud of dirt hit me in the face as the igura exploded into dust.

Taking a gasp of air, I twisted, falling away and smacking the flat of my hilt into the head of another igura.

Laughter reached me. Degamon. My hatred for the demon ignited like a flame coursing through me, a hot poison in my veins.

I was going to gut that SOB.

My breath came in sharply and I halted when an igura jumped at Danto, taloned hands reaching and an ugly sound erupting from it.

For a second, I watched, shocked, as the two grappled, both moving incredibly fast. Danto seemed to blur in and out of existence, making the igura look like it was trying to catch a moving shadow.

"Look out!" I cried when another igura got a grip on him from the back, but the vampire twisted with an inhuman speed to fix his teeth on the demon's neck. The demon screamed and went limp, and before it fell, Danto whirled and snapped the neck of the other demon. Our eyes met, his fangs shining with black blood.

I was moving again. I darted towards the red demon, towards Jax. If I could kill it, all of this would be over.

Desperation filled me as I pushed my body harder than ever, twisting, rolling, ducking. I assailed my way through the mass of igura, my sight never leaving Jax's pained features.

I'm coming.

It wasn't courage that fed my body with strength, it was fury and fear.

"Rowyn!" Tyrius cried. "Behind you!"

I jumped and spun in midair, catching the sight of two iguras coming at me with frightening speed.

291

Hunger marred their faces. They wanted to kill me. But I wanted to kill them more.

Eyes widening, I curled my body as I fell and made contact with the ground. I hurled myself onto it, rolling and keeping low until I was right up under two iguras that were still trying to come straight for me. They screamed as I disemboweled them both in two swipes.

I came back up. Danto was crushing another demon's head with his hands, given his supernatural strength. He snarled, his teeth still dripping with demon blood. I winced as the vampire reached up and dug his sharp talons into the demon's eyes. Screaming, the demon flung itself back, but the vampire was after it. Two quick swipes and the demon's head was sliced right off its neck and flopped to the ground in an explosion of ash.

Tyrius leapt at the face of an igura. He was a blur of claws and teeth as he attacked without mercy, slicing into the soft demon's flesh with savage intent. Black blood flew everywhere, showering the cat's light fur.

A growl sounded near me, and I whirled, heart skipping, as I saw an igura charge for Father Thomas who had his sword plunged deep into the gut of another.

"Father! Duck!" I shouted before throwing my soul blade at the creature's approaching face. The priest barely moved fast enough to avoid the blow, and the demon's blood splattered on his shirt.

As Father Thomas pulled his sword from the other dying igura, I looked up and saw an opening.

A clear path right to Degamon.

Half of his igura army were dead and the rest were busy fighting off a priest, a cat, and a vampire. That left me.

"Gotcha," I whispered and lunged.

I was almost there. I could reach out and touch Jax. His eyes were closed. He was out cold.

With a savage howl, I threw myself at the red demon, my death blade inches from its repulsive, blistering face.

My ears popped at the sudden shift in pressure— and then I fell flat on my face.

I pushed myself off the ground and whirled around.

Degamon and Jax were gone.

CHAPTER
28

"**R**owyn, this isn't going to work," argued Tyrius as he sat next to me on the floor of my apartment. "I applaud your creativity, but I think you're out of your freaking angel-born mind!"

"It *has* to work." *God help me, it has to.* I reached over and flipped the next page in the dark witch grimoire, careful not to rip the pages from the bulky tome. The smell of dust and leather tickled my nose as I read the next instructions.

I wiped the sweat from my brow with my arm, blinking at the page. I had done a few summoning rituals before, but I wasn't confident enough in my conjuring abilities to try and do it on a whim. Besides, this summoning ritual was particularly hard and was a tad different from the other times I'd done it.

Tyrius huffed out a breath and muttered, "It's astonishing, really, that on one hand you can be so clever and on the other... so bleeping stupid!"

"Tyrius."

Tyrius's face turned incredulous. "Don't you remember what happened the last time we summoned a demon? Shit hit the fan. Literally."

I sighed through my nose, trying to control my temper. I knew Tyrius was only trying to protect me—from myself and my own stupidity. But I was confident this was going to work. It had to work. I was running out of brilliant, or in this case, stupid ideas.

"We're not summoning a demon this time," I said. "We're summoning Jax."

Tyrius swore. "What if you hurt him? Did you think about that? What if you can't summon him? He's a freaking human!"

"He's not," I snapped. "He's an angel-born. And Degamon has to have altered Jax's essence with something to withstand the Netherworld. Otherwise, he wouldn't have been able to pull him with him. Or sell him, for that matter. He needs Jax to be able to stand and function in the Netherworld." I knew it to be true. If Degamon had buyers lined up for Jax, it meant he had fixed him up somehow, altered his essence or maybe even added something to it, hopefully not the latter.

Degamon had done something to Jax, and it was my key for bringing him back.

I exhaled a long breath and then took a calming one. It was crucial that I read the spell right. If I made a mistake, I could really hurt Jax, but I could also kill him.

"You think it's wise to be playing with the man's life." Tyrius was just not letting this go. "He's a jackass with really good taste in cars—but he doesn't deserve to die!"

I spun around. "Do you think it's wise to leave him in the Netherworld?" When the cat said nothing I added, "He's not going to make it. He's not a demon, Tyrius. Demons live in the Netherworld. Not angel-born. What do you think will happen to him if he stays? Turn into a butterfly?"

Tyrius made a face. "If he doesn't die, or they don't kill him, then the only thing left… is that he'll become a demon."

"Right," I said, having heard the stories of that exact thing happening to angels who'd been trapped in the Netherworld. "I can't let that happen. Not to Jax. He didn't deserve this. He only wanted to find his sister's killer. What was happening now… wasn't fair. Not to him."

I turned away and yanked out my soul blade before Tyrius saw the moisture in my eyes. My necklace slipped out of my t-shirt, the coin that hung from the black leather cord bouncing before coming to a rest against my chest.

"It keeps doing that," I said as I reached out and grabbed the leprechaun coin, feeling its rough surface on my skin. It was warm and I took that as a good sign as I slipped it back down the front of my shirt. "It doesn't seem to want to stay put."

"I don't know why you want to keep it," said Tyrius. "It was only spelled to show us the way out of Elysium. There's no use for it anymore, unless you want to go back there."

"No, thanks." There was no way I was going back to Elysium, but I didn't want to get rid of the coin. It was a visual reminder of the crap I'd stirred and of what I still had to do.

"Do you even know which summoning spell to do?" Tyrius edged forward, his eyes moving along the Latin scriptures on the pages. "Is there one to summon humans? I've never actually seen a witch summon a human before. I mean, what's the point, right? They summon demons for power. Summoning humans would probably cost them more to do it. I can't count the times I've seen witches curse humans—mostly other females because of a male involved—but I've never seen them summon a real human into their circles."

My gut clenched. "Well," I breathed, trying to control my fluttering stomach so that Tyrius wouldn't see how nervous I was. "I haven't found one either. Not exactly."

Tyrius looked up at me, alarmed. "Then, what are you doing?"

I screwed up my face. "Improvising?"

Tyrius jumped to his feet, eyes wide. "Have you lost your mind, woman! I wish you'd never stolen that dammed book!"

"That damned book might be the only thing that can save Jax."

"How?" Tyrius was practically screaming. "You just said you're *improvising*? How's that going to save him if he shows up in your circle warped with his balls on his head!"

"It's *going* to work," I repeated, as though I was trying to convince myself. *It has to.*

With my soul blade in my right hand, I lifted my left palm. Using the small white line of my previous summoning cut as a guide, I slashed through the soft flesh.

Blood oozed from the deep cut, and I pressed my palm against the floor as I dragged my hand around in a circle, using my blood as though it were ink. Then, still using my blood, I drew a closed triangle within the circle—The Seal of Solomon.

And this time, instead of drawing three demonic symbols, I leaned over and drew the archangel's Michael sigil three times—Jax's archangel marking— one inside each triangle corner.

Using the same oval-shaped mirror from my bathroom I'd used to summon Degamon, I placed it in the middle of the triangle. Lastly, I squeezed a small puddle of my blood in the middle and wrote the name Jaxon Spencer.

Tyrius made a noise deep in his throat. "That's blood magic. You drew the circle with your blood, just like the dark witch. If I didn't know any better, I'd think you were trying to curse him, not save him."

I leaned back on my heels. "The spell requires blood as payment. I had to use blood because Jax is alive and The Seal of Solomon because he's in the Netherworld and is probably under some demon curse."

Tyrius looked at me. "This is you improvising. Isn't it?"

I knew dabbling in blood magic was dangerous. Hell, summoning demons was dangerous. I'd heard the stories, the witches' souls slowly eaten away to pay for the blood magic they'd played with. Most of the time, blood magic and necromancy got mixed together. I knew the dangers. But I wasn't using this to gain power or have power over someone or something.

I was trying to *save* a life.

Now, peering down at my circle, I wiped my bloody hand on my jeans and reached out to grab the three candles. I put them on top of the three archangel sigils before I lit them.

"Maybe Father Thomas was right," said Tyrius, the pitch in his voice high with tension. "Maybe the Legion can help. It wouldn't hurt to ask."

"They could," I said, "but they won't. You know I can't trust them. They made me, remember? Changed me into... into whatever I'm supposed to be. I have to do this." I sighed. "I have to try. Just let me try, okay. Just this once and if it doesn't work, we'll figure out something else. But I can't do nothing."

"I know." Tyrius nudged beside me. "It just sucks is all."

"Sucks demon balls," I added and gave him a smile. Tyrius laughed, and the sound filled my heart with joy. Just for a moment.

"Is it finished?" asked the cat as he peered at the circle.

"Almost," I said as I reached inside my jean pocket. "I just need to add one more thing." *And pray to the souls that it will work.*

I pulled out a set of keys, jingling them as I set them on the mirror.

"Where did you get those?"

"They're Jax's car keys. I took them after Father Thomas and Danto left. It's the only thing I could find in his damn car. It's so freaking clean. I tried to find a hair or something else, but this is all I got."

"And the keys symbolize Jax? I'm not following."

Breathing deeply, I exhaled loudly. "For the spell to work, I need a taglock, which is basically a piece of that person, or something they have close emotional or physical tie to, which can be used as a targeting system by the spell. The grimoire says taglocks are usually the person's blood, hair, teeth, skin, or nail clippings—but it's all I've got."

"Jax's DNA," Tyrius exclaimed softly.

"In a way, yes." My breath came in a slow, controlled sound. "I just hope there's something on those keys."

I reached out and pulled the grimoire closer. My heart pounded against my ribs and inside my head. I felt dizzy and nauseated. *Please. Let this work.*

Tyrius shifted nervously next to me, his lips moving in a silent prayer or curse.

Calming my breathing, I let the words flow off my lips. "Jaxon Spencer invocabo. Qui nos venimus ad te veniat nosque hic habitare. Et sanguis sanguinem meum et vocavi te. Et sanguis sanguinem: revertere ad me. Jaxon Spencer antrorsum intra te voco."

And then again carefully in English. "I call upon Jaxon Spencer. Come to us who call you near. Come to us and settle here. Blood to blood, I summon thee. Blood to blood, return to me. Jaxon Spencer, I summon you in the space in front of me."

I held my breath and stared at the keys without blinking. I could feel the blood pounding through me, hear my heart racing. After a minute, my face went cold.

But nothing happened.

"Damn it!" I slammed my fist on the wood floor, hearing something snap. Shit, I'd broken my own finger.

I moved my hand away, trying to fight off a feeling of depression. My eyes widened. "It's the keys. The keys didn't work," I said, as a frustrated sigh shifted through me.

Tyrius snuggled next to me, put his head on my arm, and blinked his big blue eyes at me. "Sorry,

Rowyn. You did what you could. Cheer up. We'll find another way. I promise."

Tears of frustration spilled down my eyes as I shook my head. "This isn't over yet. I need something better. I need—"

The pressure in the apartment changed, followed by a loud pop.

"Did you hear that?" said Tyrius.

My heart pounded as sweat broke out on my arms. I turned around towards the sound. Standing in my kitchen wasn't Jax, but an angel.

CHAPTER
29

There she was, glowing, as angels always did. Her coffee-colored skin was a stark contrast to her modern white pant suit, and I wondered if she had dressed all in white just for an added "angel" effect. Probably. Her black hair was clipped short against her head and she looked to be in her late thirties.

I might suck at demon summoning, but I was sure I didn't summon an angel. Not this time.

Her eyes moved around with the cool precision of making herself aware of everything surrounding her at all times, a predator.

Her eyes met mine, her dark eyes smoldering with barely contained contempt. And she smiled, not a kind nice-to-meet-you smile, but the smile a predator gives before it kills its prey. Her right arm moved, and a long silver blade slipped to her right hand.

"Rowyn, she's got a blade in her hand," whispered Tyrius, his blue eyes flashing. "Why does she have a blade in her hand?"

The angel's eyes moved to Tyrius and her smile widened into something downright scary, revealing her brilliant white teeth.

I scrambled to my feet, the hairs on the back on my neck standing on end. What the hell was an angel doing in my apartment? When angels showed up, it was because they wanted something. And yet I couldn't shake the deep feeling of dread that twisted in my gut. There was nothing holy about the looks she was giving me, or that long dagger in her hand.

"What do you want?" I asked, my voice hard. There was no way I'd let the angel sense the fear in me.

Still smiling, the angel crossed my apartment and moved towards me, speaking in a loud voice as she did. "Rowyn Sinclair. The Hunter." Her eyes moved to the blood circle on the floor. "Summoning demons, I see. How very irresponsible of you. Summoning demons is considered blasphemy. Demon magic violates the angel laws."

I gritted my teeth. "I don't give a rat's ass about your laws." I raised my brows and smiled. "I'm no angel."

The angel cocked her head as she took me all in, her eyes rolling over the death blade at my hip. "No.

You're no angel. But you were once angel-born. But it doesn't matter now."

I frowned. "Your point being?" *What the hell is going on?*

"Either tell us why your angel ass is here," growled Tyrius, his tail slashed behind him. "Or get the hell out. This is a private home. You can't just beam yourself up uninvited. There are rules."

"I don't need an invitation," answered the angel.

I went cold. "What the hell are you talking about?" I asked, my mouth dry.

The angel laughed hard and deep. "You're charged with the murder of the archangel Vedriel." She lifted her dagger and rolled a finger over the sharp edge. "A charge punishable by death."

My mouth dropped open as Tyrius cursed. "What?" Shit. Shit. Shit. "Wait a minute. This is a mistake. I didn't murder anyone."

Yes, I had killed the archangel with the help of my friends, but it was either him or us. And we had chosen him. A nauseating mix of dread and nervousness shook my knees, and I held my breath to try and calm myself.

"No further violations of the angel laws will be tolerated." The angel lowered her blade. Her dark eyes danced with excitement, which gave me the creeps. She *wanted* to kill me. "The sentence for committing murder, for the death of an archangel no less, is death by the blade, to be carried out at once."

Tyrius lowered his ears. "The bastard had it coming. Do you even know what he did? What he did to Rowyn and the others? No, you don't. That is punishable by death. Rowyn only tried to save herself from Dr. Frankenstein."

The angel gave him a chilling look.

I nudged the cat with my foot. "Tyrius. Don't. It's not helping." I stuck out my chin at the angel belligerently and moved my hand to my waist. "This is a mistake," I protested. "The archangel was trying to kill me. He killed others like me. I wished it didn't happen," *yeah right*, "but he gave me no choice. It was either him or me. It was self-defense. He was going to kill me. Don't I get a trial or something?"

The angel laughed. "There is sufficient evidence to back up the claim of murder. You miserable, meat-suit, wannabe angel. You murdered an archangel. There's no way you're getting a trial. It's simple. You're going to die. That's all there is to it."

I licked my lips. "What evidence?" I said, my voice low so it wouldn't shake.

The angel's smile never flickered. "There were witnesses. Enough to put a bounty on your head."

A bounty on my head?

I stiffened as a volley of curses flew out of my mouth. "Damn you and your Legion." Now I was pissed, really, really pissed. "Let me guess… you're getting something in exchange for my life. Aren't you? Not money. Must be something else. What do you angels want?"

"A promotion," she answered, her eyes gleaming. "Elevation. Status. Power. I can have it all, once I bring in your soul."

DARK BOUND

"Damn angels," muttered Tyrius. "Killing mortals to move up the freaking angel ladder. Brilliant."

Anger flashed through me, fed by the memory of Vedriel trying to kill me, of my parents' deaths, of the deaths of the Unmarked.

The angel continued to stare at me. The pleasure and excitement in her eyes was disturbing.

I met her stare and yanked out my death blade. "Get out. Or so help me God, and all the gods, I will end you."

The angel beamed. "You must die, Rowyn Sinclair. You must pay for killing an archangel."

She shot forward in a blur of white and black. Her blade out and swinging, a battle cry rang from her lips as she lunged at me swiftly and deadly.

But I was ready for her.

I pushed Tyrius out of the way with my foot and darted back, dodging each swipe of that sharp and lethal blade. *Damn angels. Can't they just give me a break for once?*

I jumped back as she circled around me. "You can leave now, and I'll forget all about this. Deal?"

The angel pitched forward and jabbed with her long dagger. I sidestepped her, only to feel the side of her dagger along my neck. I ducked and spun, but the blade grazed my skin. Blood warmed my neck and shoulders.

Bitch. She's going to pay for that.

307

The angel grinned at the sight of blood on my neck. She was so damn fast. And one hell of a fighter. But so was I. And this was a fight—fight or be killed.

And I wasn't dying today.

"Guess you really want that promotion, huh?" I teased, grinning at the loss of a smile on her lips. "Tell me, what happens if I don't die? What if I win? What happens to your promotion then?"

"You won't." The angel snarled as she feinted left and slashed right. She came at me, whirling with cold grace, an onslaught of her flashing blade. I ducked and rolled aside, crashing into the kitchen counter. Plates and dishes smashed. The tiled counter shuddered as the angel's blade gouged deep into the tile.

The angel pulled out her weapon, cursing.

"You missed." I smiled at her frustration. I too could play this game.

The angel hissed and lashed out at me, but I ducked and spun, driving my dagger into her side.

Shit. I'd just stabbed an angel with my death blade. But she *made* me do it.

The angel screamed as I yanked out my weapon and leaped back, the tip covered in a white liquid, the angel's essence.

She turned around, her face darkened and livid. "It's going to take a lot more than your death blade to kill me. A trip back to Horizon and I'll be as good as new."

"You can still leave," I said, my gaze going over her shoulder to Tyrius who was crouching on the back of my sofa, ready to pounce if I needed help. "No one has to die."

"I'll leave when you're dead."

The angel's blade glinted in the candlelight as she lifted it over her head. With a wild rush of strength, she flung herself at me. I dove, and the blade buried into the cabinet door. The angel drew it back again as she leaped toward me.

I spun and cried out as her knee drove up into my gut. The air knocked from me in a whoosh. Coughing, I kept my grip on my weapon.

Without air, I couldn't cry out when she kicked me again in the gut. I went crashing onto the floor with the powerful blow, the mirror in my circle crashing under me. So much for seven years of bad luck.

I heard a crack as the back of my head hit the hard wood floor, and agony arced through me.

"Rowyn!" warned Tyrius.

"Stay there!" I shouted. I didn't want him to get hurt. He was still not fully recovered, and I didn't know what the angel was capable of.

Speak of the devil, she loomed above me, her smile more terrifying when seeing it from below. "I'm going to carve out your soul, little mortal. Nothing personal. I just really want that promotion."

"You're a sick bitch. You know that?" I snarled, spitting blood from my mouth and fighting a wave of nausea as I tried to stop the room from spinning. I felt as though the back of my head had exploded like a melon.

"I've been called much worse," remarked the angel, her dark face twisted in a sneer.

My lips curled. "I believe that."

With a scream of fury, the angel swung her blade, the tip whistling as it came around directly for my face. I rolled and sprang to my feet. Grunting with effort and rage, I ducked and dodged her swift attack.

She was lean and strong, but she was nothing compared to the terrifying force and speed of the archangel Vedriel.

The angel female had skills, but she wasn't a trained Hunter like me. She was too cocky, too brash. Soon she would make a mistake, and I'd be waiting for it.

"You move like a bloody accountant," I jeered, waving my blade. "Is that what you do in Horizon? Have they put you behind a desk to count numbers? It's why you're all worked up like that. Isn't it? While your friends are out in the world saving mortal souls, you're sitting at a desk pushing numbers. You must really suck as a guardian angel if I'm your ticket for an advancement."

I knew I'd hit a mark when her eyes narrowed. Her laugh didn't meet her eyes as she looked at Tyrius. "I think I'll kill your cat for an added bonus." She smiled turning her attention back to me, but in the depths of her eyes I could see for the first time into the core of her despair, her anguish for a damn promotion.

Anger bubbled alongside the pain in the back of my head. "Now, why did you go and have to say that."

She raised her barely-there brows. "I hate cats. You could never truly call a cat a pet. They always had that superior look in their eyes, as though they were the masters and we were their pets."

"Nothing wrong with that," mewed Tyrius.

"Plus," she added, "I'm allergic." The angel hurled off with a twist so swift I could barely follow. She was a mist of white as she plunged her long blade. The angel was so damn fast. Too fast for me to block her.

I ducked and rolled, but the angel was already there. And she sent her killing blow straight to my heart.

In that moment, all I saw was her eager, twisted face.

But instead of the soft tear of flesh, there was a faint thud and a stinging reverberation in my chest as her dagger struck something hard and unyielding.

My leprechaun coin.

Her hand shook with the blow of the force. The angel cried out and stumbled back, the whites of her eyes showing. Her mouth dropped open, but she said nothing. Her eyes, full of shock and hate, remained on my chest.

But I'd had about enough of her crap.

I pitched forward as fast as a fae arrow. The angel's eyes went wide as I buried the end of my death blade up through her chin and pushed it up into her brain.

I sprang away as she toppled back, her shocking and terrible gasps dying out in heaving pants. The angel dropped her weapon, her eyes wide and her mouth open in a silent scream. White light poured from her eyes, nose, mouth and ears, until her entire body was enveloped in a sheen of light.

And then she exploded into a million brilliant particles.

The clang of my death blade was loud as it hit the floor. The last of the angel vanished as a mist before the sun, until there was nothing left of her but the pounding at the back of my head.

"And then there were two," said Tyrius as he came up beside me. "Damn, Rowyn. And just when I thought things couldn't get any worse, we kill another angel."

My legs and arms shook with the last effects of the adrenaline. "You mean, *I* killed. This is on me, not you." Ah, hell. Damn those angels. I didn't need this crap right now with everything else that was going on.

Tyrius's sigh was loud. "You know what this means. Don't you?"

I snorted. "That my life sucks?"

"You've been officially charged with murder." Tyrius's voice was distant as he looked at the floor and what was left of my botched-up blood circle. "The Legion is going to come after you for killing the archangel."

"It was self-defense," I snapped. A surge of anger rose in me, but I quickly stifled it seeing as I didn't want to direct any of my anger at Tyrius.

"Not according to their witnesses."

"Screw their witnesses. *We* were the witnesses." I remembered that night like it was yesterday. Apart from Degamon and his minions, there hadn't been anyone else inside Devil's Mouth, one of the abandoned attractions on Fox Island's amusement park where we'd killed the archangel Vedriel.

"They're lying," I said, shaking my head. This entire thing smelled bad. Rotten. I had to find a way to prove to them that I was innocent, or I was as good as dead. "I've spent my entire adult life with the council looking for a chance to accuse me of things I didn't do, and now I've got the Legion of angels trying to set me up and entrap me when I was only trying to defend myself."

"It sucks. I know," said Tyrius. "But we can't stop now. We need to keep moving forward."

"That's all I've ever done," I said. "Move forward. *Keep going, Rowyn. You can do it.* But forces out there just keep pushing me back. Like I'm doomed to fail."

"You're not doomed to fail."

"Feels like it." I found myself clenching my fists, my mood turning utterly black.

"I know that," said the cat, soothingly. "We'll find a way to remove these baseless accusations. But until we can prove your innocence, you can't stay here anymore. It's not safe."

A shiver rose through me. I sank to the floor, angry and depressed. "Great," I said, staring at nothing. I knew Tyrius was right. Any minute now there could be another pop followed by another angel, hungry for a goddamn promotion.

My chest contracted as I fought off the tears. Jax was still Degamon's prisoner. I had to get him back. Just as Tyrius said, the Netherworld's air was toxic to non-demons, so Jax didn't have much time.

"You know there'll be more." Fear lay deep in his eyes, the rim of blue glistening as he snuggled next to me. "And they won't stop until you're dead."

"I know." The Legion of angels thought I was a murderer and wanted me dead. What could be worse?

My eyes darted to the circle, to the set of keys on top of the broken mirror. The summoning hadn't worked. But I hadn't failed Jax, not yet at least. Hope strummed through me, almost painfully.

There was still a chance to save him, and I knew exactly what to do.

CHAPTER
30

"Rowyn, you know I love you. But this is crazy-ass stupid!" exclaimed Tyrius. The stress in his voice only intensified the pounding of my heart. "Have you forgotten what happened the last time?"

"Of course not. I was there." My heart hammered inside my chest as if I had just finished a race. And it wasn't from excitement.

"Crap, I'm sweating like a freaking pig," I hissed. "And now I probably stink."

"Right," agreed the cat. "Stress sweat."

"Stress sweat."

"Then try to relax before you give yourself a heart attack," said the baal demon.

"I can't relax, Tyrius. You were there. You saw what happened to Jax. I have to do something. Plan A didn't work."

"So we're off with Plan B."

"Yup."

"We can still turn around and figure out another way to save Jax." Tyrius's warm breath tickled my cheek. "We haven't even consulted the priest or the vampire. I'm sure if we put all our heads together, we could come up with something a lot less suicidal."

Tyrius's body bounced against my shoulders as I strode down the street at a fast pace. "I've gone through everything already," I said, admiring the cat's ability to hang on without impaling me with his sharp claws. "And this is it. There isn't another way. Right now, a dozen or more demons are torturing him. Doing things to him that I can't even bring myself to say out loud."

Tyrius flinched. "I know."

"You look me in the eye," I told him, "and tell me you think we should let him suffer when we have the means to save him."

Tyrius's whiskers grazed my neck as he shook his head. "Degamon would have never accepted the trade, you know," he said quietly. "Probably because it wants to come back and grab you too."

"I'd like to see it try." I said. "And if it does, I'll be ready for it."

"Rowyn," Tyrius said gently, "we're taking a terrible risk."

"I know," I breathed, my gut tightening. "But Jax is worth the risk."

Tyrius shifted his weight around my shoulders. "I just want to make sure you know what you're doing," Tyrius mumbled under his breath.

"I always *know* what I'm doing. It's just that it doesn't always turn out the way I want it to."

Tyrius was right. What I had planned was suicidal, but there could be no other way. I had to move fast. Every minute wasted was one more minute Jax had to endure the tortures of the Netherworld.

Unshed tears made my vision blur, but I wasn't going to cry, damn it. Not now. Not with what I was about to do.

Pulse fast, my boots clunked on the sidewalk amidst the spotted pattern of sunlight that made it through the colored leaves still clinging to the dark branches. The cool morning mist was damp and pleasant, and I breathed in the smells of fallen leaves, earth, and freshly cut grass.

"Those leper-chaun coins are curious things. Aren't they?" said Tyrius, his voice careful and a little uncertain.

I turned my head to look at him. "What do you mean?"

Tyrius was silent for a moment. "Strange how things played out, eh? I've been playing the scenario over and over in my head, trying to shake out the kinks in the chains of logic."

"Spit it out, Tyrius. I can't read minds."

"Well, I know you hate yourself for accepting the Tooth Fairy's job," he said, and I felt him nudge a little closer, "and how you're going to blame yourself for what's happened—forever."

"Yes. And…"

"But if you hadn't accepted the job," he added, his voice pensive, "you would have never entered Elysium."

"What's your point?" I grunted and slowed my pace marginally.

"And if you hadn't entered Elysium we wouldn't have gotten lost and we wouldn't have met the leper-chauns—which are still dicks in my book. But if we hadn't met the leper-chauns, you would never have gotten that coin." He took a breath and said, "Without that magic coin—"

"I'd be dead." A chill fell over me, sharp as a winter wind.

"Exactly," said Tyrius cheerfully. "Now, try and wrap your head around that."

Crap. I hadn't thought about it. Not really. I turned that over in my head a few times, and the more I did, the creepier I felt.

We fell silent as I continued to walk down the street. The cool air slipped easily in and out of my lungs as I walked, and I kept a steady pace. My heart thrashed inside my chest and I felt as though I was at the edge of a cliff.

We were almost there.

"I can't believe the Legion's put a bounty on your head," commented the cat after a moment of silence. "That's freaking nuts. It means any minute, day or night, sleeping or not, an angel can pop up anywhere and grab you."

"Or kill me." I shuddered at the thought.

"But that makes no sense," said the cat. "Shouldn't there be a trial or something. How can all of Horizon want you dead?"

"You heard what that angel said," I argued. "Maybe those other archangels Vedriel told us about lied to the Legion. For all we know, they've told them that I was a demon spawn, out to kill all archangels. He wanted me dead, and so do the others. They'll make up whatever excuse to kill me."

"It's not fair," hissed the cat. "When do we ever get a break! We're trying to do good here, people. Cut us some freaking slack."

I laughed. "You're so cute when you're angry."

Tyrius puffed out his chest. "Darling, I was born cute."

My smile faded as my boots hit the gravel walkway. My blood pressure rose dangerously. Damn. My face was probably tomato-red, but there was nothing I could do about that now.

Pulse throbbing in my ears, I stepped up to the doors and rang the doorbell. I felt a brush of fur against my cheek as Tyrius leapt off my shoulders.

"What are you doing?"

"I need elbow room if there's going to be a fight," said the cat as he crouched low.

My answer froze in my throat as the front doors swung open.

A beautiful woman with honey-colored hair stood in the doorway. She wore a fitted black dress and a surprised expression. Her large green eyes pinned me for a moment, hard and with a deep revulsion. Then she angled her glass of red wine carefully and leaned against the doorway.

"Well, isn't this a surprise?" said Mrs. Spencer as she crossed her legs. "You're the last person I'd expect to see at my front door, especially after your rude behavior, *demon*." She said the last part with a smile, as though it gave her immense pleasure.

I swallowed, ignoring the slight. "Trust me, not as surprised as I am." I braced myself, hoping I hadn't made a mistake coming here. "May I come in. I need to speak to you about Jax."

For a moment she just watched me. A slight crease formed on her perfect face as she took in my words and worried manner. Then, in a tone of dawning comprehension, she said, "Something's happened to him?"

A cold spot formed in the pit of my stomach, despite my sweating. "Yes. Something bad. Something really bad."

Jax's mother stepped from the threshold. "Then you better get inside," she said. Her eyes moved down to Tyrius and her lips parted.

"Don't worry," said the cat. "I know the drill. I'll wait here outside with the flower pots."

Mrs. Spencer raised a manicured brow but said nothing else as she turned on her heel.

Holding my breath, I followed her into the den.

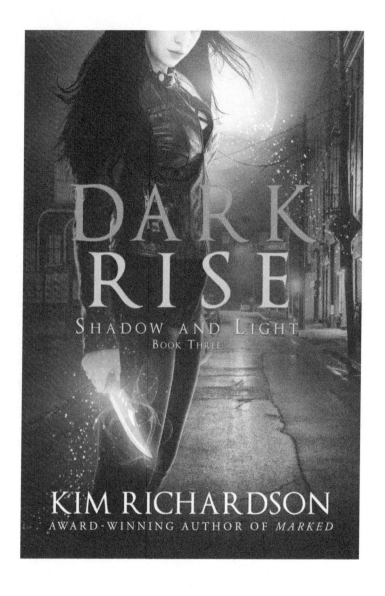

CHAPTER
1

My life was a disaster. There was no denying it anymore.

I sat in a leather armchair, whose owner made me want to gouge out my own eyeballs, breathing in the scent of wine, polished wood and musty antique rugs of her lavish home.

Yup. I was off my rocker.

But what else could I do? Jax had been abducted by the Greater demon Degamon and dragged to the Netherworld. I had tried and failed to summon him back to our dimension. Then, I almost died when an angel showed up and attempted to collect the bounty on my head—a gift from the Legion of angels—thank you very much. Like I needed more drama in my life.

Every minute I sat in this stupid, expensive chair was like a week of rigorous torture for Jax. The longer he spent in that world, the harder it would be to get him back out. If Degamon really was going to sell him off to another demon, it would get a hell of a lot harder.

I couldn't go to the council, the angel-born group of elders and leaders. I didn't trust them, and I couldn't give them any information about Jax without the risk of exposing him and myself. Conjuring demons was taboo. It was the sport of half-breeds, specifically witches, and forbidden to all angel-born. If the council found out, Jax would be shunned or worse, sent to Silent Gallows—the only angel-born prison in North America.

Summoning demons was also a dangerous game. The occasional stupid human did it, and they always ended up possessed or disembodied. That's why conjuring demons was mainly a witch's thing as a means to increase their power by borrowing demon magic. But the catch with tasting demon power was they always took a piece of you—a few fingers, your teeth, eyes, your soul. It didn't matter to them, as long as they had a piece.

When Jax had told me he'd been working some dangerous demon summoning rituals to try and break his contract with Degamon, I'd wanted to beat him with a shovel. But when I mentioned this to his mother, her expression had been carefully blank. I was willing to bet Mommy Dearest had known all along that her son had been dabbling in something seriously illegal.

The woman hated my guts, but she loved her son.

I knew there was nothing she wouldn't do for him, not when she'd already lost a daughter to a demon.

I sat at the edge of the chair, my feet planted strategically in front of me, just in case Mrs. Spencer changed her mind and I had to make a break for it before she set her rich friends to kill my demon-born ass. She'd left me sitting in the den alone at least a half hour ago to make some calls.

Maybe Tyrius was right. Maybe this was the stupidest idea I'd ever had.

Tapping my foot on the rug, my blood pressure skyrocketed, and I wished Tyrius were in here with me. To have him sitting on my lap would have been a real comfort. He'd criticize the plush furnishings, rub himself on the rug to leave his scent and hair, and maybe even spray a few spots. Mrs. Spencer would love that.

It would have brought a smile on my face. But I'd left my best buddy outside by the front door like a pair of muddy Wellingtons. I was an ass.

"You should be nervous," said a male voice in a slightly mocking tone, and I turned to see a tall man standing in the doorway. His short black hair nearly grazed the frame as he watched me, and his dark eyes held a glint of contempt and sly amusement, like I was the butt of some inside joke.

"I'm not nervous. Just anxious to get things going." I narrowed my eyes. "It's Louis, right? How long have you been standing there watching me? That's really pervy, you know?"

The light wrinkles around Louis's eyes deepened with his frown. He was dressed in a similar style to when I'd first met him, with an expensive-looking gray business shirt and a pair of black pants. The P-shaped birthmark I spied through his collar was the same as Jax's. The archangel Michael's sigil was common to all angel-born from House Michael.

He watched me for a beat longer and then sauntered into the den, rubbing his hawk-like nose with his finger. Nervous? I didn't think so. I think he wanted me to think he was nervous. He reminded me of a scarecrow, a very well-dressed scarecrow. Saying the dude was creepy was an understatement.

He moved with the precise and twisting grace of a snake, and I could almost imagine a gray, forked tongue in that large mouth to match his scheming eyes. The slight smile on his lips was conniving. A keeper of secrets? Probably. His over-the-top concern for Jax's mother told me the creepy man had misplaced affection for the married woman. That could come in handy.

There was a smile on his lips, but not in his dark eyes, when he turned around to face me with his back against the mammoth-sized fireplace.

Louis eyed me beneath his thick brows. "You said Jax was abducted by a Greater demon?" He crossed his arms over his chest. "Is that so?"

I sighed really loudly. "I should have seen this coming. You don't believe me."

"Demons lie all the time."

I twisted in my seat and matched my smile to his. "So do the angel-born." No point in denying that I was part demon, though these angel-born seemed to keep forgetting that I was also part angel-born.

I leaned forward in my chair. "Tell me, L-o-u-u-u-is," I drawled, "do you get dressed up for Halloween or do you just go as you?"

Louis glanced over my shoulder at the sound of the front doors shutting followed by the soft murmurs of voices in the hallway. Straining my ears to catch every nuance, I stiffened at the nervous pitch, the rise and fall of their voices mixing with their restless energy. That was because of me. The uneven tread and sound of soles scraping the polished floors told me there were about three.

My thoughts went to Tyrius. If any of them tried something stupid, like kicking him, I was going to go full out Rambo on their asses.

Louis looked back at me. The smile on the man's face twitched. "You're either really brave or really stupid by coming here." His tone wavered somewhere between sly and derisive.

I pursed my lips. "I'm thinking… probably a little bit of both."

"Arrogant child," mumbled Louis as he pushed off the stone fireplace and stepped closer. "You think you're clever. Don't you? You think you're smarter than everyone else?"

"Nah," I shook my head, anger heating my face like a sunburn. "Tyrius is the clever one. I'm just the snotty sidekick with a tight ass."

Something ugly flickered far back in Louis's eyes. His voice turned rougher, and the smile on his face sent a chill licking up my spine.

"You want to know what I think?" pressed the tall man, his face darkening and his smile growing to show a slip of teeth.

"If I say no," I intoned, curling my fingers into fists, "will you stop talking and go away?"

"If Jax was abducted by a Greater demon," continued Louis as though I hadn't interrupted him, "it was because of you, Rowyn. I think you did this. I think you had your demon friend take him."

My mouth dropped open, my anger replaced by shock for a half a second. "You're out of your freaking mind." I shivered, not knowing if I had saved Jax or damned myself by coming here.

"Don't think I don't know what you're trying to do," accused the man, his jaw tightening.

"Oh, yeah? And what's that, Einstein?"

His face was an ugly mask of anger. "To infiltrate our angel-born community by getting your dirty demon fingers around the necks of the great houses."

I stared at my fingers. "I wouldn't call them dirty, but they could use a manicure—"

"This is just a ploy to get close to Celeste," spat Louis, so close to me now that the smell of cigarettes and old coffee made my stomach churn. "You can't have her." This guy was seriously demented.

"I'm trying to save an angel-born, you halfwit," I growled, my nails cutting into my shaking palms. It was my turn to raise my voice. This idiot believed I was responsible for Jax's abduction by the Greater demon. And since he and Mrs. Spencer seemed to be besties, I had the awful feeling she might agree. Swell.

Louis leered down at me. "And when I find out how you did it and can trace it back to you, don't think you're going to live long enough to set in motion whatever demon scheme you had going with your kin."

"Is that a threat?" I growled, my blood seeming to burn under my skin. I barely managed to resist the part of me that wanted to jump up and kick him in the balls. Once. Twice. Okay, lots of times.

"The only reason you're still breathing is because Celeste believes you," said Louis, seemingly pleased at my distress, almost feeding off of it like a specter. "I don't know why, but she does."

"Guess she's not as stupid as you," I answered, feeling a tad relieved that Mrs. Spencer wasn't orchestrating my death as we spoke. She had told me to wait here while she made some phone calls. What was taking her so long?

A deeply satisfied grin came over Louis, and his breath quickened. "You're not as clever as you think, demon," he whispered. His eyes rolled over me, very slowly, and I had the sudden impulse to take a hot shower. "You might have fooled Jax and seduced him with your pretty demon flesh while you flaunted your sexuality at him," he added. "It's hard for men to resist the temptation of flesh. But your whoring demon ways won't work on me."

"Thank the souls," I laughed out loud, smacking my thigh and wishing I knew a spell to make him disappear. The hair in his nose was unnaturally long and touched his upper lip. Yikes.

Louis's smile shifted, becoming wicked. "You're nothing but a cheap, demon succubus imitation."

"And that's why you were voted Personality of the Year." Furious, I gathered myself and jumped to my feet. I had had enough of his crap. I put myself right in his face and leaned in. Louis was a head taller than me, but I didn't care. Flipping my jacket back, I cocked my left hip. When I was satisfied that he'd seen my death blade, I pushed my chest out until I forced him to take a step back if he didn't want to be soiled by my tiny demon breasts.

I smiled, making a point to look down at his groin. "You know what I think, Louis? I think you're all worked up and angry because you haven't gotten laid in a while. Probably because the one you want... isn't on the market."

Louis's ears turned red, and I swear I saw some steam coming out of them. "You don't know what you're talking about."

"I think I do. We always want what we can't have, right?" I raised a brow. "Oh. I get it. Even if she wasn't married, she'd never give you the time of day. Not up to her standards, eh? Never desired you the way you've been lusting over her for years. I'm right. Aren't I?" Creepy perv.

An ugly noise came from Louis's throat. With a slight flick of his wrist, a blade appeared in his hand. Impressive. He might actually be worth the sweat of a fight. Almost.

The blood washed from Louis's face, and his chin trembled in anger. "How about I kill you now and save everyone the hassle of getting their hands dirty with your demon filth. You don't believe me? I'll do it."

I wrapped my hand around my death blade. "Do you see me trembling in my trendy yet economical boots here? Exactly." I didn't want to kill the bastard, but he was asking for it. Mrs. Spencer wouldn't be too pleased if she found her manservant bleeding out on her expensive rug with my death blade in his gut.

Resolved, I took a calming breath and tried to rein in my emotions. But if the idiot moved, he was toast.

"What's going on?" came a voice from behind me. Female, but not Mrs. Spencer's. I waited for Louis to sheathe his blade back in his wrist strap concealed under his shirt before I stepped back, sheathing my own blade before it got me into some serious trouble. I turned around slowly.

In the doorway stood a young blonde woman, probably in her early twenties, athletic in a cheerleader-type way with a voluptuous chest and a face that could have been on the cover of Vogue. She had on too much makeup, like she was trying hard to hide her true beauty. Her long hair was styled in a French braid that fell past her shoulders. She had on a pair of tight jeans and a short, motorcycle-style black leather jacket that almost had me drooling.

Tension hit me hard, and I clenched my jaw when I recognized who she was.

Ah hell. I knew who she was just by the venomous look she gave me.

I was staring at Ellie, Jax's fiancée.

ABOUT THE AUTHOR

KIM RICHARDSON is the award-winning author of the bestselling SOUL GUARDIANS series. She lives in the eastern part of Canada with her husband, two dogs and a very old cat. She is the author of the SOUL GUARDIANS series, the MYSTICS series, and the DIVIDED REALMS series. Kim's books are available in print editions, and translations are available in over seven languages.

To learn more about the author, please visit:

www.kimrichardsonbooks.com

Made in the USA
Las Vegas, NV
10 September 2022

55021945R00198